PRAISE FOR *A CLIMATE OF CHAOS*

This isn't just a novel; it's a glimpse into our near future. The political machinations and technological challenges in this book feel like they could be pulled from tomorrow's headlines.

Tamara Nall | CEO & Founder

As climate disasters escalate and water becomes the world's most valuable resource, a leaked report on Spontaneous Mass Migration thrusts scientist Mark Wells into a dangerous global crisis. Extracted from Ethiopia by a high-tech space jet, he is pulled into a web of political intrigue, hidden agendas, and the fight for survival.

From drought-ravaged landscapes to the halls of power, *A Climate of Chaos* is a gripping thriller that explores the urgent realities of our changing world—and the choices that will shape our future.

Carl Grant III | Author, *How to Live the Abundant Life*

This work speaks to contemporary and very topical macro and micro level issues. It blends individual, societal, economic and political levels of analysis in a very engaging narrative that is in sync with modern day frontier logics. At the same time beautifully working to requirements of what could also be classed as a thriller driving across multiple contexts and vantage points.

Pushkar Jha | Professor of Strategic Management

A Climate of Chaos: This Parched Earth is a rare combination of technical expertise and masterful storytelling that not only keeps you on the edge of your seat but also illuminates one of humanity's greatest challenges—our changing climate.

With a compelling narrative that weaves personal and political intrigue, it presents a thought-provoking and gripping exploration of the future we may face. The writing is smart, fast-paced, and frighteningly plausible, making it a must-read for anyone interested in climate change, global politics, or simply an electrifying thriller.

Warning! This book will leave a lasting impact on you as a reader and beyond, sparking important conversations about the human path ahead.

Monique Blokzyl | HeartPowered Business

A real thriller that throws the reader into a deeply engaging storyline of human endeavour and power games, intertwined with the complexities of global climate politics. Artfully futuristic, and yet thought-provokingly contemporary.

Ricarda Baldock | Leadership Coach and Trainer

An excellent and intriguing debut that goes beyond mere fiction by providing a timely, compelling and prospective warning about our immediate future.

Julius Brookman | Law Firm Partner

Prescient and unsettling, Nawtej Dosanjh's storytelling in *A Climate of Chaos: This Parched Earth* stirs the conscience and asks the big question on global water security. It's a brave subject and a gripping read.

Anna Persson

A CLIMATE OF CHAOS

This Parched Earth

Nawtej Dosanjh

ISBN 978-1-63735-377-6 (pbk)

ISBN 978-1-63735-379-0 (hcv)

ISBN 978-1-63735-378-3 (ebook)

Library of Congress Control Number: 2025934293

TABLE OF CONTENTS

DEDICATION

Dedicated to Joanna, Ellie and Lottie

FOREWORD

In a world brimming with boundless possibilities yet teetering on the brink of environmental chaos, few voices manage to strike a chord that resonates deeply across continents and generations. Nawtej Dosanjh's *A Climate of Chaos: This Parched Earth* is one such voice—a stirring narrative that is as much a call to action as it is a masterful tale of human resilience, political intrigue, and environmental reckoning.

As someone who has dedicated my life to the art of storytelling, branding, and building authority for entrepreneurs and thought leaders, I have encountered stories that inspire, provoke, and transform. But seldom does one come across a work that does all three with such clarity and urgency as this. Nawtej's portrayal of a world grappling with the dire consequences of water scarcity and climate-induced mass migrations is not just a cautionary tale, but a blueprint for survival, adaptation, and hope.

What makes this book stand out is its profound human element. Amid the chaos of political machinations, resource hoarding, and environmental breakdowns, we meet characters who are flawed yet heroic, caught in the crosshairs of survival and morality. Their journeys reflect the struggles and aspirations of billions today—people confronting the harsh realities of a warming planet while clinging to the hope of a better tomorrow. As a strategist who helps leaders craft their messages and legacies, I am struck by the depth of authenticity and relevance in this story. It forces us to confront uncomfortable truths while leaving room for possibility and change.

Nawtej has woven a narrative that not only mirrors the challenges we face as a global community but also urges us to think about solutions that transcend borders. Through vivid prose and meticulously researched scenarios, he has offered readers a chance to reflect on the choices we must make today to ensure a livable future for generations to come.

It is not an exaggeration to say that this book is essential reading for policymakers, environmentalists, and anyone who wishes to understand the stakes of our time. But it is also a deeply personal journey - a reminder of our shared humanity and the responsibility we all bear in safeguarding this earth, our shared home.

As we stand at this critical juncture, *A Climate of Chaos: This Parched Earth* serves as both a wake-up call and a beacon of hope. It challenges us to act, to think, and most importantly, to care. I am honored to lend my voice to this remarkable work, and I urge you to dive into its pages with the curiosity of a learner and the resolve of a changemaker.

Nawtej has given us a gift—a story that speaks to the very soul of our times. Let us not merely read it, but let it move us to action.

Alinka Rutkowska
International Bestselling Author
Cofounder, Leaders Brands

ACKNOWLEDGMENTS

Writing a novel—or any book—is a long and demanding journey. It requires persistence, imagination, and, most importantly, the support of others. I am deeply grateful to those who have contributed to this endeavor; my heartfelt thanks to Amanda, Alinka, Andy, Anette, Josh, Martin, and Paula.

This novel is the product of fifteen years of dedication, shaped by a singular vision about our near future human story. It carries the subtle imprints of countless conversations, insights that deepened my understanding of character and voice, and the collective wisdom of storytellers. I am profoundly grateful for both the emotional and practical support I received along the way. Your wisdom illuminated corners of this narrative I might never have explored alone, enriching its texture with perspectives I would not have found on my own.

Writing is both a solitary act and a deeply connected one—a testament to persistence as much as to creativity. To Joanna, your unwavering belief was the quiet foundation upon which this book stands. Your support meant everything.

PROLOGUE

Jorge Jimenez looked out over the vast expanse of the plateau as he readied himself to make a call on his phone. Where once an expansive lake had sat at the center of the landscape in front of him, there was now only dusty, dry land—five years of stifling drought had blighted the land in this area so that very little remained of the tree-studded grasslands that had once filled the plateau. All that remained were a few skeletons of trees visible here and there on the otherwise desolate plain.

He had resisted the allure of some of his fellow farmers who had taken up work of a more illicit nature. Many had turned to the drug cartels for work. His wife, Maria, had warned him against such work.

Early one morning, Maria shouted out from the window to Jorge, "What is that on the horizon?"

Jorge looked toward where Maria was pointing and saw a long object moving across the landscape. As the image continued to grow, he shouted back to Maria, "It is cars, hundreds of...no, maybe thousands of cars."

"Are they heading for the United States, do you think...like the one last month?" she said, wondering if they should be doing the same.

"Probably," replied Jorge as he too wondered what he and his wife should do.

"Is it spontaneous again?" she asked. She had heard the news that hundreds of thousands, even millions, in Mexico and South America generally and around the world were migrating to find water.

Jorge walked over to her, looking at his phone. "I don't know Maria. But look at this," he said, showing her his phone, flicking through multitudes of social media videos and posts. "There is water in the United States. They are hiding it in giant underground reservoirs, stopping it flowing into Mexico."

They looked at one another in silence, both instinctively knowing that they were going to join the migration. "Let's pack and go, Maria," Jorge said.

***

The new Chinese ambassador to Mexico, Zhang Wei, had arrived in Mexico City a month ago. He sat in a meeting with Foreign Office officials who delivered the news about the latest mass migration to the US.

Zhang Wei looked at the information displayed by hologram from a small digital device. Without commenting on the movement of so many people, he launched into his rehearsed words: "The People's Republic of China is delighted to aid the Government of Mexico with our AI technologies augmenting our aquaponics and hydroponics systems. Mexico will increase food production by eight percent in the next year alone. Since 2035, your food production has risen 11% in just over 18 months, after a decade of year-on-year decline. For ease of labor movement and logistics, we request that borders be opened in the south."

The Foreign Minister of Mexico, Hector Baldini, knew precisely what Zhang Wei was requiring rather than requesting. He wanted refugees and migrants from South America to have easy passage to the US border. Without speaking, the minister waved his hand to one of his subordinates, who, understanding the order, immediately walked out of the room to make arrangements.

Zhang Wei sat expressionless but gently nodded and left the building. Later that day, he directly contacted Beijing on his encrypted device in the Chinese embassy: "They will not interfere in Taiwan...they will have their own border problems. They think they were clever by using bitcoin to eradicate their deficit, but it's made them fat and lazy."

***

Alexander Mihajlovich Medvedov, the Head of Cyber Psychology Operations, sat directly opposite President Pavlova.

"Well?" she enquired without elaborating further.

"We have enhanced the number of people on the move to the US border by at least double. People are aware that the US is storing huge amounts of water in giant underground aquifers and chambers after removing it from the Colorado River."

"How much water has the US government removed from the Colorado River?" she asked.

"We have no idea if they have or haven't, nor if it is being stored or not. But it is possible, I suppose."

"Mr. Medvedov," said President Pavlova, sternly. "The US government is removing water and storing it. We have evidence from our satellites that that is the case. Is that correct?"

"Yes, President Pavlova. It is my mistake. Of course, I now recall the briefing where the irrefutable evidence was presented to all of us." Medvedov remonstrated to himself internally for being so lax. It was critical that the façade of this false reality was maintained at all times.

"Please have the briefing documented and make sure those who were present sign to confirm their attendance. Today, please. The US needs to deal with its southern border problems rather than take an interest in the assistance we are providing to Belarus in restoring order. I also understand that a spontaneous migration of our people has begun, to Kyiv...to take back the water Ukraine stole from our aquifers."

"Of course," he said. And with that, he was ushered out of the large room.

CHAPTER 1

"Mark, are you asleep?" Aida whispered. "Do you hear that noise?"

There was no answer, but she felt the body next to her tremble slightly. Maybe he was dreaming, or perhaps the contact of her skin had produced a shiver.

She raised herself up on one elbow and, in the half-light, looked at the face of the man beside her. His eyes were closed, and his straight, auburn hair was flowing in multiple directions. Beneath them, his dry and chapped lips were parted, giving a glimpse of neat white teeth. She blew on his hair, making it flutter slightly and free some strands from the sweat that shone on his forehead. As she turned towards him, her slight frame came to rest on his torso.

Somewhere, a rooster crowed. Aida smiled and slowly moved her hand towards the familiar tuft of chest hair, where gray began to show. Just as her fingers made contact, her lover shot to life. As she squealed with fake fright, Mark grabbed her wrist, made a lunge for her other hand, and, spinning her slender brown body over, sat astride her waist, pinning both of Aida's arms above her head.

"So, you are awake then," she giggled. "Pretty good reflexes for your age."

With a straight face, Mark said, "That cockerel doesn't feel good about himself when I'm around."

Aida smiled. She liked his humor. No one else at Stanford had made her laugh so much.

"His cockereling is embarrassingly poor…I've noticed it has declined rapidly since I was here. I am fast, and the cockerel knows it."

"There's that noise again." Aida pricked her head up a little at an angle as though that would help her hear more clearly.

"I don't hear anything," replied Mark, lifting his head to the sky as though his hearing would pick up more sound from that angle.

"It sounded a bit like a plane, but it was so faint I couldn't make it out." Aida seemed unsure whether she had heard anything at all. She became distracted by his shining green eyes.

"We don't get planes in this part of Ethiopia," Mark said confidently. "It must be a truck or something."

"Yeah," Aida said. She wasn't sure what it was, but she felt strongly that she had heard something.

They stayed in each other's embrace. Aida arched her back as Mark bent his head towards her. They kissed as the day broke, and the temperature began its inexorable climb.

By six in the morning, they had rolled up the bed matting, swept the floor, and eaten a little kocho bread. Enset, the plant used to make kocho, would have been a wonder food in a time of climate change and rising population. But with rising temperatures came new viral diseases that impacted plants and crops along with humans. The enset plant had not been spared.

Aida turned to Mark, holding the bread before taking a bite. "When I was a child, we ate this every single day."

He nodded.

"What a difference twenty years can make. Who would have thought kocho would become almost a rare delicacy."

So many things had changed in the world at that time that Aida supposed the rarity of kocho didn't make all that much difference in the big scheme of things. Still, it was emblematic, at least to some degree, of the situation her community and the wider world now faced. The old ways of doing things, or the resources those ways had relied upon, no longer sufficed in the current era. The result, at least in this part of the world, was often a crisis of one type or another. Aida looked beyond Mark and out the window, eating her bread without speaking as she thought.

For her, what the locals called the *fake banana* plant had been the essence of these mountains. She had eaten kocho almost from birth. Like the other children, Aida had also taken delight in the same plant's fruit seeds—a favorite snack. As she grew, she helped the other village women harvest and cook the fake banana's roots and bulbs.

Now a tall, slim, striking woman, Aida finished eating and sat in a plastic chair in front of the two-roomed home her grandfather had built almost 70 years ago.

"Tom should be here soon," Mark said as he emerged from the hut.

"The water pipeline interchange is getting urgent, no? What is the delay with the AI?" Aida asked.

Mark sat down next to Aida, his frame dwarfing hers.

"You and I know it's been urgent for a while already," Mark said, a tone of exasperation in his voice. "This is the place where pipelines from the coast and Uganda merge, with those from Kenya and Somalia. It's from this point that we can control the flow and the direction. It's the most complicated part of the infrastructure, and there are some delays getting the artificial intelligence and sensors to work."

Aida put her hand on his arm. "There's no place for us to go," she said. "It has to work."

She pulled her dress away from her legs—the heat made everything sticky—as she stood up, swishing the garment to create at least a sense of cool.

"Yes," Mark said. "And fast."

"I just pray that it does," Aida said.

There had always been the possibility of a catastrophic drought every ten years or so. But now, the semi-permanent water shortage had become critical. The people of this region had nowhere they could easily migrate to. With their long experience of droughts, they knew that many would die on the way to neighboring countries. Despite this, at some point, they would indeed have to walk long distances to find food and water. The locals knew from their social media feeds that tens and even hundreds of thousands of people were moving worldwide, not for a better life, but for a few more liters of water a day. Simply to get away from this parched earth.

Mark stretched and swatted away a fly. "Please don't be anxious, Aida. Tom and I are doing everything possible." Mark understood Aida's concern for her community, but he could not help but feel mildly irritated that he had to explain this with such regularity, almost every day.

"The leaders of Uganda, Kenya, Somalia, Eritrea, and Ethiopia are seeing sense and trying to work together rather than risk a situation of permanent conflict. And if we can show that people can work together across national boundaries in one place, particularly in East Africa, we can make it work everywhere. It will create the political will to share water; I am sure of it."

Aida cupped his chin in her hands. "I love you, and your passion about water equity," she said, kissing him on the tip of his nose. Then, feeling a bit bruised by Mark's irritation, Aida gathered her things to go to the hospital where she worked.

Before she left, Tom Van Heusen arrived in his Jeep, turned off the engine, gave a little wave, and got out from behind the wheel with a large plastic bag swinging by his side.

"Mark, Aida," he said, a little nod in the right direction accompanying each name. "I brought breakfast."

"That's nice of you, Tom," said Mark, "but we've already eaten. You go ahead."

"Ah, well, it's not for me. It was for you. The UN crew gave away extra muffins and coffees. I've got a doggy bag of stuff here. Even got some yogurt and chili peppers they were serving with that Ethiopian fit-fit stuff they used to eat in the mornings round here."

He paused for a moment. "Thought it might make a nice change from kocho for you guys."

"Thank you, Thomas, but I have no time," said Aida as she stood up, looking at the two men side by side. They were both a little under six foot, and while Tom was much the stockier, Mark was more muscular. "I have to get to the hospital. Good luck with the work. We are all counting on you."

"Listen," Mark said to Tom. "I'll bring my gear out, and we'll get moving. Pretty soon, it'll be too hot to do anything. You can drive."

After the three-mile drive, Mark and Tom were mentally and emotionally drained. In normal times, the Jeep would have bumped through the mountains of Ethiopia's Gamo Gofo Zone in around fifteen minutes; the two men would have shared the muffins and a few jokes and arrived at their destination happy. However, these were not normal times.

The Jeep journey took just over an hour. During it, the defense mechanisms of humor and playfulness Mark employed to cast a protective blanket over Aida's home, evaporated. Out here, away from UN and NGO aid centers, the harsh reality of the situation was all too clear.

Drought was leading some people to leave their communities already. The muffled sound made by the shuffling feet of countless men, women, and children moving while they still had the strength to do so echoed through the oppressive heat. The throng of people kicked up squalls of dust as they walked slowly along the dirt road. Babies, hanging from their mothers' shoulders, wailed with hunger. Parents, unable to give them what they needed, let them cry.

Mark, without turning to look at Tom, muttered, "This is what the initial stages look like."

"They are moving," Tom said grimly, "but most of them know they won't make it."

"We are in a race against time," Mark said. "This is just a trickle compared to the numbers we'll see trying to migrate if

5

we don't get this done. It's already happening all over the world, particularly from Latin America to the States."

Tom nodded his head in agreement.

The women were dressed in the brightly woven robes their mothers had worn, and their mothers were before them as far back as anyone could remember. Today, on this trek that took them from their homes, these colorful clothes seemed mockingly garish. The women and the men carried large bundles. With the heat and the lack of food or drink, some had let their belongings fall to the ground, where the billowing dust quickly covered them. Tom had to sound the horn almost constantly to make any headway. Despite the pain, no pleading arms were thrust into the Jeep, just hollow eyes.

The Gamo highlands, Mark knew, had once been a greener landscape than most people might have thought possible in this part of Africa. Aida and the other 30,000 or so members of the Dorze people had grazed cattle and sturdy sheep here. Now, Mark and Tom crossed a depressing landscape. Deep swathes of tropical trees lay in dried-up and rotting piles. The crumbling soil, almost as red as the precious chili peppers nestled in the doggy bag, bore few new shoots. Instead, the ground was scattered with the bones of farm animals as well as those of the jackals that, for a while, had feasted off them.

"When even the jackals can't make it, you know the time to get out is getting close if it's not already here," Mark said. Tom again nodded to indicate agreement.

"Without this project," Mark continued, "the people in this part of Ethiopia face the choice of staying and facing certain drought and starvation or moving to a neighboring country where the probability of survival can't be calculated." Mark now looked at Tom and said, "I know you know this already, Tom. I suppose I'm just motivating myself by restating the reason we're doing what we're doing."

"My guess is that the possibility that we can transport water from Uganda and the Somali coast is keeping most of them from leaving for the time being," Tom said.

Mark hoped that the faith the people of this region placed in the water pipeline project would soon be rewarded. Given the progress they were making, he had every reason to believe that it would.

Mark had learned from Aida that her grandfather's home had once stood among forty or so near identical homes, but the village had now dwindled to just a handful of families. There was barely a drop of milk or a mouthful of meat to be found. The false banana trees were very close to becoming just a fond memory. Lakes and water holes were empty and cracked, which was precisely why his team was there.

"When I heard what you were proposing, I thought it was both crazy and made a lot of sense at the same time," Tom said after they had passed through the multitude of migrating people.

"Thanks, I think," Mark said with a grin. He had been more than a bit uncertain himself—not at the feasibility of the plan, but at the reception it would receive among the leaders and relevant NGOs in the region.

"It was and is an audacious plan," Tom said. "And now that it is so close to getting off the ground, I would say the common sense far outweighs the craziness." Mark and Tom shared a grin at this. "Of course, your reputation for solving issues like this and the fact that you were a former climate advisor to the US president didn't hurt when it came to getting people to support the project."

"Luckily for us, the right people took an interest. It's great if my experience, whatever that means, helped with that, but at the end of the day, what matters is that we get it working. That support will disappear as fast as it materialized if we don't produce."

"Yep," agreed Tom as, at last, the Jeep came to a stop in a cloud of dust in the area where the water tanks were being erected, mostly below but also above ground. As Tom exited the Jeep, Mark surveyed the giant futuristic tanks in silence for a few moments, doubt creeping into his thoughts: *Are we really going to move water via a pipeline from Uganda to Ethiopia and from the coast to the countries where it is needed? And the security that Kenyan troops will provide. Will the multilateral agreement continue to be held?* Mark snapped himself back into the reality of the moment, dismissive of his doubts.

Thrusting any remaining worries about the success of the project from his mind, Mark got out of the Jeep and walked to where Tom was standing. The tanks rising from the ground ahead of them and the pipeline supplying them were just part of the extensive water infrastructure project Mark was working on with several countries in the region. When complete, it would connect these countries' coast and inland areas to multiple water sources. To optimize flexibility and ensure that water flowed to where it was most needed, AI switches when tripped, could move the water in multiple directions. The final agreement was reached when leaders of the African countries involved became convinced that the AI would provide the precise amount of water needed and no more. They had all worried about scare tactics from some opposition parties that water was being given away to enrich the leaders themselves. Hard-fought elections in some countries had been won against candidates who had sought competitive, aggressive, war-like rhetoric over this collaborative approach. For now, the disinformation of some had not worked in East Africa.

Looking over Tom's shoulder, Mark noticed the workmen by the water towers looking up at the sky and gesturing.

"What's that noise? What are they pointing at?" he asked Tom, who had also turned to look.

They followed the pointing fingers of the men as they gazed, mouths agape, at what appeared to be some sort of oncoming craft. The snap and roar of its engines had cracked above the men's heads before they sighted it. Now, though, they could make out a fast-approaching shape.

"Aida said she heard something," Mark muttered to himself in a barely audible whisper.

The airship came to a surprising and almost abrupt mid-air stop. It seemed to hang briefly and then descend vertically to the ground. The word SpaceForce One, painted on the side of the craft, was now visible. Mark and Tom turned away and covered their faces in an effort to protect their eyes from the billowing dust caused by the ship's engines. Anyone watching from a distance would not have been able to see either the vessel or the storage towers: the whole scene was now simply a huge dust storm.

"Tom, did you ask the President of the United States to visit me in Ethiopia to have a cup of coffee and some kocho," said Mark, drawing a laugh from his friend.

Mark tried to dust himself off a little and was about to step forward when the door of SpaceForce One opened, and an automatic step system unfurled. Two figures emerged from the open door, followed by a third. The first two were clad all over in body armor and wore visored helmets that hid all but their mouths. Guns nestled on their shoulder cladding, with the weapons pointed ahead of them, ready to fire if necessary. The third figure appeared to be a woman dressed in civilian clothes.

The work unit froze as the soldiers scanned 180 degrees with their guns raised. Satisfied that their smart visors found no danger, one spoke just loud enough for the other two to hear. His colleague nodded, and they all moved forward toward Mark. Six feet from Mark, they stopped.

"Recognition confirmed," one of the soldiers said after the reading the same words from the corner of his visor, lowering his gun. His fellow soldier did the same.

"Mark Wells?" the woman dressed like a civilian said, stepping forward. She was much shorter than the two soldiers, and her assertive tone was incongruent with her sleight build.

"Yes," said Mark. "Who are you?"

"My name is Lorraine Betts." Her brightly colored pants and blouse stood out sharply from the soldiers' uniforms.

"I am the President's National Security Adviser, and we would like you to accompany us to Washington to meet with President Poulter."

Mark and Tom instinctively glanced at one another, both more than a bit surprised by this turn of events.

"You will not need baggage or a passport. Take-off is imminent. SpaceForce One has only temporary clearance to be on the ground in Ethiopia."

"Wait a second. Wait just a second," Mark protested. "Can you explain what's going on?"

"Mr. Wells," Lorraine said, an impatient look on her face. "The President of the United States has sent her own aircraft to take you to Washington to meet with her. It's about a report you wrote, but more importantly, we believe you are in imminent danger."

"Who am I in danger from?" Mark replied.

"I will explain further on the plane. This is in your best interest," Lorraine replied sharply.

"Oh, come on, what danger am I in? And from who? I have a partner here. Is she in danger? Are my friends in danger? Is the pipeline in danger? If you can't tell me, who can I talk to?" Mark was hesitant to trust this woman, however impressive her entrance had been.

"Mr. Wells, we have confirmed intelligence that foreign-backed forces are in Ethiopia to abduct you and question you about your report. No one else is in danger if you are not in Ethiopia. Only you are in possession of vital information about international security."

Mark looked back at Tom and the other men who stood motionless a little distance behind him. Tom simply shrugged. Mark shrugged back, then swiveled to face Lorraine Betts again.

"Okay, remove all the water and food from the aircraft and give it to my friends, and I will come with you."

The soldiers were silent for a moment and then, with a nod from Lorraine Betts, they returned to the plane. As he watched, most of the water and any food on the plane was removed.

Mark felt a hand on his shoulder. Turning, he stood face-to-face with Tom. "Maybe this will be useful. It feels important," Tom said, pointing to SpaceForce One with a nod of his head. "We'll keep working here. Everything will be okay. You might be back in a couple of days."

"I have to see Aida first," Mark said.

"I'll let Aida know what happened. Call her from the plane," Tom said.

"Mr. Wells," interjected one of the soldiers, "We must embark now. The Ethiopians have given us clearance to be on the ground for less than an hour. Kenyan troops may be close by, but our safety cannot be guaranteed. Russian backed proxies are active in the area and SpaceForce One would be huge prize."

"I have a call with Henry later today and with Mikeo tomorrow. What will they think if I leave without a word?" Mark said.

"Who are Henry and Mikeo?" asked Lorraine.

"Henry is the President of Uganda, and Mikeo is the President of Kenya," Mark said.

"We have secure video and audio on SpaceForce One, even when we briefly leave the atmosphere."

Evidently, she had an answer for everything. But Mark still hesitated.

"Mark, listen," Tom said, "the UN security people are trained in handling any security issues we might face here. I will make sure that Aida is guarded...from these foreign-backed...guys, or whatever you call them. But listen, you are really the only one with the expertise to explain what, how, and why we are doing this to the President. This could lead to something even bigger than our East Africa Water Transfer Project."

11

Lorraine nodded her head in agreement with Tom. For his part, Mark couldn't deny the logic of what his friend was saying.

"Okay," he said, relenting at last. "Let me get my things."

He made his way across to where the Jeep was parked. One of the soldiers fell in alongside him. The other soldier said something into his microphone, then stood still, watching for any sudden movements among the men assembled in front of the group.

When the first soldier and Mark returned, the second soldier took his place on the other side of Mark. Lorraine Betts had already boarded SpaceForce One. Together, the three mounted the steps and joined her on the airship. As soon as they were inside, the steps recoiled with a whir, and the door closed. Minutes later, the huge engines began firing, and the silver shape rose into the air. In another roar of noise, accompanied by a cloud of blinding dust, the President's jet lifted off and streaked across the sky toward the United States.

CHAPTER 2

"Guttenberg, are you alone? I need to speak with you. I have an update."

Temir Bousson was straight to the point, as always.

Guttenberg was equally terse. "I need to drive somewhere away from my home. I will call you back in precisely fifteen minutes. Leave your normal phone where it is but switched on and take this phone with you."

"I am already several miles from my office, and my work phone is in my desk drawer. I will wait for your call," replied Temir.

About twenty minutes elapsed before Guttenberg called back. His deep, strong voice gave an accurate impression of a physically large and confident man. "Sorry, there was some traffic. I didn't expect a call from you today. Is there a problem?"

"Maybe. I don't know," Temir replied. "I leaked Wells' Spontaneous Mass Migration report. The New York Times will report that the President kept the report secret as she plans to agree that the US and American companies will take the lead in funding climate change initiatives and water projects across the world —"

Guttenberg interjected. "As you said you would. So why are we talking?"

"The President sent SpaceForce One for Wells," Temir responded. "He may already be on his way. I'm not sure yet. I don't know if this is a problem or not."

"How do you know she sent SpaceForce One?"

"Because she sent my boss, Lorraine Betts, the National Security Adviser, to go and get him. None of us had any time to prepare. She seemed to have a CIA briefing and ordered Betts to get on with it. Betts didn't even have time to tell me."

"I don't think this is a problem," Guttenberg said. "In any case, I told our friend at the Gudonov Group about Wells a couple of months back, and he told me he planned to ask President Pavlova for the authority to abduct him."

Temir sounded stunned. "I didn't realize it was you."

"What do you mean?" replied Guttenberg.

"We have intelligence that Wells is going to be abducted by Russian-backed mercenaries," Temir said in an agitated tone. His anxious and soft voice made him sound much smaller than he was. "President Pavlova obviously gave the go-ahead."

Guttenberg recognized that Temir was agitated but ignored this and continued, "As I said, I don't think this is a problem, but we need a contingency plan. It is conceivable that Wells could drum up some support and inadvertently disrupt our plans for the US government."

"What about your daughter?"

Guttenberg did not flinch at the question. "What about my daughter?"

"Well, Ingrid is still married to Wells. Perhaps she could be in DC on business and get close to him to find out what he's up to. I can't think of a better contingency plan right now."

There was a brief silence, then Guttenberg spoke. "Can you speak to Ingrid on my behalf, Temir?"

"Sure," Temir said before abruptly changing the conversation. "You know that getting mixed up with Gudonov could get us killed. They are responsible for the deaths and disappearance of a lot of prominent people around the world—Russian or otherwise. They don't even bother pretending it's not them anymore."

"The replacement American government will not have any problems with Russia or Gudonov, Temir. We will have a very good working relationship."

"You are always very confident that she will be impeached. I don't understand why." Temir hoped Guttenberg was right but could not understand how this would come about.

"Temir, it is better that you don't know too much, in case you make a slip. But this much is in the public domain; the House Democrats are itching to get back at us for impeaching President Macmillan four years ago. It failed in the Senate, but they are pissed with us."

"Well, it was a pretty frivolous reason. A half-brother's connection with a Chinese tech company. But even if they do succeed at impeaching her, they don't have the numbers in the Senate."

"There are some courageous Senate Republicans who will do the right thing when the time is right," snapped Guttenberg.

Temir did not question any further, not only because he knew Guttenberg wouldn't tell him the whole plan but also because he had something else he wanted to discuss.

"One more thing, Guttenberg," Temir said, his tone calm but laced with intensity. "My daughter Sara. I need you to convince me somehow that the recording you have is going to be destroyed and that you haven't made any copies. I don't know how you do that, but I have done what you asked and leaked the report. And we are on the same side in wanting to remove this president. You don't need this hold over me."

"I don't know how I can convince you either," Guttenberg responded, his tone measured but direct. "Whatever I say can be doubted. But I have destroyed the recording. Besides, I don't think that sex with three guys simultaneously carries any shock value in this day and age. Like it or not, times have changed."

Temir tried an emotional appeal. "If this recording ever becomes public, she will never become a lawyer."

"I don't have it, Temir. I destroyed it. We share the same disdain for this President." Temir could hear Guttenberg's car starting.

"Why would you make the recording in the first place, in your own home, if you didn't intend to use it against me?" Temir's tone became a bit more frantic, which was unusual for him. "I trusted you enough to send my daughter for an internship with Guttenberg Mining, and you went so far as to offer her the chance to stay at your home."

"Temir," Guttenberg's tone remained calm, "I didn't ask her to bring those guys to my house while we were all away. I didn't do anything. The facial recognition cameras automatically record when faces aren't recognized by the system. The guys she brought home didn't match any records."

"But you still used it as leverage against me."

"Goodbye, Temir."

Temir hardly heard the electric car, but he surmised that Guttenberg was on the move just before the phone went dead. Temir switched off his phone, took out the battery, hid them in their usual separate spots, and decided to drive back to the office. He was agitated about how the meeting ended and wanted to have some kind of hold over Guttenberg. However, he knew Guttenberg was protected by people, not just through his own resources but also by people in government, the FBI, and the CIA. He didn't know their names, but these people had been planted in important positions over a decade ago, ready to topple an elected American President if he or she stepped out of line in terms of their vision for the US. But then he had an idea. He turned his car around and pulled a different phone from his glove box and made a call.

"Mendez," he said. "I need to see you now."

"What, right now?" Mendez replied.

"Yes, right now. I won't talk on the phone. Meet me in the usual place and bump into me. We can talk about my divorce from your sister, and I can then fill you in."

Within twenty minutes, Temir was walking along the Potomac, which was where he gave Mendez his last surveillance job.

"Temir, is that you? How are you?" Mendez walked toward Temir with his hand held out, feigning surprise.

"Robert, hey," feigned Temir, with equal surprise in his body language.

Within minutes, after some brief words about Temir and Diane's divorce, Temir started talking.

"A man called Guttenberg has something on Sara... your niece. And I need something on him. But you cannot follow Guttenberg, as he is heavily protected. His car has smart cameras installed and is linked to his personal data center, which analyses every vehicle that comes in contact with him. He also has a miniature drone overhead sometimes. So obviously, don't put a tracker on his car."

Robert Mendez butted in, "If I cannot surveille him at all, I have no idea how I can get anything on him."

Temir began to speak again. "He has some sort of low-grade fix-it type of guy called Carruthers. I don't know if that's his real name. I only saw him once, but I managed to take this photo with my wrist embedded camera." Temir held up his forearm and showed Mendez the photo on his wrist.

"Okay, it might dig up something, but don't bank on it, if I have to be as careful as you say."

"I know. And Robert, if you get caught, as usual the buck stops with you. That's why I pay so much." And with that, he handed over a device with of a 24-password code, which was a twentieth of a bitcoin, equal to about $100,000, with a promise of more to come.

"Make the transfer to your own code, and there will be no trace of a transaction." Temir belatedly added the obvious instructions.

"Wow, where did you get that much?" Mendez was eager to know, but without answering that it had come from Guttenberg, Temir said goodbye.

He then continued to the office, and once there, he ascertained that Mark Wells was on his way to DC and would land within three hours. He then drove back to pick up his hidden phone and went to one of his usual spots to make a private phone call.

"Ingrid. Ingrid Guttenberg."

"Yes, this is Ingrid," she recognized Temir's voice from her one previous encounter with him.

"Your father wanted me to let you know that Mark Wells is in DC meeting the President, and he needs to know what is going on. He will be at the Conrad."

CHAPTER 3

"I am on this fucking plane, and I cannot do anything about Aida being threatened."

"Mark," Lorraine's tone radiated concern. "We didn't know about her uncle Jebal."

"Jemal," Mark corrected her. "Why didn't you know? You knew about the Russians."

"We should have known. Jemal seems to be small time, and he has no history of terrorism. But you're right; we still should have known. I am truly sorry."

"Yes, you should have," Mark said emphatically, turning away from Lorraine to gaze out the window of the spacecraft.

Jemal was a large man with a recognizable permanent scowl. His resentment was understandable. Five years ago, the region had been hit by a famine. It wasn't as bad as some of the others they'd been through in the area, but it was bad enough to kill tens of thousands. Among those that died were Jemal's wife and children. He was the only one to survive. Jemal had blamed the US for climate change and causing the famine that killed his family.

Mark's phone rang, and he could see it was Tom. He turned back to face Lorraine.

"Anyway, I don't want to talk about my fucking report right now. What is there to understand? People are going to move if there isn't enough water. What don't you get about that? I need to take this call."

"I will give you some privacy, Mark," the authoritative and calm National Security Adviser said, then left the room.

Mark clicked the button to accept the call from Tom, but there was only silence on the other end of the line. Even with advanced technology, atmospheric conditions alone could sometimes make air-to-ground communications difficult. As he waited for Tom to call again, Mark thought about Jemal. In the aftermath of the famine-caused death of his family, he created a protest group called Al-Haqa. He'd already let Aida know what he thought of her working in an American-funded hospital, but this morning's events had pushed things up a notch. Aida had been shaken up, and it took a lot to do that.

In their brief call a few minutes earlier, she had told Mark that Jemal and his men had come down to the hospital waving old AK47s around and shouting about bloody retribution. Aida had explained that the people at the depot were terrified. They thought Jemal and his cohorts were going to open fire, take hostages, or even blow the whole place to pieces. In the end, they simply left. Thankfully, Aida was okay, or at least she had not suffered any physical harm.

As if the lack of water and food wasn't enough, now she has to deal with an uncle who'd do something like this…and who knows what else.

Mark's phone rang again, and this time, the call from Tom went through.

"Mark!" Tom exclaimed.

"What's happening, Tom?" Mark said impatiently.

"It's all under control. Aida is safe. I just left her."

"Why did you leave her?"

"It's fine. She is with the armed guards from the UN. They're insisting she goes through some security protocols right now. She will call you straight after."

"Okay, thank God."

"Mark, why didn't you tell me about Jemal?"

"There is nothing to tell. He is Aida's uncle. He is a nobody, really."

"He isn't a nobody, bro. There were at least a dozen guys with guns shouting Al-Haqa stuff."

"Yeah, he often tries to set up Al-Haqa protests. But I've never seen him with a gun or any other men. And where would he get AK47s? He has always just vented in the past. I didn't tell you because, well, what would I say? 'Oh, hey Tom, Aida's uncle, Jemal, came by and said fuck America.' Years ago, some people joined him in protests, but that's it. So, I am sorry, bro, but I could not have seen this coming. He has just vented his anger before."

"Yeah, venting. That's one way of putting it."

"Tom, he lost his entire family in the famine five years ago."

"Oh. Shit."

"Anyway, the poor man must have been full of guilt at being the lone survivor. Plus, he blames the US for climate change...for causing the famine.... All that hate, guilt, and anger must have finally pushed him to become violent. Where does a lonely, bitter old guy get AK47s?"

"Okay, I hear you. But you still should have told me. You put me in danger."

"I really didn't know that he would do something like this..."

"Al-Haqa. Come on, Mark."

"Al-Haqa has been nothing ever since he founded it. It's always been just a protest thing. You can't even call it a movement. It's been just him."

"You still should have told me."

"I am sorry, Tom. I really am. I didn't think it through. Even now, it seems totally out of my experience with Jemal. Guns and men. And if Jemal was that important, why didn't Betts know about this? They knew about everything else. Anyway, Betts told me she will get Al-Haqa put on the terrorist watch list."

Tom had no answer to Mark's question. He was in the dark as much as Mark when it came to what exactly NSA Betts and her team knew and why they were so eager to bring Mark back to DC with them.

A few minutes after his call with Tom, Aida called, and they talked briefly. Despite the day's events, she reassured him that he had done the right thing by leaving without saying goodbye to her and that Tom had organized some security from the UN. He tried to tell her not to go to the hospital for a while, but he knew he was wasting his breath.

Earlier, he had spoken to the President of Uganda. Far from being worried that he was on his way to Washington, Henry had thought that any engagement with the US President was a positive because of the attention it could bring to the water issues facing East Africa.

As he settled in for the flight, reassured that Aida was as protected as she could be given the circumstances, Mark contemplated how he had adapted so quickly to the futuristic scene of the world's most advanced passenger jet. He had been in the country for months that had begun to seem like years. During that time, he had grown used to a simpler way of life, and far from the 24/7 culture of his homeland. He had adopted Ethiopian alcohol, like tella or areki. He had worked long hours in the heat with little in the way of creature comforts. Then, there was Aida. He wasn't looking forward to waking up without her next to him.

As he pondered the question of how he had adapted to these various circumstances, he soon realized he already knew the answer. *I adapted quickly because, much of the time, everyone adapts quickly. We adapt to technology, wars, famines, and climate change, and now we are adapting to Spontaneous Mass Migrations. Except when we don't. Which is when we become irrelevant or disappear.*

His musings on adaptation were interrupted by the ringtone of his phone, which indicated an incoming call from Mikeo Thundilayskila, the President of Kenya.

"Mark, how are things, my friend?" Mikeo said in his customary hearty tone.

"They are a bit topsy-turvy at the moment, Mikeo. How about you?"

"As good as can be expected. I suppose I could complain, but what good would that do?" Mark has always enjoyed Mikeo's fatalistic but somehow still optimistic take on life. "But what is going on with you? Is the pipeline with its intersections still on schedule?"

"It is, but I've now turned supervision over to Tom Van Heusen for the moment. That's why I called you; I wanted to let you know that I'm on a plane, a space jet, sent by the President of the United States to bring me back to Washington, DC."

"I hope you're not in some type of trouble, my friend; you always struck me as a law-abiding citizen." Mark also appreciated the Kenyan President's dry sense of humor.

"No, she's not imprisoning me, not that I know of, anyway. Apparently, a report I co-authored on spontaneous mass migration is making waves in Washington years after its publication. The report was classified but it isn't anymore. It was leaked. Anyway, I hope you don't mind that I may not be there for the completion of the pipeline link."

"Not at all, my friend. In fact, this could be a good thing for you and the project, and for East Africa."

"How do you mean?"

"With your passion and persistence, I am confident you will be a highly effective ambassador for this project in your country's capital."

"I appreciate your faith in me, Mikeo. I will do my best. I was thinking earlier about how people have had to adapt to drastic changes throughout history, and certainly in our time. I suppose that is what I must do now."

"You must indeed."

"Pardon me for being a little philosophical, but it seems to me that, perhaps for the first time in the history of the species, it's not about some groups of people adapting while others don't. The whole human race is adapting. It makes me wonder if there will be a far-off future where historians and others write about this period of history. And if so, what will they say?"

"You are truly a philosopher, and a historian my friend, and this is why I believe your trip to Washington represents an opportunity for you to explain to the President just how vital this project is."

"I will do my utmost to adapt to the strange circumstances I'm likely to find myself in on this trip to the jungle, otherwise known as Washington DC. Hopefully, I'll do as well as you've done in navigating the corridors of power in Nairobi."

"Flattery is just the way to do it, my friend. I can tell you are well prepared for your visit to DC." They both laughed at Mikeo's jibe. Mark heard the president's name being called on the other line.

"It seems my duties call me away. I wish you the best of luck on your important journey, Mark. Please keep me informed."

After hanging up, Mark felt an urge to see more of the futuristic airship on which he was a passenger. Leaving his room, he headed down the corridor in the direction of the front of the plane. After passing the three doors to his left, of what he imagined were cabins similar to his, he entered the jet's main galley. It contained seats for eight or so people. However, only an attendant and a young man staring intently at the computer before him were present. Beyond the galley were the cockpit doors. It seemed much smaller than the AirForce One of old.

Mark assured the attendant that he didn't need anything and just wanted to see more of the plane. Closing his computer, the young man rose from his seat and shook Mark's hand as he introduced himself.

"I'm Nick Drazen, Deputy Director of Communications for the National Security Adviser. Thank you for joining us on short notice, Mr. Wells."

"I was convinced that the need justified the abruptness of my departure, Mr. Drazen. I hope that turns out to be true."

"While only you can determine if that is the case, I certainly think it will be. These are trying times, and I think the sudden attention your report is enjoying, given its none-too-cheerful subject matter, attests to that."

"Indeed. Please excuse my directness, but your job title makes me wonder if Director Betts didn't bring you along to help her convince me to get on this marvel of transportation technology if her initial entreaties failed to bear fruit."

Nick smiled at Mark's comment. "I can see how you might think so, but Director Betts has little reason to doubt her own persuasiveness. She is very good at getting people to see her point of view. The truth is that with all the...excitement, or chaos, some might say, going on in the world these days, my job has become even busier than usual. Director Betts was kind enough to let me use some of the time on the flight to talk with her about some other issues."

Mark appreciated Nick's candor. The young man had a low-key but affable personality that doubtless served him well in his role. At least he was willing to acknowledge the troubles that beset the world. Some people were still in denial about what was happening. It seemed almost unbelievable to him, but in many developed countries, the crises caused by near-worldwide drought and multiple spontaneous mass migrations had not significantly impacted large sections of the public consciousness yet. Even though these problems were impacting their own countries. *Knowing that the good times would end soon enough, it was as though the wealthy were doing all they could to enjoy the last years of the good life.*

"It sounds like you are up to your eyeballs in alligators, as they say. It's not my subject of expertise, of course, but I can imagine that the national security implications of these crises are attracting attention at the highest levels," Mark said.

"You would not be wrong to surmise that, Mr. Wells. Although it's not a secret that there are different views on the matter among those with influence in this area. As can be seen in several recent opinion pieces circulating on social media."

"I've been immersed in my work in Ethiopia for many months, so I can't say I've read them. But it's hard for me to believe that anyone could argue against America doing its best to help solve the underlying causes of SMMs, given how beneficial it would be for the USA and the world as a whole," Mark said.

"I believe those who advocate against direct action argue that we have enough issues of our own to deal with and that trying to solve the world's problems means less of an ability to take care of pressing matters at home," Nick said.

"That is a ridiculous position. Apart from the humanitarian context of withholding assistance, our prosperity at home vitally depends on the prosperity of the countries we trade with." Mark knew that Nick was not necessarily expressing his own opinion on this matter, but he could feel his ire rising nonetheless as he contemplated the folly of the USA attempting to remain aloof in such a situation.

"After reading the paper you co-authored, I fully understand your position, Mr. Wells," Nick said diplomatically.

"Yet here we are in this high-speed airship where we are afforded every luxury, while millions, even tens of millions, all over the globe, including in our own country, could soon be living under Mad Max-type scenarios of crushing poverty and a near total breakdown of law and order and basic services and infrastructure."

Mark did not press the point further but thought that was already the case for so many around the world. Tom's parting words came back to him. "This feels important," he had said.

"All of which explains why your report has caused such a stir in DC and why you are on this high-speed jet," Nick said.

"A friend of mine said he thought it was important that I take this trip," Mark said thoughtfully. "I sure hope he was right; otherwise, what was the point of getting on this flight?"

"Your friend sounds like a wise man," Nick said.

"I hope so," Mark said.

He turned to look out the window beside them. Below them, the Earth appeared blue, calm, and timeless. Mark became semi-hypnotized by the elegance of the scene and found it hard to focus on the urgent problems the world faced. Nevertheless, the preternatural beauty of the panorama could not entirely force them from his mind. *It was undeniable that the planet was in the depths of the deepest of multiple crises perhaps in human history, at the very least in recorded human history.*

Mark pushed thoughts of the world's troubles away for the moment. He had no doubt there would be plenty of time to ponder them before they arrived in DC. A thought occurred to him, and he turned back towards Nick. "What is our ETA in DC? I get the feeling that it will be faster than usual."

Before Nick could reply, a man emerged from the cockpit and walked in their direction.

"Mr. Wells, let me introduce you to Captain Gehrling."

Mark shook the captain's hand, and after the two had greeted each other, Nick repeated Mark's question to the captain.

"We'll land in Washington in just over four hours."

"Without refueling?" As fast as the jet was, Mark was certain it had used a significant amount of fuel to get to Ethiopia.

"We refueled mid-air before landing in Ethiopia. President Poulter informed us of the urgency of this mission, so we are making every effort to conclude it promptly. That's why we exited Earth's atmosphere as soon as was feasible on the return trip. That enabled us to switch to space flight."

"I'm no physicist, but I can imagine that escaping the friction generated by the earth's atmosphere would make for faster travel."

"That is exactly it. Anyway, I wanted to say hello, Mr. Wells, and welcome you to the flight. My copilot is more than capable of handling all functions of the jet, but I must get back to the flight deck as we get ready to return to the earth's atmosphere. Protocol dictates that there must be two pilots at the controls during the procedure."

Mark told the captain he understood completely. The two shook hands again, and the captain departed to return to the flight deck.

Back in his cabin, Mark found himself admiring the craft's interior. In the States and elsewhere, he had experienced a fair amount of luxury, but this took things to another level. Had he not known he was in a speeding airship, he could have believed he was seated in a state-of-the-art virtual reality studio. Mark lay back in his chair with his seat belt fastened tightly as the plane was returning to Earth's atmosphere. He put on the barely perceptible lightweight glasses and flicked through the instant touch holographic buttons, which took him through various virtual and augmented realities. He settled on the roofless floating spherical object, initially circling over San Francisco Bay and then switching to the Himalayas.

Everything was impeccable. Every detail was a jewel of design. Every surface, every fabric was just right. The aesthetics were allied to functionality. Nothing in these virtual and augmented realities was there just for the sake of beauty. Instead, the soothing curves and noble materials brought to life by master design were a key part of just how pleasant and efficient everything was to use.

He took off the glasses to examine the airship's interior. Mark adjusted his position in the generously padded chair and stroked the smooth, polished leather surface of the armrest panel. All at once, sitting in luxury, he realized how grimy and sweaty he must be. On entering this airborne bedroom-cum-office-cum-meeting venue, he had been shown a button with which he could summon a flight attendant. Mark's finger hovered an instant over the button, then, with resolution, pressed it.

Thirty seconds later, the crewmember who had shown him to his seat spoke into the room on some kind of surround sound intercom. "Yes, Sir," he enquired with just the right mixture of deference and solicitude.

"I was wondering," Mark answered, "if I could freshen up somewhere."

"Certainly, Sir," the attendant replied. And then the small shower room opened. "Please remain in your seat until we re-enter Earth's atmosphere."

"Great. Thanks." Mark hesitated, then added, "And maybe a change of clothes? I really need to get out of the ones I'm wearing."

"I'm afraid that might be a little trickier, sir. You see, the only clothes we could offer you are those belonging to Mr. Fisher. I am sure I could phone Mr. Fisher to see if you could wear his clothes, and I am equally sure that he would not mind, but I am even more certain that you and he are not nearly the same size."

"Mr Fisher?" said Mark.

"The President's partner, First Gentleman Ari Fisher," came the reply.

"Of course, of course," said Mark. This seemed like a hurriedly scheduled journey. How could they possibly have arranged clothing for him? When SpaceForce One re-entered the atmosphere, the attendant knocked on the door.

"Yes?" said Mark, as he opened the door.

"Mr. Wells," the crewmember continued, "I talked to the captain about clothing, and he told me that once in Washington, you will be taken to a hotel where new clothes are already in your room. The captain called ahead earlier to confirm arrangements when we land."

"That's great; thank you so much."

The multi-jet high-pressure shower with touch-sensitive temperature control was almost enough to make him forget the chronic water shortages that most of humanity was facing.

His sheer pleasure at standing under a stream of warm, refreshing water lasted a minute. Then, the flow of water ceased. That was the cycle time. He thought about using it for another minute but, admonishing himself for considering using more than he needed, quickly got out of the shower.

He had no desire to climb straight back into the dusty, sweaty clothes he had worn when boarding. On the back of the effortlessly sliding door, he found a man's white bathrobe. Mark slipped it on and could not resist burying his nose in one of its fluffy, clean-smelling sleeves. He took a pair of matching open-toed slip-ons from under the sink and ambled back to his seat like a visitor at a seaside spa resort.

He spent the rest of the flight gazing out of the porthole and channel-hopping on the TV. He settled on the AI Film channel where he could create his own story, with his favorite Hollywood actors playing the characters. He chose Nathan Cruise, grandson of the legendary Tom Cruise, to play the hero saving giant underground carbon capture plants from destruction. He slipped into restless sleep for a while, then woke with a start when the flight attendant returned with food: a bed of scallops and tiger prawns. Mark ordered a glass of La Cuadrilla from Santa Barbara. He didn't care much that the wine didn't match the food. To his surprise, they already knew all about his favorite wines, and all of them were on board. This is how AI-augmented supply chains had become the norm. In a sign of how acclimated he had become to the region he had just left, he found himself thinking that some kocho would be a great addition to the meal.

Before the attendant left, Mark asked about the high-tech shower he had recently experienced. "Pardon the question if this isn't your expertise; the shower I used was very refreshing but used very little water. Is that correct?"

"I've had the chance to learn quite a lot about this spaceship, sir, and you are correct," the young man replied. "The showers use a low water output technology that maximizes the utility of every ounce of water used on the plane. It is by-product of the technology used to provide just enough water for crops."

"I thought so. We have introduced something similar in our pipeline system so that each country gets a precise amount of water. I hope this journey is fruitful as I should really be in Ethiopia right now."

"I hope so, sir," the attendant said.

As SpaceForce One prepared to land, the noise grew much louder. He knew this was caused by the switch from non-fossil fuel to fossil fuel for the extra energy required during takeoff and landing. The plane approached the runway at Morningside horizontally rather than vertically, as that method of landing used much more fuel and because the standard landing approach was many decibels less noisy. Mark had exchanged reassuring text messages with both Aida and Tom all through the flight. Then, he had reluctantly swapped the cozy bathrobe for his own clammy clothes.

After landing, when the space jet's main door opened, the heat felt as though Mark was still in Ethiopia. As he left the plane, Mark let out a startled sound. "What the hell is that thing?"

"I am IAWP; Identity Authentication Without Passport."

The attendant stepped forward: "I am sorry, Mr Wells. We have become used to the drone verifying identity as we board or leave SpaceForce One. It's the same at the White House and other government buildings now."

"Identity Mark Wells confirmed. Please place your fingers and thumbs on the console and look straight ahead. Welcome home, sir." With that, the drone moved away from the door.

"Now, you never need to have your passport at a US airport, Mr. Wells," said the attendant, seemingly impressed with himself at delivering this news. "Your iris, fingerprints, and photo mean that you can move freely within Japan, Canada, and the United States."

At the foot of SpaceForce One's steps was a huge, black Hummer. Its rear passenger door was open, and next to it stood a man of refrigerator-like stature dressed in a black suit. The man remained silent and immobile as Mark luxuriated in the feeling of being back on American soil. Another White House staff member of slimmer build, with a similar suit, perhaps a couple of shades lighter, stepped forward with right hand outstretched. He was visibly sweating, as was the silent man, Mark, and everyone else at the landing site.

"Mr. Wells," the man said with a brisk handshake. "Welcome, sir. My name's Hancock. Let's get you to your hotel. I hope you had a good flight?"

"A little…" Mark searched for the right word. "…it was a little odd. A real experience. But yes, I did, thank you."

Mark looked down. "Regarding clothes…" he said.

"Of course," Hancock said, suppressing a smile. "It's just a short drive to your hotel and a closet with plenty of clothing for you to choose from."

Mark walked the forty feet or so to the hunk of metal with tinted glass. When they reached the Hummer, Hancock turned and gestured towards the very tall man in the suit. "This is Special Agent Gortsky, Mr. Wells. Not that you are in any sort of danger, but his job is to keep you safe."

"I don't get it, Mr. Hancock. Why do I need a security guard if I'm not in danger?" Mark asked, careful to adopt the same ultra-polite tone as the White House functionary.

"Any guest of the President must have a security detail, Mr. Wells. Your safety is Gortsky's concern. He'll be in the room down the hall from yours at the hotel and will accompany you anytime you leave the building."

"A sort of bodyguard."

"Definitely a sort of bodyguard," Hancock replied with a smile. "Any guest of the President has needed a security detail since 2026. Or they provide their own security. You might remember the awful incident in 2025 where a schoolteacher who was invited to the White House to see the president was murdered by a relative of hers an hour before she was due to arrive. It caused negative publicity for the then President, and we don't take any chances now."

"I suppose you don't need a security detail after seeing the President. Being murdered afterward doesn't create the same news headlines." Mark seemed to be the only person impressed by his wit.

"There is no security detail after your business with the President is concluded," replied Hancock.

Mark nodded as an acknowledgment that security was important. Moments later, Hancock raised his hand to his ear and, after a moment, said, "If you follow me, sir, we are ready to leave."

On the drive to the Conrad Hotel on New York Avenue, Gortsky was the prototypical secret service agent. Even though the car was self-driving, not a word passed his lips. His eyes projected intensity and vigilance. He sat straight-backed and attentive in his seat. Next to him, Mark looked out the window: *Air-conditioned driverless electric cars, so many drones of multiple sizes, some of them single-person taxis.* While he did so, Hancock filled him in on the program. Two or three times, Mark said, "Sorry, Mr. Hancock, could you repeat that?"

"I imagine, Mr. Wells, that you're tired and need a little time to rest. As mentioned previously, new clothes are in the closet at the hotel, and if there's anything you need, just let us know. The President has asked that we send a car for you in two hours."

"I will be ready, Mr. Hancock," Mark answered.

"Good. Well, here we are. I'll leave you with Gortsky, but we'll no doubt run into each other again. Pleasure meeting you, sir."

The Conrad's design, Mark thought, had been conceived almost as work of art. The interior atrium was high, with a folded well of light with a honeycomb of circular windows on its roof. Marble floors, sweeping curved walls, and minimalist spaces dotted with discrete armchairs equipped with holographic computers emphasized the message of space and modernity. The physical design did as much to keep the place cool as the actual air conditioning.

Mark walked over to the reception. As they progressed across the wide expanse of floor, Gortsky was so discreet that he hardly noticed the agent. When they arrived at the desk, Mark introduced himself.

"The name's Wells," Mark said to the woman behind the desk. "I've, well, I've been—"

"Good afternoon. Sir. Say no more, Mr. Wells," the receptionist interrupted with a polite smile. "We're expecting you. This sort of thing happens quite often at the Conrad. We're close to the White House."

Mark wondered whether the last statement was a comment on the hotel's physical proximity or some set of shared values when the woman asked him to gaze into the iris verification system at the counter. Once this had been done and a discreet buzzer had rung, verifying his identity, she handed him a card. "You're in room 820, Mr. Wells. Your swipe card to access the room is now on your phone. If you need anything, please don't hesitate to call reception."

Mark thanked her, and she began checking in Gortsky. Her smile and friendly demeanor remained constant as she dealt with the stoic agent. Mark wondered if she ever got tired of having to be so friendly all the time, but figured if that were the case, she probably wouldn't have taken the job. Gortsky thanked her and took his room card from the woman. Although not obliged to do so, Mark waited for Gortsky. The two men started to head for the elevators, but after just a few steps, the receptionist called out to him.

"Mr. Wells, I almost forgot; I have a message for you."

Mark stopped and turned back to face the desk, but instead of giving him the message while he stood there, the woman motioned for him to approach again. Gortsky remained where he was while Mark walked back to the desk.

"Sorry, sir. I didn't want to shout across the lobby. It's your wife, Mr. Wells."

"My wife?" Mark asked. "There's nothing wrong, is there?"

"No, Sir, well, I don't think so," the woman said, still smiling. "It's just that she wondered whether you'd be free a little later."

"Er, yes, I suppose so," Mark said, unsure what all this meant. "Did she leave a number?"

"602, Sir."

"Okay," Mark said, looking puzzled. "What sort of number is that? Did she say where she was? At the office, at home?"

The woman let out a fake peal of laughter. "No, Mr. Wells, you misunderstand. It's not a phone number. She's in Room 602 here at the Conrad and wanted you to know she'd be free anytime today."

CHAPTER 4

A large group of people were gathered on the White House lawn in the late evening when it was cooler.

"And this is a picture I drew of you for the whole class. And I'm going to give it to you. It's a present because you are a...an... inspiration...er, Madam President."

The president bent down and took the painting from the six-year-old girl. It was a bright splash of color, with a huge yellow sun dominating the scene. Below it was Christine Poulter in a scarlet red trouser suit with exaggerated blondness covering her thinly lined short hair.

Having done her duty, the little girl stood there gaping at the country's leader. Christine Poulter thanked her and asked her name, how old she was, and if she liked school. All the usual questions presidents run through when faced with children. The girl answered in monosyllables, then awkwardly looked behind her for help. Cameras clicked, TV crews filmed, and reporters scribbled. Finally, a teacher stepped forward with a knowing smile at the president and, taking the girl by the shoulders, led her back into the gaggle of schoolchildren assembled nearby.

With the public relations exercise now over, children and teachers were ushered out of the grounds with the media in tow. The president waved to them as they left, a true politician's smile on her face. As the doors closed, the smile evaporated, and she looked down at the picture she still held in her hands. She walked swiftly into the Oval Office.

Several people were in the room, including Deputy National Security Adviser Temir Bousson. The Chief of Staff was trying to organize the room.

"Now," President Poulter said, "Let's get down to it. Brian, Rachel, …Mark Wells will be here in a few minutes. You have read the report. I want Ari along with us, too. We need three things from Wells. First, how was he so accurate with where these SMMs would occur, including getting the timing right? Second, what else is to come? And third, what can be done in the short term?"

"Yes, Madam President," the two aides answered in chorus.

The President continued, "Let me set the scene. In the spirit of bipartisanship, I have asked Republican and Democrat leadership in Congress and the Senate, the National Security Adviser, the Deputy National Security Adviser, and the Vice President to attend. The Secretary of State is in Uganda and will be Zooming in."

"Madam President," said Donald Crest, the Chief of Staff. "I didn't know the Democrats were coming. It is an open secret that they will use any excuse to impeach you in revenge for what the Republicans did to the Democrat President. Everything you say in that meeting will get leaked. Including that your partner Ari will be in the room."

"Precisely," she said, without explaining further. "Okay, let's do this. I need to clear the office now."

While President Poulter, her partner Ari Fisher, and the two aides remained in the room, as they had been instructed to, the rest of the staff began filing out in a murmur of conversation. However, one person hung back. Temir stood still as he watched his colleagues go.

President Poulter had turned her back on the departing staff and was already in deep discussion with Ari and the aides. As the last person to leave the room closed the doors, the president still did not notice Temir standing in the center of the Oval Office. He moved uncomfortably from one foot to the other and waited. After a few long seconds, he took the initiative and coughed.

The president looked around and raised her eyebrows with surprise. She and Ari exchanged quizzical glances before the president asked, "Was there something else, Temir?"

"Yes, Madam President," Temir replied, "Might I have a word?"

The president turned to Ari once more. Ari shrugged. Poulter turned back to Temir and looked into his eyes for a few seconds. Temir pulled his collar away from his neck as if to signal that the silence was oppressive. Then she let out her breath, waved her hand as if chasing off some invisible foe, and addressed the two aides. "Okay, tell me."

"The report."

"The Spontaneous Mass Migration report," Poulter said, as though trying to hurry Temir along.

"There are significant national security issues. The Russians…," said Temir.

"I know, that's one of the reasons I got Wells out of Ethiopia. To get him to safety. He is a treasure of information to them. What is the issue?"

"The security issues, the possible advantages Wells' report and thinking give us, may outweigh the climate change issues…"

"What? How?"

"Let me restate that. We don't have specific intelligence to this effect yet, but the Russians' purpose in trying to abduct Wells was likely to weaponize climate change to undermine our national security. Not to understand climate change impacts for themselves."

"Why are you telling me this now?"

"We have to be careful about what we tell Wells and what we commit to in terms of American aid," Temir said. "It could be used against us."

Christine Poulter said nothing for a moment. She sat perfectly still. Behind her, Ari was busy on his forearm-embedded phone. Had Temir worked out what she was doing?

"Okay, we will be cautious about what we commit to."

"Thank you, Madam President."

"Get Rachel and Brian back in here," Poulter said into the mobile console. Poulter looked up as Rachel and Brian walked into the Oval Office. "Could you just give me a few minutes with Ari, please?" she said to her aides. "Why don't you both get to the meeting and take Temir with you? He will brief you on national security issues we need to be aware of."

Rachel said, "Madam President, are we rowing back on our climate change investment effort?"

"No, but we won't include Wells in the most classified national security discussions."

"Madam President..." Rachel said, realizing that her tone of voice sounded like pleading. "Of course, Madam President."

The aides nodded in unison and left the Oval Office with Temir. Ari and President Poulter watched them go and then turned to face the window that looked out onto the neat hedges and high trees of the White House grounds.

Beyond the greenery, police were holding back a glut of protesters. Some were chanting for more action on the climate; some were screaming that the climate should be left alone. Others were marching on behalf of the hundreds of thousands heading for the US-Mexico border, trying to sway the president to open the border to the US and avert a human tragedy. Others still were protesting against more South Americans crossing into the US, voicing their anger about the open border. On the fringes of the crowd, pro- and anti-abortion activists were struggling to make their voices heard amongst activists for and against gun control, for and against nuclear weapons, and for and against the president.

"Not a pretty picture, is it?" Ari said

"I don't get it. Economically speaking, we have moved way ahead of China. Europe is stagnating, but we seem to have so many problems. But it's the picture we've got, I suppose," replied the president.

"So, what was all that with Temir?"

"I don't know, to be honest," Christine Poulter said. "He has this ability to bring confusion to clarity. He is difficult to figure out."

"What do you mean?"

"Well, his point about national security means we cannot share too much information with Wells...maybe Temir has figured out what I am trying to do. But how could he? And why would he care if I am trying to bring centrist Democrats and Republicans into a new alignment to deal with climate change? He is the Deputy National Security Adviser, not the Republican Party Chair."

"It is puzzling."

"Something about this doesn't sit well with me, but I can't put my finger on it."

"You are doing nothing different, certainly at the moment. It feels like a coincidence. I have not seen him act differently myself, but I don't spend much time with either of them. Let me ask you a question. What is the worst that could happen here?" asked Ari.

"Nothing. I don't think he would deliberately undermine me. Actually, he couldn't undermine me. There are so many people in the room that someone is going to leak something anyway. And I want a leak to happen, which is why I have so many people in the same room. I want the American public to start feeling comfortable with the idea that we are talking to everybody to solve these SMM crises. We need to get past the polarization we've had for so long now, otherwise we are not going to be able to deal with climate change. But it has to be an organic approach, not directly explained via someone in the administration talking to the media. I want it to be observed and reported on."

There was a period of silence as they both considered what had just been said. The President felt that articulating her thinking had given her internal clarity. The conversation with Ari had been useful, as usual. And no one else had been present to observe how her mind worked. "Let's get to the meeting," she said, her confidence in her plan bolstered. "Wells will be here shortly."

The Hummer carrying Gortsky and Mark Wells drove along New York Avenue NW in the direction of the White House. Gortsky said nothing during the journey. That suited Mark. He needed quiet to compose himself and organize his thoughts.

He wondered if he should review the report on SMM. Where earlier he had been enmeshed in his own emotions, he was now, just thirty minutes later, excited and eager. Without thinking, he took out his phone and tried Aida once more. The ringtone began.

Just as Mark prepared himself to listen again to the recorded message, Aida's drowsy voice came into his ear: "Mark, I am very tired and don't have the energy to talk. Is everything okay?"

"Aida!" Mark almost shouted, no doubt with too much enthusiasm for the woman half-asleep in southwest Ethiopia. "It's so good to hear your voice. I know you must be so tired, and this is a totally selfish call. I had to talk to you. Just to hear your voice. I'm sorry. I did try to get through to you earlier."

"I know," came back the fuzzy reply, "I was very busy at the hospital. Late nights....as you know."

"How late?"

"We are supposed to close earlier, but how can we tell people to come back tomorrow?"

"And your uncle?"

"Jemal and those other men have not returned," Aida said in the staccato voice Mark already missed so much. "He is troubled. I have never seen him with those men before. He has got himself mixed up with some unsavory people, it seems."

"God, I wish I was there with you," Mark said in a half-whisper. Gortsky showed no sign of having heard or taking any interest in the conversation.

"How is it going?"

"I still feel bad about leaving without saying goodbye."

"I know you do, but you told me that on the plane. Please don't worry. How is it going? What is going on? What does the President want?"

"I'll be able to answer that later. I'm on my way to the White House now."

"I have faith in you."

"I love you, Aida," Mark said, cupping his hand around his mouth as he spoke.

"I love you too," came back the voice from over 7000 miles away.

"We're getting near the White House; I'd better hang up," Mark said, suddenly feeling awkward speaking to Aida in front of Gortsky. "I'm in a luxury car built like a tank. I even have a bodyguard. It's obscene. I'll have to tell you about the presidential jet next time. And the hotel."

"I am tired…I know it's only 9:00 p.m. but I am exhausted," Aida said without energy.

"Sure, sure. Listen, I'll call you back tomorrow and let you know how it went. Get some sleep. I love you."

"Good night," Aida said before hanging up.

Gortsky gave Mark a nudge and lowered the electric windows on both sides of the Hummer. They were at the entrance to the White House, and the security drone was already hovering at the level of Gortsky's head, ready to carry out the facial recognition process. Mark watched as the machine emitted its white beam across the agent's features. Ten seconds later, the drone flashed a green light to confirm Gortsky's identity. It then disappeared from view above the car before reappearing on Mark's side. Again, the beam flashed; a few seconds passed, and the green light lit up once more.

The driver edged forward and parked the Hummer in a short tunnel-like shelter that covered its entire length. A full-length scanner on wheels ran along the car forward, then backward. Another larger green light lit up: the car was clean. Mark was cleared to enter the White House.

Mark was ushered on his own into the West Wing lobby of the White House to wait. This was the only time that Mark was not in view of Gortsky. He sat down on one of the blue, straight-backed couches. Behind him hung a reproduction of Leutze's *Washington Crossing the Delaware*: another president facing an obstacle.

Thankfully, he did not have to wait long. After just a few minutes, he was shown into the Roosevelt Room, where the meeting would take place. As the aide turned the doorknob, Mark took a deep breath.

During his time with the first Macmillan administration in 2029, he had never been in the room he was now entering. To his surprise, it was somewhat of a disappointment. Like the lobby he had just left, the Roosevelt Room had a relatively low ceiling and a lack of light, making it a little dark. Here in 2037, the room looked as though it had seen better days. What was impressive, though, were the fifteen or so people gathered around the 16-foot black cherry conference table.

At the head of the table sat the president. Among those around the table were Ari, Temir, the two aides who had been in the Oval Office, Lorraine Betts, and members of the Republican and Democrat Congressional leadership. Surely, Mark thought, leaders from Congress are invited only when a policy is close to being decided? Are they part of the policy-making group now? It was confusing to him. Over the next few hours, it would become clear who among them was prepared to listen to Mark's arguments and who had already pinned the label of foe on him.

As Mark entered, the president stood up. "Mr. Wells," she said. "Glad you could join us. Please come in and sit down."

While she spoke, she approached the door so that she was able to shake Mark's hand before he slipped into the only vacant seat. All eyes were on him for a moment. The president returned to her place and remained standing.

"Ladies and gentlemen, thank you for attending this meeting on such short notice. We face an unparalleled situation as we attempt to address a number of crises all over the world. We know what they are, so I won't waste time describing them again. And let us be honest. We did not see this coming. Well, that is not quite right. Mark Wells authored a report in 2029, which until yesterday, I had never seen. And if it had not been leaked, perhaps I would never have seen it."

"A group of extraordinary people authored the report, Madam President," interjected Mark. "It was not just me."

Unruffled by the interruption, the President nodded to indicate she had heard him and continued, "As you see, Mark is here today. The report that he helped to author predicted spontaneous mass migrations in general and, specifically, in nearly all the places where we see it happening now. It's not just these crises that we are fighting. We are also up against terror groups using the movement of desperate people to further their anti-American objectives. And there is a tremendous amount of disinformation or fake news out there, for example about how we buy up and hoard water supplies or drain wells for our own purposes. This means that…well, let's not kid ourselves… whatever we do, there will be many who question our motives or don't believe us."

After a brief silence, she continued, "I have invited all of you here so that we can find out from Mark firsthand what is happening and what we can do about it. Without any spin. Together. All of us. Republican and Democrat."

President Poulter left it at that without explaining what she meant by 'together.' She continued, "Many of us may not agree with Mark's views, but his credentials, his report, his work in Ethiopia and with the Ugandan and Kenyan leaders make him amply qualified to aid our reflection on what is a subject of the utmost importance. Mr. Wells has been good enough to fly in from Ethiopia—"

"On the presidential space jet," said one of the Democrats disapprovingly.

"Indeed, on the presidential space jet," the president resumed, with a nod and a polite smile in the direction of the man who had interrupted her. "SpaceForce One is the only way to get Mr. Wells in time for this meeting. In Ethiopia, Mr. Wells is working on a water infrastructure project that could offer a partial solution to the dire water issues the region faces. His work in Africa is a direct result of his research of almost a decade ago, which pointed with remarkable accuracy to what we are experiencing today. I would like to ask him to give us an overview of the context of these mass migrations and what we can expect in the coming weeks months, and years, and what we can do about it. Mr. Wells." The president motioned to Mark and took her seat.

Clearing his throat, Mark looked around the table, then began addressing the assembled leaders and staffers in a measured tone.

"Firstly, Madam President, I'd like to thank you for the invitation. As you said, I have been in Ethiopia for months, and we are nearing a situation where at least some water can flow within this region. The leaders of several countries in that region have seen the wisdom of working together to share water resources, knowing that anything less will result in semi-permanent war. Let me say first that this is not just about water pipelines. That is one partial solution for one part of Ethiopia and East Africa. There will be different solutions in different parts of the world. There will be different ways to move water. To grow food. But if we do not move water where people need it at certain times of the year, people will continue to move. In my estimation, and I have talked this through with several colleagues, the next large-scale spontaneous mass migration will happen in Spain as people move toward France. That's what our model predicts. I can give you direct access to our supercomputer if you like. There is already a trickle from Spain, but tens of thousands are likely to join.

"Let me turn to the word *spontaneous*. As we said in our report, and as I will say now, at some point, the movement of people ceases to become spontaneous. It becomes semi-spontaneous and even planned. Planned because information and disinformation are easily accessible now. Planned by people with different motives. By terrorists, by extremist groups, by anti-capitalists, by anti-left and anti-right groups, by nations, by non-state actors, and even our secret services may adopt the technique. Without some type of adaptive action, it very quickly becomes unmanageable. This disinformation at scale becomes possible through the almost limitless social media platforms. So again, this is not about water pipelines just because that is what I am working on in a particular geography. This is about thinking about water differently. Or thinking about how we manage and distribute it differently. To do this properly will be costly. Beyond the means of all but a handful of the wealthiest nations."

Mark paused for a few seconds, surveying the room. All eyes were on him, whatever they thought of the points he was making.

"There are more obvious high-tech solutions," he continued, "which will be useful in California and other parts of the developed world so that we use only the level of water needed and no more, and only the crops that are most drought resistant. But again, that's delving into the details. The principle here is that we need to move water to places where the local population may otherwise move away. Overall, in terms of how water is managed, I recommend that we do two things: first, the United States guarantees that every human on the planet has the right to a minimum supply of water every day. We believe that the minimal guarantee is 15 liters. We are not saying that there should be a maximum. Most of us in the US will use more than 250 liters of water daily. The second thing is that we need to de-commoditize water."

"Hold it! Hold it right there!" The interjection came from one of the Republicans, Senator Clark, sitting opposite Mark. "I thought we were here to gain information. We don't want his opinion." The senator turned to face the President as he spoke. "We just want facts." Turning back to Mark, "Why doesn't Mr. Wells just hand over the supercomputer so we can do our planning?"

"I am going to ask that we let Mr. Wells finish," said the President, taking control of the situation. "I am under no illusions that we don't have our differences on this topic, but there will be plenty of time for everyone to express their views. But we should direct our questions to Mr. Wells; he is the subject matter expert."

After mumblings of agreement greeted the president's words, she turned again to Mark. "Now, Mr. Wells, before you continue, I have a question for you."

"Of course, Madam President."

"I can't remember the exact date, but didn't the United Nations some twenty or thirty years ago already agree on a resolution that every human on the planet should have the right to 15 liters of clean, safe water a day, at a minimum, for cleaning, sanitation, cooking, drinking, etc.?"

"That's right, Madam President. It was thirty-five years ago, almost to the day, back in 2002, that the UN passed such a resolution. But that is not the same as a guarantee. That modest goal, which is well below what is needed for basic human dignity, has not come to pass. A guarantee of financial backing from the wealthier nations and a technology transfer would make it closer to reality. In the meantime, what has happened is the opposite. Many investors, realizing that water scarcity is the basis for a lucrative opportunity, have invested in water and related products, particularly in the US. That makes it harder to achieve the goal of 15 liters per day for every human. And it makes any technology transfer impossible. If we, the United States, take the initiative, we will create a reason for people not to move. Whether it is Mexico, Spain or Ethiopia."

"Okay, I cannot pretend to understand the connection completely," the President said, "but I see your reasoning. Of course, everyone should have access to a minimum amount of water. Please continue with what you were saying."

In truth, the president did understand what Mark was saying but instinctively felt that this was not the moment to play her hand. There would be different views around the table, and some of those would be vehemently opposed to Mark's assertion.

Mark continued where he had left off. "Thank you, Madam President. In these past weeks, my worst fears have been realized. Today, we are seeing what our report of 2030, seven years ago, warned us would happen. A lack of water and food linked to acute temperatures, mainly in the summer months, is driving large populations to leave their homes in search of basic resources.

"Until a few months ago, you may not have been familiar with the term 'spontaneous mass migration,' but today, it is probably the most used phrase on the planet. The sheer weight of the numbers involved means that SMMs are almost impossible to stop once they start. This is what we have seen in China, Central America, the US border, and Southern Europe. It is possible even here in the USA, especially after five years of crippling drought in the desert southwest. It seems that SMMs will be here as long as a chronic lack of water is felt in certain regions. As we have not managed to reverse climate change and the crippling droughts that have accompanied it around the globe, we, therefore, need to address how to better share the water we have and use it more sensibly. That's what I can tell you," Mark concluded.

A short silence followed as those present considered what Mark had said.

"Madam President," began Senator Clark, breaking the silence, "This is socialism. Communism. That system failed. We beat it. Several times over. We beat the Soviets decades ago. And when everyone was telling us that China would overtake us, it was American ingenuity in creating the bitcoin reserve that took us ahead of them...probably for the next thousand years. De-commoditize water. A free technology transfer. Who will pay for that?"

49

The Democratic Speaker of the House gently chimed in, "Let's just explore everything for a little while longer. There is no danger of us becoming a communist country, so let's just talk and get everything on the table."

"With all due respect to Mr. Wells, Madam President." Everyone turned to look at the woman speaking. Besides her position as special assistant to the Secretary of Defense, Gretchen Dann also had experience with climate war games, which merited her inclusion in this meeting. "For years, we have been trying to stop temperatures from rising, and nothing has made any difference. What does this show? That the world is getting hotter whatever we try.

"Whether or not it is a natural trend is almost irrelevant in this context. It's not what we want, but we have failed to stop it. Governments have failed to come to any international agreement. Perhaps, if they had succeeded, it would have made a difference. Perhaps it would not have. I don't know. There is nothing we or anyone else can do about it now, and it's going to get worse. That may sound heartless, but in such a situation, I don't know that anything can be done. To be brutally frank, with the climate changing as rapidly as it is, people will die. The issue today is how the United States can protect itself from the collapse of large parts of the world."

"That sounds like a compelling point, Ms. Dann," the President said. "Mr. Wells, your response?"

"What Ms. Dann is saying is that we should oversee the permanent state of conflict that the mass movement of people leads to. Conflict in the USA as much as anywhere. But if we need people to stay put, we must give them a reason to stay put. We cannot have a situation where millions of people do not have water while large numbers can invest in water. The people of Arizona, Texas, and New Mexico are in every bit as much danger as the rest. That is not socialist. That's just basic humanity. I'm not trying to stir up trouble for us nor bring socialism in the back door. Make your returns from investing in gold or crypto, or anything else. Make as much as you want. I could not care less. But water? Who will we trade with or sell our goods to if they don't have enough water?"

Mark did continue to make his points rather than wait for anyone to answer. "All I'm trying to do is point out what we have to deal with. If we don't find ways to move water, we will have millions moving around the world. There will not be an economy that can survive this. Millions will march, walk, and move to where they perceive the water. They will probably get it wrong, and many won't be able to cross the national borders they reach, but the damage will be done; the conflicts have started, and it will be difficult to put out the fires. Besides, we are already seeing evidence of massive disinformation on social media that authorities are lying, that there is plenty of water in the USA."

He turned to Gretchen. "The policy option of doing nothing leads to spontaneous conflicts in border regions and even within countries. Not only does that not protect America, but it also destroys America's economy."

"That misinterprets what I said—" Gretchen replied.

Talking over her, Mark continued, "… or we can adapt and make it preferable for people not to move like the East African countries are trying to do. Look, we are not going to be solve this problem completely; people will die regardless of what we do. But this buys us time to figure out what else we might do."

While he felt strongly that his point was valid, Mark instantly regretted talking over Ms. Dann to make it. *I shouldn't have been so dismissive of her opinion. My fatigue is taking a toll. I need to build consensus. If the opportunity arises, I need to show her I value her opinion, even if I disagree with it.*

"Mr. Wells," said Ari, above the increasing chatter among the group, "for argument's sake, let's say that we choose this adaptation. I know you have mentioned this already, but we may have lost the essence of it, so it is worth repeating—what could be done concretely and right now?"

"As I said earlier, in the very short term, there must be a concerted effort to get water to the people who are involved in these SMMs. If we can bring them water, we can at least slow down population movement. And simultaneously use social media to make the consequences of moving far worse from the point of view of receiving water rather than staying put. Moving water will require different solutions for different areas. We can work on that. Most importantly, we also need quick examples of some kind of success, like in Ethiopia, where we are so close to getting water moving over long distances during the dry, hot months. Examples of success will give policymakers and the public hope. In the meantime, we send a signal that access to water is enshrined in the United Nations charter as a basic human right. As I said earlier, 15 liters of water is needed for every human to be alive every day. And the United States makes this commitment, not just the UN. Finally, later on, a coordinated massive investment across the world. We're still talking years, rather than months, to do this, and the diplomatic bargaining behind the scenes would be difficult."

Mark turned to Ms. Dann as he spoke, noticing she still looked unconvinced. "Ms. Dann, I want to apologize for cutting you off earlier. I just wanted to make sure the point I was making was understood. I really am sorry."

Gretchen accepted his apology graciously, and Mark continued. "Perhaps we could think about this situation as analogous to the aftermath of the Second World War. We invested massively in Japan and Europe, essentially to stop them from turning communist. It worked, and it aided our economy. We need to lead the investment similarly in this case, however difficult it will be to deal with Russia, China, India and Europe."

A hand gently rose three chairs from the president as though to provide a dramatic introduction to comments that would follow. It belonged to the Poulter administration's National Security Adviser, Lorraine Betts.

"If I may," she said, hand slowly falling to the table, "I'd like to add a little pragmatism to the debate."

"Go ahead, Lorraine," said the President.

"Thank you, Madam President. I like to think I'm an open-minded person, but we must accept that we live in a competitive and untrustworthy world. For how long has the US propped up countries that needed help? When we invested in Europe and Japan, we got something in return. However, most of the time we have invested in other countries, we have become hated as a reward."

"But we went about things the wrong way." Mark didn't really mean to put it that way, but he couldn't seem to express his meaning in a better way at that moment. Normally, he thought of himself as a quick thinker, but he was exhausted, and that, combined with frustration, could cause such mistakes. *If I can't get a hold of myself and avoid this type of verbal clumsiness, I'm going to lose this argument, and thousands, millions of people will suffer as a result.*

"We went about things the wrong way," the National Security Adviser repeated slowly for emphasis.

Mark apologized for his choice of words, mentioning how tired he was. Just as he was saying the words "SpaceForce One journey," he knew he should stop but somehow couldn't keep himself from continuing to talk.

"I'm just trying to say that the investment that we need to make protects us from people at our borders and protects our economy from catastrophic instability." He was seriously unimpressed with himself at this moment, but at least this was a succinct statement of what his plan could accomplish. Hopefully, it would be enough to turn things around in his favor.

"I think this makes sense. And we can attach conditions to our investment," said Rachel, one of the two aides the president had briefed before the meeting. "Since the SMM report was leaked, Mr Wells seems to have a huge following, not only here in the US, but all over the world. There seems to be public appetite for what he is proposing. He has become a hero figure to so many in our country."

"Our self-interest is about achieving a fair distribution of water, and that will involve a technology transfer," Mark continued, essentially making the same point but using slightly different words. "We should do this not because we want favors from other countries but because our economy, like all others, is predicated on stability in much of the world. There is no stability when large, unprecedented numbers of people move in such a short period of time. It's not so much about helping others, although it will do that, as much as it is about helping ourselves."

The National Security Adviser spoke again, once more very calmly, but this time without raising her hand. "Madam President, as sincere as I believe Mr. Wells to be, there is no sense in what he is saying. We know that SMMs are now being secretly encouraged by malevolent state and non-state actors through various social media channels. We know there is an oversupply of water in Canada and Northern Europe. Perhaps getting water to these places was a good idea before SMMs started. But this is now going to play out no matter what we do. We have to let it play out. We can work through the scenarios, but it is too late to prevent them."

The National Security Adviser spoke with such calm expertise, like Ms. Dann, but with additional authority and gravitas, that Mark found himself impressed, even though he disagreed with her.

"Well," said Christine Poulter after a moment, "this has been a good discussion. I suggest we take a break now. Thank you all for attending. Now, I need to take care of something. Rachel, Brian, come with me please."

As everyone filed out of the room, Temir was grateful that Lorraine Betts had put in some strong counterarguments. His boss had essentially done Temir's work for him. Otherwise, Mark Wells had sounded very convincing. He was clearly not some type of anti-American socialist.

CHAPTER 5

"Did you get anything of use, Mendez?" asked Temir with a forlorn tone in his voice.

"I don't think so, although there was one incident," the private detective said. "One day, Carruthers left Guttenberg's mansion in Alexandria, Virginia, and made a series of turnbacks and maneuvers designed to rid him of any tail. Which is suspicious in itself. Luckily, I had flown a self-destructing miniature drone tracker on Carruthers' car the day before and was able to surreptitiously monitor him as he doubled back to the State Park abutting Guttenberg's country estate in Virginia. As it happened, I know the park well. While it would have been too risky to attempt to trail Carruthers throughout the park, once I saw the direction Guttenberg's assistant was taking, I guessed he was heading to a meeting spot on or near Bearskin Hill. A heavily wooded, slight incline in the middle of the park that would be a perfect place to meet without being observed.

"To avoid notice, I took the long way around, running until I was near enough to the spot. I had just made it to a vantage point opposite Lookout Hill when I saw Carruthers and a bearded man wearing a grey flannel shirt walking together down the hill. I snapped photographs while they had shaken hands and departed, each heading in a separate direction. Here are the photos. I don't know who this bearded guy is."

"Okay, I didn't really expect anything, to be honest," said Temir, taking the photos. "It will be worth seeing if I can find out who Carruthers was meeting from a retired FBI friend of mine. Were you spotted?" asked Temir, who now seemed a little worried.

"Not a chance. I followed the tracker drone, and I was careful. As it was pre-programmed, it moved a few miles from the car and then dissolved. There is no evidence that this thing ever even existed. This thing is smaller than a wasp and looks like a screw."

"Okay, thanks, Rob. Let's leave this now. I don't think it is going to give me anything, but I will run the photos through the FBI guy I know."

"Sure thing."

CHAPTER 6

The day after the meeting with Mark Wells and the President, Temir was in the lunchroom of the National Security Agency watching television coverage of a new SMM originating in Mexico. Drone footage revealed a massive throng of humanity headed to the US border from the driest areas of Mexico. Drought was not only affecting Africa, the Middle East, and Southern Europe; it had now spread its tentacles to South America. Temir wondered idly how long it would be before it reached even the more northerly climes of North America. As he was watching, the Director stopped beside him after finishing her lunch.

"President Poulter will not be happy about this," Lorraine said.

"Do you think it will help Wells make his case?" Temir asked.

"Well, he has quite the public following. He is getting wall-to-wall media coverage. So, it may. It's hard to tell with the President. She can play her cards close to her chest when she chooses. The Democrats hate her, or hate all of us more accurately, but this is the sort of thing they could get behind."

"Do you think she has something planned?"

"I think she's trying to formulate a plan."

Lorraine was as cautious as ever, Temir thought. She didn't like to speculate on people's intentions unless she had a great deal of confidence in her analysis.

"I suppose we'll learn more at the meeting tomorrow."

"Yes, we will. If you'll excuse me, I have a meeting with our CIA liaison. I'll read you in at our three o'clock."

Temir could guess what the meeting was about. This latest SMM appeared to be inspired, at least in part, by a massive

Russian disinformation campaign centered on the claim that the US was hoarding water, as well as Mexico opening its border to the south to allow easy movement of people to the US border. The intelligence appeared to suggest that the Chinese government was behind this, but there was no hard evidence. The Poulter Administration had cracked down on the utilization of social media sites for such purposes, but it was impossible to prevent these campaigns completely. Organizations with sizable funds at their disposal, such as the Russian FSB, could work through proxies to mobilize large numbers of accounts to parrot whatever propaganda they wanted to disseminate at any given time. Additionally, there was little that could be done to restrict Russian social media from propagating such disinformation. The CIA's sources could help provide context regarding the cyberattacks.

He would learn more when he met with Lorraine. Right now, he had something else on his mind. He was having difficulty reaching his daughter. While she could be slow to respond if she was out somewhere having fun, she always got back to him eventually—generally within a few hours of his call or text. But he had texted and called her last night, and she still hadn't gotten back to him. He dialed her number once again as the TV coverage shifted to a large protest outside the White House. The call went to voicemail, and he hung up. He had left a message the last time he called.

The protestors outside the White House held holographic signs with messages such as "Water rights are human rights," "Let them in," and "There is enough water for everyone." President Poulter had made it clear that restrictions on crossing the US border would not be relaxed for what the press referred to as "water refugees." This policy was supported by the American Glory groups and hated by others.

Temir was worried about Sara. She was at a critical point in her career, with pending applications to several top law schools. But she had seemed unfocused the last few times he had seen her.

It wasn't just the episode Guttenberg's cameras had captured. She had taken several trips to various places around the country and overseas in recent months. At first, he had thought she was traveling for pleasure with her girlfriends, but she had been evasive enough about what she was doing to arouse his suspicions. He had the resources at his disposal to find out what she was up to, but he had hesitated to use them—if she really was up to something, he wasn't sure he wanted anyone else to know.

Finally, he decided to take matters into his own hands and have her followed. He had used Mendez again to discover that she was involved with a protest group intent on changing the country's policies on various issues. Mendez would be discreet as he was Sara's uncle. The group was avowedly anti-capitalistic, which wasn't all that unusual these days, he supposed. Anyway, he was relieved it wasn't something more nefarious—dealing drugs or something like that, not that he believed she would do such a thing. She certainly didn't need money, considering how much she received from her mother and father.

He had found a way to get her to own up to what she was doing without revealing he had followed her. It had taken a concerted campaign of expressing worry about all these trips she was taking and then threatening to stop funding them and her, unless she told him what was going on. Eventually, she told him the truth. She had kept her protest activities secret because she was worried he wouldn't approve of her support of the anti-capitalist movement. In truth, he didn't, but he knew better than to tell her that. As long as she didn't do anything too crazy and jeopardize her law school admittance, he told her she could do what she wanted. However, he had advised her to avoid protests that might lead to her arrest, at least until after she had been accepted to law school, and she had seen the logic in his advice.

The protesters outside the White House had grown in number, and the White House security force, bolstered by the Capitol police, was hard-pressed to keep them in check. There didn't appear to be any violence at this time, but if the numbers swelled any further, he wasn't so sure that would hold true. As he watched the coverage of the Mexican SMM and the protests, for and against, at the border, Doug Rollins, the department's chief cybersecurity analyst, stopped beside him.

"These protestors never learn, do they?" Doug said.

"Never learn what?" Temir asked.

"That the more they protest something, the stronger the support becomes for whatever it is they are protesting."

Temir couldn't see the logic of what Rollins said. But given the source, he wasn't surprised by the sentiment. Doug had expressed support for some of the ideas of the American Glory movement in previous conversations, and this sentiment was congruent with their beliefs.

"Wait a second," Doug said excitedly. "Isn't that your daughter?"

Temir's attention had strayed from the television, but when he looked up at the screen, he saw, to his shock, that Doug was right. The protest at the border was getting chaotic, and there was Sara holding a sign saying, "Open the Border for Water Refugees!"

"No, that's not her. Not unless she can be in two places at once. She's on a trip to Kauai with her girlfriends," Temir said, thinking quickly. It was partially true—she had been there a week ago, and he had pictures of her on the beach to prove it. Luckily, the news channel they were watching cut from the White House protest to show the SMM refugee column continuing north.

"How would you know what Sara looks like, anyway?" he asked Doug.

"You brought her to the Christmas party a couple years back, Temir, don't you remember?" Doug answered, giving him a speculative look.

He was right about that, Temir realized. Diane couldn't make it, so he brought his daughter instead. "I did indeed. Well, that woman looked a bit like her, but I think I would recognize my own daughter, and that wasn't her."

Doug laughed and agreed. He recalled Temir saying she was considering attending law school after college.

"That's the plan," Temir answered, relieved to change the subject. "She's applied to several law schools and is waiting to hear back."

"Well, I wish her luck. My kids are a long way off from college, but with the amount of homework they're getting in elementary school, I'm hoping they'll be well prepared by the time they get there."

"Maybe I should have sent Sara to your kids' school. She might have got better grades and saved me some money by earning a scholarship or two to pay for college."

"I hear ya," Doug said, his mirth at the joke possibly tempered by the thought that he would eventually have to foot the bill for sending his children to college someday. "Well, time to get back to work before Lorraine catches us watching TV," Doug said. Temir and Doug shared a grin at the comment—the NSA Director was known for working long hours, and she expected the same of her subordinates.

Temir was worried about what he had just seen on the television as he walked back to his office. *At least I know where she is now.*

CHAPTER 7

Mark reclined in a stylish but comfortable sitting chair in his hotel room. The television was tuned to a news channel covering the latest SMM, a wave of people moving from the Mexican interior towards the border of the United States. He was stunned to learn that a new SMM of tens of thousands of Russians had marched across the ceasefire line at Sumy into Ukraine, heading to Kyiv, and simultaneously Russian troops mobilizing on the Belarus border. His model had not predicted this Russian SMM, and he doubted it was anything other than something orchestrated by President Pavlova herself. He ran the SMM program on his laptop, which projected a holographic image at his eye line. He moved the windows around, and there were no scenarios in which a Russian SMM to Ukraine would emerge. He was only half watching the action on his screen, which had now turned into a large protest outside the White House. The President's reluctance to open the border to the fleeing masses was doubtless designed to discourage any more such events. Still, it was viewed as inhumane by some picketing in front of the White House.

Still feeling the effects of his trip yesterday across multiple time zones, Mark closed his eyes to rest. Aside from the travel, the meeting with the President and assorted Washington power players had been grueling. After a half-hour break, the meeting continued, with Mark tasked with walking the assembled politicians and bureaucrats through various scenarios associated with the SMM phenomenon. He had found himself besieged with questions about his assumptions, his methodology, and even his political ideology. Despite the pressure, he felt he had done a decent job of staying on topic and delivering the message that doing nothing was not an option—at least not a good one.

Mark's phone rang and he answered eagerly, happy to get a chance to speak with Aida again.

"Aida, it's so good to hear your voice," he eagerly greeted her.

"And to hear yours," she said. "I wanted to hear how the meeting went."

"I think it went as well as could be expected. The President and some of her advisors seemed to understand the gravity of the situation the world faces and the need to bold steps."

"Only some of her advisors?"

"Not everyone sees things the way we do, Aida, you know that."

"I do, but I'm hoping that someone as smart and passionate as you can change their minds."

"I share that hope. We'll have to see what happens. I'm scheduled to meet some military brass later today and the Deputy National Security Adviser tomorrow. Hopefully, I can convince them that the USA's security depends on taking steps now to prevent further SMMs."

"I hope so, too. The American public seems to be supporting you, Mark. I have to go now, as I have a lift home with a UN soldier."

"Yes, of course, babe, but first, tell me how you are doing. How are you holding up?"

"I'm fine; I'll call you later. He's waiting."

"Great. Any sign of Jemal?"

"He has not been around. I have to go. Goodbye Mark, I love you."

"I love you too, babe."

It was hard for Mark to believe he'd been in Ethiopia just a day ago, living with Aida and working on a water project for the region. It all seemed so far away now, but he knew he needed to return there as soon as possible. He wasn't sure exactly what to expect from his meeting with Temir. The President had said that some of her staff would contact him for follow-up meetings. Given NSA Betts' dismissal of his warnings, he wasn't sure that he should expect all that much of her deputy.

Gretchen Dann had also approached him after the meeting. They had scheduled a meeting for today with several high-ranking military officers. The US military was unlikely to be blind to the dangers to the country from the spiraling chaos, home and abroad. Mark hoped that this meeting would enable him to convince them that the US could not stand apart and wished to ride out the storm easily.

Things were getting chaotic at the protests in front of the White House. Mark watched as the Capitol Police, reinforced by DC Metro officers, moved forward to push the protestors back. Arrests were being made as some protestors refused to retreat, while some threw water bottles and other objects at the oncoming officers.

Mark had one further call to make before the meeting with Temir. He dialed Tom's number.

"How was the flight, Mark?" Tom greeted him with a question.

"Good, thanks. And I think you were right about the importance of this trip. I feel like the President really listened to my views. She hasn't articulated this exactly, but I believe she understands that only the US can provide the leadership and financial backing to have any sort of impact against climate change."

"I'm glad to hear it."

"What made you so certain I should go?"

"Just a feeling. I suppose you could say I didn't want us to miss the forest for the trees. What we are doing here is important. But much of the world is experiencing similar crises, and the President of the United States is one of the few people, really the only person, who has the power to help."

"You're right about that, bro. How are things there? Aida said Jemal hasn't made another appearance."

"He hasn't, thank God. And with the UN guards, he'll find a different reception awaiting him if he tries. But tell me more about the trip. What's your sense about what the President will commit? And when?"

"As I said, she seemed to understand what I was saying, but I'm down to speak with some of her advisors personally to get them on our side. If I can do that, hopefully, her understanding will turn to action."

Just then, a call from a DC number came in, so Mark told Tom he would keep him up to date on his progress, and the two said goodbye. The call turned out to be from Temir's assistant, who asked if he would be amenable to pushing their meeting tomorrow back an hour. Mark told the assistant he was happy to do so.

With the call finished, Mark leaned back in the chair once more. He picked up the remote control, planning to find a show to watch until it was time to leave for the meeting with Temir. Suddenly, a thought crossed his mind; he put down the remote and picked up the hotel phone by the bed. In all the excitement of the meeting, he realized he had forgotten the message his wife had left for him in the hotel lobby. He wasn't sure why Ingrid was in town or why she wanted to see him, but he figured it was at least worth a phone call to find out. He dialed the hotel lobby and asked them to put him through to room 602.

Two hours later, Mark opened his eyes with a start. After getting no answer from Ingrid's room, he closed his eyes briefly, hoping to get a few minutes' rest before preparing for the meeting with Gretchen and the military leaders. His fatigue had turned a few minutes into a couple of hours, and now he had to hurriedly ready himself for the meeting. Just as Mark opened the door and stepped into the hall, a voice came from behind him.

"Follow me, please," Gortsky told him as he walked down the hotel corridor towards the elevators.

Forty-five minutes or so later, Mark found himself seated in a conference room at the Pentagon with Gretchen Dann and four military leaders. They were: General Stuvers of the Army, Rear Admiral Conover of the Navy, General Caruso of Army Intelligence, and General Rutherford, Chief Deputy to General Johnson, Head of the Joint Chiefs of Staff. It was an impressive array of the nation's military brass, and Mark reminded himself to choose his words carefully before answering the first question directed his way. It came from General Stuvers.

"Mr. Wells, I've read your report, and I am not sure why we were not privy to this information several years ago. We have the necessary clearances. I know you couldn't have leaked the report, as there is no way you could have retained a copy. These SMMs started a year ago and I wonder if you think the leak is helpful or unhelpful?"

"President Poulter says she wasn't aware of the report, and I have no reason not to believe her. I just don't know if it is helpful or not. I can't work it out. It was certainly designed to embarrass the President that she knew about the Mexican SMM at our border but didn't do anything about it. An SMM on our own doorstep is certainly creating some urgency around policy response, I suppose. Whether the leak was designed to help or hinder a particular policy response, I don't know. What I have gleaned from my earlier meetings is that there is support for an interventionist and American leadership approach, not just within the administration but also from the public, but there is also resistance from some to American know-how and financial resources being shared. I must you tell you that without American leadership, our economy will suffer like everyone else. Let's think about this way; it seems that our enemies do not want America to do anything about climate change. They believe it will damage their long-term interests more than ours. By not intervening, I believe we are playing into Russian and Chinese interests. The chaos that SMMs cause is a cover for them to expand their territories."

"Mr. Wells." Rear Admiral Conover now spoke. "I don't disagree with your analysis about how these SMMs can be used by our enemies. But I am curious to hear more about why you think they will continue. Isn't it possible that a good year of rainfall or the intercession of international bodies like the UN, supported by the US and other nations, will put an end to them?"

"Our model, as any good model does, presents probabilities, not absolutes. A good year of rainfall would ease the situation. But it is certain to be temporary. In addition, in large parts of the world, precipitation is increasingly in the form of extreme events, and water capture needs major investment." As he spoke, Mark looked out the window of the second-floor conference room at the extensive Pentagon parking lot and the burst of green beyond. Northern Virginia, where the Pentagon was located, was home to a significant expanse of picturesque foliage.

"So, I presume your model would change if the political situation changed?"

"With a time lag. That is correct, Admiral. If the United States, for example, mounted a concerted effort to enlist the UN and other nations in a program to eliminate or at least reduce SMMs, our model would certainly reflect that change in the variables. We will need different initiatives in different areas; for example, better water capture during extreme events would be helpful."

"That is all well and good, Mr. Wells," General Rutherford said, "but taking such action presents risks in the current threat environment. As you intimated yourself, Russia has already weaponized these movements as a cudgel against us and our NATO allies. If we act too aggressively along the lines you suggest, they are likely to use that as further fodder for their propaganda campaigns. Their disinformation machinery knows no moral or ethical boundary. I hate to say it, but it works."

"That is why the report I co-authored stresses the importance of building consensus and working with other nations in a collaborative fashion. But I am afraid that whatever the consequences of Russian disinformation, doing nothing is not the answer. As I said it has become clear to me that the Russians want us to do nothing. It is in their interests for us to do nothing."

"Well, I certainly think it is in our interest to minimize the chaos in the world," General Caruso said, "But I take your larger point about working with international bodies as a means of making such actions more palatable to our friends in the world community. It would also, as you suggest, provide less ammunition for our enemies to use against us in any propaganda wars. But all of this assumes we *can* do something to stop these SMMs, at least at an acceptable cost. I'm sure you realize that some voices advocate simply letting them run their course."

"I've met some here in Washington who take that very tack, General," Mark said. "But I simply disagree with their analysis. We can change the conditions on the ground in the areas where SMMs are most likely to take place, and by doing so, we can eliminate them or, at the very least, reduce their prevalence. Doing nothing or letting these areas go to hell will land at our door ultimately, and, well, quite frankly, it is un-American."

"I see," the general said. He shuffled some papers in front of him on the table for a moment.

Mark felt the meeting was going well so far, with none of the rancor that had marked his meeting with the President and her advisors. That, of course, didn't mean the military leaders would agree with what he suggested at the end of the day. Still, his impression was that they were less focused on the political repercussions and more on the security implications of SMMs, making them more likely to be receptive to the points he was making.

"Tell me about this project of yours in East Africa," General Caruso said. "I understand that you have partnered with area governments there to deliver water from places where it is more abundant to areas where that is not the case at different points in the year."

"That is correct, General."

"How difficult has this project been to build, and when is it expected to begin operations?"

"It certainly hasn't been easy, but once it gained critical mass among key leaders in the region, things started moving fast—faster than you might think. My take is that the clear consequences of doing nothing and facing the results that would bring—an increase in the number and frequency of these SMMs—helped give impetus to that momentum. The critical point was when we demonstrated, through our technology partner in California, that the AI infrastructure would ensure that water flows would be fair, provide just enough water and not a drop more, and only if there were sufficient reserves. It was part of a wider trade agreement so that those countries with more water received other benefits. As for starting operations, we are hoping to be operational within a month or two for the most critical element of water flow into this part of Ethiopia. But full operational capability is four years away. It was the leadership of the countries in the region that made it happen. That leadership was borne out of a realization that without collaboration, there would come a time when they were permanently at war."

"Impressive," General Rutherford said. "Your model, I understand, has been remarkably accurate in predicting these SMMs to date. Would you be willing to share—"

A knock on the door caused General Rutherford to stop mid-sentence. "Enter," he said. The door opened, and an aide entered the room and asked to speak to General Rutherford urgently. Excusing himself, the general left the room with the aide. A moment later, he returned, shutting the door behind him.

"Mr. Wells, I have to apologize for leaving the meeting early. I will also request that Rear Admiral Conover and General Caruso accompany me. It will soon be on the news, so I can tell you that there has been what appears to be a terrorist attack on our navy base in San Diego. General Stuvers, would you mind remaining here with Ms. Dann to complete the meeting?"

"Not at all, General," Stuvers answered. With that, the two generals and the admiral left the room.

CHAPTER 8

"Hey, Ingrid," Mark said as he walked up to the table where she was sitting in the hotel bar the day after meeting Gretchen Dann and the military leaders.

"Mark, so good to see you," she said as they embraced.

They sat down, and the waitress appeared within moments to take their order. Ingrid ordered a gin and tonic, and Mark, rather predictably, a glass of Franciacorta to cleanse his palate, followed by a La Cuadrilla red from Santa Barbara. Over the years, the climate intensified the full-bodied reds from Santa Barbara, but the style was as smooth as ever. This was one of the few things he missed about the States.

"I've got to get to the White House in an hour to meet the Deputy National Security Adviser, but we can meet again when I have more time available if you are still in town," he said.

"That would be lovely," she replied. "You are all over the news. You are more popular than any politician right now."

"So, what brings you to DC?" Said Mark, as he ignored the comment about being so popular.

"I'm here on business," Ingrid said.

"Are you taking over your dad's firm?"

"I think so. I hope so. I think I should, in any case," she giggled as she spoke.

"How did you know I would be here?" Mark had been curious since he received the message she had left at the front desk and called her to set up this meeting over lunch.

"You know me, I hear things," Ingrid said enigmatically.

She had a good radar for what was going on with the people around her. She didn't seem inclined to spill the beans about how she had heard he was in town, so he changed the subject.

"So, what's your dad up to these days, still burning the midnight oil at the company until he decides to hand it over to you?"

"He says he's a recovering workaholic, but I don't know how much I believe him. He's been traveling the world, combining business with pleasure as he looks for places to expand, so at least he's getting some vacation time here and there."

"That sounds like your dad," Mark said, smiling. He had gotten along with Guttenberg okay when they had met at family functions, although he always had the feeling that the man didn't approve of him somehow. Guttenberg didn't talk much about his politics. Still, from what Mark had heard him say, it wouldn't surprise him if the mining magnate's views weren't all that far from those of the American Glory movement that had surged in popularity since 2029. Strangely, both the left and right had built an unlikely coalition around a set of conspiracy theories about how government planned to implant chips in people's bodies to control them or poison them.

There was silence for a moment. Mark could see Ingrid getting ready to say something, so he refrained from commenting before the silence got awkward. In an unusually frank moment, Ingrid blurted out.

"Mark, I want to tell you that I really regret having the affair. I don't know what got into me. I feel so stupid."

"It's totally fine, Ingrid," he said. "Well, you know something, actually it's not fine. It is what it is. And I should tell you that while I'll always treasure what we had, I'm with someone else now."

"Wow. You didn't waste any time replacing me, did you?"

"I don't see it that way. Besides, you had an affair. And it wasn't like it was a one-off—you were seeing the guy for quite a while."

"I know, it was just deep dissatisfaction with myself. I don't even know exactly why, but as soon as you found out, I ended it." She seemed sincere, but that didn't matter to Mark. He wanted to be straight with her and explain that he had moved on.

"Look, Ingrid, I'll always have a place in my heart for you, but I'm really in love with my partner. We've been together for almost a year now."

"Who is she? I thought I would have heard if you were with someone."

"She's Ethiopian. I actually met her in the States, first at Stanford briefly and then at the UN a couple of years back. You didn't know her at Stanford. After the UN, we stayed in touch as colleagues and then I suppose she was a bit of a shoulder to cry on. Then, she was part of the group organizing this water infrastructure project. So, we met up again and really hit it off."

"Does she know you're married?"

"Yes, of course, she knows about us. Look, we're really in love. We have a very simple life. We don't have the life you and I had. It's a different dynamic."

"I'm glad for that, Mark," Ingrid said, once again radiating sincerity. She put her hand on Mark's, and he did not immediately move away. There's no reason to offend her, he told himself. She knows I'm with someone else now. After a few moments, she moved her hand off his.

"Do you remember Tom? He's in Ethiopia with me."

Ingrid's eyes lit up with surprise. "I do remember him," she said. There was a moment of silence before she said, "I don't know if you ever knew, but I always had the feeling that he wanted to make a move on me. And I wasn't doing anything to encourage him, so please don't think I was leading him on. He always seemed super desperate to get with me."

"No, I'm not thinking that," Mark responded. "I'm not saying you're wrong necessarily, but it could have just been that he thought you were attractive. He certainly never said anything inappropriate about you to me."

"Well, he wouldn't tell you if he had the hots for me, would he?"

"Maybe not, but Tom is a very loyal guy. The most likely explanation for why he didn't tell me he found you attractive is that he didn't want to make you or me feel uncomfortable. You know it's okay for him to have just been attracted to you."

Ingrid looked doubtful at Mark's explanation. "Well, I could be wrong, but I've usually got pretty good antennae for things like that. I have a good read on these things, Mark."

Mark wasn't convinced Ingrid was right about Tom, although she did indeed have a good read on such things. And it seemed clear that other than looking at her, Tom hadn't actually done anything about his desire for Ingrid, assuming she was right. Ingrid was a good-looking woman, and she attracted more than her fair share of attention from men, so he could certainly believe Tom had found her attractive.

"So, how are things going at Guttenberg Mining these days?" Mark asked to change the subject.

"As well as can be expected. My father says he's trying to step back from the day-to-day, but I'm not seeing much of it. Mostly, it seems that he works from home or while taking a trip. He likes to work from different locations, he says. I don't even know which country he is in most of the time, and it really is potluck whether his phone is switched on or off."

"He always seemed like an extremely driven guy to me, so I can see why he's finding it hard to step away, even after appointing his daughter as executive vice president. Is he still the biggest donor by far to the Republicans?"

"Yeah, they all revere him. He has been the biggest donor to Republicans for the past decade or so. It's like he is the unofficial President. Sometimes, I wonder why he appointed me to the job if he isn't going to let me do it. But I suppose he'll have to retire someday," Ingrid said with some heat.

"You would think," Mark said. Who knew when that would be, he thought, given Guttenberg's penchant for wanting to control things, but he refrained from sharing the thought with Ingrid.

"So, tell me more about yourself," she said. "I'm still unsure exactly why you had to come to Washington. Why would the National Security Adviser be so interested in a water project in Ethiopia?"

"Good question." Ingrid had always been quick on the uptake when it came to reading between the lines. "I'm not here because of the project, per se, but rather because the classified report I co-authored on spontaneous mass migration for the Macmillan Administration some years back, was leaked."

"Who would do that? And why is it such a big deal?"

While sympathetic to the cause of helping people access water resources, Ingrid had never been all that interested in the details of his work, Mark knew, so he didn't take umbrage at the question.

"I think any number of political operators trying to make the President look bad could be behind the leak," he said. "As for why it matters, I think that besides any embarrassment it caused the President for her administration's lack of action with respect to SMMs, these migrations have grown so large and disruptive in recent years that some are beginning to consider them a threat to national security. I suppose she could be accused of knowing about the report but not acting soon enough. It would make her look weak, right? I have also been thinking that it was to draw attention to or maybe hinder a particular policy response. I don't really know what I am saying…"

Ingrid interrupted him and said, "Now I get it. They want you here to help them figure out what action they should take to deal with SMMs. And it seems like someone with access to classified reports is out to embarrass her about the southern border. American politicians cannot be seen to be soft about the southern border. It is electoral suicide."

She really was sharp, thought Mark. "That's the gist of it. I've met with the President and some of her advisors as they consider my suggestion that the US should take the lead in guaranteeing every person on the planet a fixed amount of water per day. There's a significant cost to that when you get down to it. In a way, I am suggesting that the US becomes the UN, I suppose."

"If they are smart, they will see the light and agree with you. I hope you've been polite when interacting with these...hangers-on. They have egos, Mark. You know how you can be sometimes when you are talking about the importance of your cause."

Mark smiled at her comment. She had always been quick to chide him when his passion for his work caused him to become what she regarded as too intense in conversation. He joked, "I have tried to be incisive and persuasive while maintaining an affable and charming disposition at all times in my conversations with the grand folks of the Administration."

"Good," Ingrid said, looking at him suspiciously, aware that he was gently teasing her.

Mark smiled to show that he was laughing with her and not at her, and Ingrid smiled back. He checked his phone and, with a start, realized that he needed to head out or he would be late for the meeting with Bousson.

"I've got to get going if I want to make the meeting on time," he told her. "How long are you going to be in town?"

"I'm in town for a week, maybe longer, depending on the deal I'm working on. I'd love to see you again if possible. Could we go to dinner, for old time's sake?"

"Absolutely. Of course, we can. I don't know how busy I will be, but assuming the President doesn't need me this weekend, let's plan for Saturday night if that works for you?"

"It does," Ingrid said.

CHAPTER 9

As the car drove Mark and Gortsky to the Roosevelt Office Center for the meeting with Temir, he thought about his talk with Ingrid. It had gone better than he expected. He found himself thinking about her, even though he loved Aida. He had also met Ingrid at Stanford, and until the affair, they had an enjoyable marriage. While he was happy in his relationship with Aida, he didn't see the harm in meeting Ingrid while they were both in town. It would give them a chance to learn more about what had been going on in each other's lives over the past year and a half or so.

Upon arrival at the White House, Mark was quickly ushered into a conference room on the first floor. He didn't have to wait long for the Deputy National Security Adviser, Temir Bousson, to join him.

"I understand they are claiming that the bombing in San Diego is suspected to be domestic terrorism," Mark said after they had exchanged greetings and shaken hands.

"A terrorist group called The Liberty Salvation Front has claimed responsibility, as you may have read," Temir said. "We have never heard of them. The FBI is following up on leads as we speak."

"I read an article claiming that the LSF may have links to the American Glory movement," Mark said.

"Well, as I'm sure you can understand, I can't get into any specific information I may have that pertains to this investigation."

"I understand, Mr. Bousson—"

"Call me Temir, please."

"Of course. Anyway, Temir, while I agree with your assessment, you didn't invite me here to discuss domestic terrorism," Mark said.

"No, I did not. Essentially, Mark, if I may call you that?" Mark nodded his assent, and Temir continued, "The President is relying on her National Security Adviser and myself, as the Deputy NSA, to provide an analysis of the validity of your modeling of SMMs as they relate to our security interests abroad. Of course, this latest SMM originating in Mexico brings the issue closer to home."

"I'm happy to answer any questions you have about the model," Mark said. He hoped that the President would agree to lend the weight of the US, both financial and moral, to the cause of reducing SMMs, and to increase the likelihood of that happening, he would have to do his best to win the support of her advisors.

Temir had a series of questions for Mark about how he had developed the SMM model and how it could be used as a predictive model. The Deputy National Security Adviser also wanted to know how easy the model was to replicate and who owned the underlying AI engine it used.

"Can the US government acquire your model?" Temir asked after Mark had informed him that he had full rights to use the AI engine in question along with the proprietary indicators he had developed for the model.

"The short answer is yes," Mark answered, choosing his words carefully. "I do feel that this belongs to the world rather than a single individual or nation. I'm a believer that sharing water resources is crucial to surviving the environmental collapse caused by climate change. This and other issues linked to climate change will impact anyone and everyone, no matter where they live."

"As noble as that sounds, Mark, it seems to me that what you are describing could be said to be good old-fashioned socialism. The kind of thing that might be called social democracy or something similar in failed Europe. The continent hasn't seen growth for two decades now, and the European Union is breaking apart since the Netherlands and Belgium exited a few years ago."

"As I said in the meeting with the President, I'm not at all opposed to capitalism." Mark tried to keep his voice calm in the face of Temir's attempt to label his thinking. "I own a decent amount of stocks and bonds in my own investment portfolio. But I believe water as a resource is so crucial to human existence that we need to take a broader view of its distribution."

"I see. Well, if you look at how these socialist-leaning European economies have performed in the nearly three decades since 2010, I think you can see the danger in what you are suggesting. If we look at the growth of the US economy over that period, we see a widening gap between the US and Europe, China, India, everywhere in favor of the US over that time. Your ideas, as benevolent as they seem, could set us back economically.

"This is a political position," Mark said, not happy with the direction the conversation was taking. "What does this have to with national security?"

"Well, Mark, we have to take a wide view." Temir's tone had a somewhat patronizing ring to Mark's ears. "National security is enhanced by staying ahead of our main competitors—China, for example. Despite the predictions, we're even further ahead of them. Their growth has stalled somewhat and all the predictions that China would catch us by now haven't quite materialized. Our Australia, India, and Japan Most Important Allies policy has been a complete success. The Russians are still in play, of course, but only because they possess nuclear weapons. Their economy is barely second world."

"Why is Russia in play?" said Mark, feigning ignorance, in an attempt to get Temir talking rather than having to answer questions himself.

"Their economy is nowhere near the size of ours, or China's, for that matter. They don't want to play ball on climate change because they're less negatively affected by rising temperatures than most of the world, and they can use it as a weapon against us."

"Is there any evidence of that?" continued Mark, determined that Temir should do the talking rather than allow himself to become irritated. Ingrid's reminder to him about being charming was timely.

"Don't forget, they wanted to abduct you."

"Both you and your boss have said that. But how sure are you? I'm no intelligence expert, but I know that some intelligence takes the form of rumors as opposed to what is actually happening on the ground."

"Once again, I can only say so much about these things, but I can assure you that the intelligence we gathered on this was more than mere rumor. I'll just say that we had evidence from assets on the ground, which is why we acted so precipitately to remove you from danger. You have expertise vital to our national security."

"What would they have done with me?"

"As I think my colleagues have mentioned previously, our analysis is that they wanted to learn more about spontaneous mass migration, not for any humanitarian motives, but because they wanted to know what you know to enable them to weaponize these SMMs ahead of time. If they have more data, they can make the SMMs happen faster, for example."

"How would my knowledge help them do that?" Something about Temir made Mark feel uncomfortable. Although he could not identify the issue, he preferred to continue to ask questions and let Temir speak, rather than allow Temir to use his words to paint him as being some sort of anti-capitalist. Temir seemed to take the bait and continued to answer Mark's questions.

"Take a look at how they spread disinformation about the USA storing water around the world. With the insights you could provide, we believe that their intention was to manufacture SMMs against American interests around the world. To make the US chaotic at home and abroad."

Mark thought for a few moments before speaking. "Well, if that is the case, it's all the more reason we should make this AI model publicly available, so the world knows where and why SMMs occur and how the interplay between water resources, population density, movement, etc. all combine to create spontaneous mass migration."

"Mark, they want to create additional SMMs to use them against the USA. Particularly on our southern border. Why can't you get that?" The conversation was taking a more heated turn.

After initially heeding Ingrid's word to be charming, Mark was unable to control himself.

"I see your point, Temir, but I'm not sure you're seeing mine. There is a bigger issue here than geopolitical jousting between nations. The stability of the world is at stake, and therefore, our own is at stake. One would think that it is a national security interest you would want to support. This is going to need real leadership."

Before Temir could answer, Mark's phone rang. He was grateful he could interrupt his conversation. It was Aida. "Would you mind if I take this call?" he asked.

"Not at all," Temir said. "I'll be in the lobby outside when you're done."

"Hey babe," Mark said after Temir had left the room.

"Mark, I miss you," was the first thing out of Aida's mouth.

"I miss you as well. How are things in Ethiopia?"

"As busy as ever. The hospital is swamped from morning till night, but I'm sure that doesn't surprise you."

"No, it doesn't. How about the security situation? Any sign of Jemal?"

"None at all. I'm sure the UN guards being here will make him think twice about trying anything. And I should mention that Tom has been a big help. He's been stopping by to make sure I'm okay and keeping me company. You picked a good friend, darling."

"I'm glad he's there, that's for sure." Actually, thought Mark, was he really all that sure about Tom, given what Ingrid had said? He quickly dismissed the idea from his mind. Aida had nothing on her mind particularly. She just wanted to speak to Mark as their previous call had been so short. Conscious that Temir was waiting outside the conference room, however, Mark wrapped up the call with Aida after what seemed like an all too brief ten minutes, then let the Deputy National Security Adviser know he was done.

"Everything okay?" Temir asked.

"For now. I took the call because there was an incident a couple of days back with my partner's uncle. Apparently, he is involved with a local protest group in the region called Al-Haqa. My partner's uncle, a guy called Jemal, founded the movement, and very out of character, he showed up with men and guns outside the UN-sponsored hospital where she works. The building is guarded now, and he hasn't been back since. Luckily, my friend is keeping an eye on things while I'm gone," Mark explained.

"Does your friend work for the UN?"

"No, I met Tom when he was at Stanford for a year on a fellowship, and I met him again at the UN, where he was helping with another project when I was working on getting this project off the ground. He works as a sustainable resources consultant, and his firm was kind enough to lend him to us to help with the project."

This was all interesting information, Temir thought. Betts had told Temir that she was listing Al-Haqa as a terrorist organization, but he hadn't caught on that the guy at the helm was the uncle of Mark's partner. This link was potentially gold, and Temir was sure Guttenberg would think so, too. While Temir kept his face expressionless, he was pleased with what he had learned so far. As a skilled operator, Temir knew better than to press Mark for too much information of a personal nature and risk making him suspicious.

"I'm glad to hear you've got things covered while helping us understand the potential of what you're doing here in DC," Temir said. "Speaking of which, I must say that, aside from any reservations I might have about the degree of the financial commitment involved, the more I think about it, the more involving American companies and the government in helping other countries overcome spontaneous mass migrations makes sense to me."

"That's something of a surprise, given your earlier remarks," Mark said.

"I've found that it's best to work with people who don't abandon their position on an issue as soon as they encounter some pushback. But after testing your commitment to your cause, I can see you that your ideas are robust and will withstand House scrutiny."

"I couldn't see exactly what you were doing, but I suppose that makes sense," Mark said. "To me, this is a case where helping others, individuals and countries, improves our country's security and economy."

"I concur. Certainly, the security implications are complex. We will need to proceed cautiously if the President chooses to enact a policy supporting other parts of the world to prevent future SMMs. But I think the humanitarian and national security case for adopting such a policy is convincing."

Mark left the meeting somewhat surprised at Temir's turnaround, and at the same time congratulating himself that he was able to convince Temir about the value of his ideas. It made sense that in his position Temir should explore the details carefully, thought Mark. Perhaps he had been too eager to jump to conclusions about Temir.

CHAPTER 10

Temir sat in the passenger seat of Guttenberg's late-model Mercedes SUV. He had left his phone in his car in the park's parking lot. Temir, as usual, had run an electronics detection device over the car's interior to make sure there were no other electronics that could record them in the vehicle. After he had called Guttenberg to set up the call, he had driven a few miles out of DC to rural Virginia. The state park where he had parked his car abutted a vacation house Guttenberg owned nearby. A walk of about fifteen minutes had brought him through the wooded paths of the park to Guttenberg's house and the car parked behind it.

"I can go over it again, but I'm sure I didn't miss anything the first time," Temir said. He had just recounted Mark's explanation of the situation in Ethiopia after his departure. Guttenberg had been particularly interested in the familial link between Mark's partner and the Al-Haqa terrorist group. Temir felt he would please Guttenberg with what he found, but that didn't seem to be the case. Guttenberg required a very precise retelling of aspects of a conversation or event he was interested in, but he took no notes. No documentation ever changed hands between the two men.

"You're sure he said the lead terrorist was his partner's uncle and that Betts has already classified it as a terrorist group?" Guttenberg asked for the third time.

"Yes, I'm sure," Temir said, trying to keep the irritation out of his voice.

"This is excellent. We can use this."

"Why don't we leak it?" Temir suggested.

"Not just now," Guttenberg replied. "The time is not quite right. This information will be useful in undermining the President's efforts by revealing that she has links to someone who is closely connected to terrorism. But we want her to play her hand first. I don't know what she is up to exactly, but I know her plan is to give American know-how, technology, and resources to the world. Which is fine but it will not be on a business footing. It will be a giveaway. And she will ultimately make water and related investments very difficult for us. We will lose billions, and America's lead over the world will be undermined. She is a wet Republican. She is talking to the Democrats. We get one shot at impeaching her, so we wait. She first must tell the world that she will use American companies, innovation, and our financial might to build water infrastructure projects around the world. That's when we undermine her. This alone is not enough to topple her. It needs to be the straw that breaks her back. And now we have to get rid of Wells, too. We can't have his water connectivity project in Ethiopia succeed and set an example for the rest of the world to emulate. He must be removed too."

"Would that be so bad? As long as the President is removed, how would Mark's water project hurt us?" Temir asked.

"We need these projects privately funded to have financial returns factored into the calculus. We can't have UN-funded or American government-funded projects succeeding. With Wells in DC, we need an additional plan to undermine him."

"How?" Temir asked.

"I am not sure yet. I have an idea, but I will hold off on suggesting it for now."

"Can you at least give me a hint?"

"Never mind. I will let you know." Guttenberg turned to look at Temir. "Why don't you speak to Tom in Ethiopia in the meantime? See what you can glean from him. Could we use Tom in any way?"

"I suppose it would be legitimate for the Deputy NSA to follow up and acquire more information about Mark's project," Temir said, half thinking aloud. "Speaking to people on the ground would be a logical way to accomplish that. I'll give him a call."

"Good," Guttenberg said.

"Any thoughts on this bombing in San Diego? The President's numbers have taken a severe hit." Temir asked after a moment.

"I would think you would know more about it than me." Guttenberg was as terse as ever.

"You might think that, but we've discovered precious little so far. With a name like the Liberty Salvation Front, you might think the terrorists would be easy to find or would want to be found if only to publicize their ideology. But we have never heard of this group."

"Maybe so. But blowing a hole in a cruiser and killing eight sailors will get them sent to prison for a long time, if not the death penalty," Guttenberg said. "That may diminish their ardor for fame, or at least their inclination to provide any clues that investigators can use to identify them."

"I suppose. And given that this is the first time the LSF has committed an act of terror or claimed to, anyway, it does make you wonder who might be behind the group."

"Is there any evidence this might be a false flag event?" Guttenberg asked.

Temir paused for a moment before speaking. "There's very little evidence at all at this point. Someone with an underwater speedboat got close enough to the vessel to disembark a couple of frogmen who attached bombs to its hull, then swam back to their boat and sped away. That's all we have at the moment."

"Roger that, please keep me informed of any significant developments."

"Do you think this group, or this bombing, could affect our plans?"

"It seems unlikely." Guttenberg turned to look at Temir as he spoke. "But you never know. We need to control what we can control and be aware of any wildcards that might impact us. Wells is our focus for now. Find out what you can about his friend in Ethiopia and let me know when you have something."

"Will do," Temir said. "One more thing." He paused to receive Guttenberg's agreement to continue. "Can I ask why you are always precisely seven minutes late for our meetings?"

"My vehicle is fitted with miniature drone detection radar, and it takes five to seven minutes to do a sweep of the area around your car, Temir. These smart drones are the size of a fingernail and look like they are part of the car. They've been developed by our military recently. Very few people know of their existence."

Temir's heart sank as he exited the car. He didn't look back as Guttenberg started the engine. He wondered if Carruthers' vehicle was also fitted with some radar; he hadn't even heard of such a thing. Then he realized Carruthers would likely have abandoned the meeting with the bearded guy if it was fitted with such a device, given the precautions he had taken, doubling back and forth. Temir entered the State Park outside Guttenberg's compound and headed back to where he had parked his car on the other side of the park.

As he left, Temir wondered what Guttenberg meant by this should the 'straw that broke the camel's back.' *What else was Guttenberg up to and not sharing with me?*

CHAPTER 11

Mark looked over the menu with interest. Tivoli, the fancy Italian restaurant he and Ingrid had selected for dinner, had a fairly wide selection of gustatory delicacies. He had his eye on the sea bass, which he duly ordered when the waiter arrived. Ingrid had gone with the gnocchi, an old favorite of hers, as he well recalled. And they shared a side of the artichoke hearts.

"So, I didn't get a chance to ask you much about what you're doing in town when we met last time," Ingrid said. "I feel like that was impolite of me unless you are on some sort of secret mission and can't tell me, of course."

Mark laughed at that. "Hardly. You asked a lot of questions. I already told you. It's about the water pipeline project I'm working on in East Africa. With these spontaneous mass migration—SMM—events around the globe attracting attention, my paper on the subject has apparently become a hot topic on the Hill. I'm talking to a guy called Bousson, who is a bit of a strange fish; by the way, I was told it's all about national security. There you go. Exactly what I told you last time."

Ignoring Mark's comments, she continued with her questions. "I've been thinking about what you said about not understanding why your report was leaked. You did this work years ago. So why now?" Ingrid asked.

"I've asked myself the same question as have some of the military top brass I met. My report was classified. But it was leaked by someone, perhaps as a way of spurring the President to take some action or of showing that she knew what was happening and should have taken action, or to stop her in her tracks, or... you know what, I have no idea. I guess it could make her look weak or be used to manipulate her somehow. Either way, she seems to be on a footing to take some kind of action."

"I've always admired your work, so however it happened, I'm glad that people with the power to put your ideas into effect were made aware of it." Ingrid placed her hand on his as she spoke, and he, like the last time they met, did not pull his hand away. After a moment, she moved her hand away.

"Well, as gratifying as that is, she is getting mixed advice. Some of her advisors are clearly against any decisive costly action, so we will have to see how it plays out. I think I did make some progress with the Deputy National Security Adviser in our meeting the other day, for whatever that's worth."

"Isn't the NSA Director Lorraine Betts?"

Ingrid had always had a keen interest in politics, taking after her father, and she was usually up to date on who was who in DC. "Yes, but Temir Bousson is her deputy. After we talked, he seemed to come around to my way of thinking. Initially he seemed to focus on national security issues, then turned to the economy and told me I am a socialist. Then suddenly he said that he hoped the President would commit American companies and the government to finance several initiatives."

"That's good news. I met him once at a cocktail party, and he seemed nice enough, although those security and intelligence types can be quite hard to read when they choose."

"I've found the same myself." Mark hesitated for a moment before launching into a new subject. "Ingrid, we don't have to talk about this if you don't want to, but I wondered if I could ask you something about Tom."

Ingrid was unfazed by the request. "Ask me anything you like."

"You said Tom was an 'admirer of yours,' or something like that. What exactly did you mean by that? Or what exactly did he do that made you think that?"

She smiled. "It's not like he groped me or anything if that's what you're asking."

"I'm glad to hear it, but I wasn't suggesting anything quite so crude. Did he proposition you? What made you think he was hot for you?"

"No, he didn't outright proposition me. It was more the vibes he gave off when you weren't around. Always when you were not around, and he did make a couple of what you might call oblique passes."

Mark was all ears. "How so?"

"Well, he offered to help you and me learn to scuba dive, with the proviso that if you were too busy, he could just teach me. A couple of times, when you were out of town, he came round to make sure I was okay, suggesting we might have a drink. I mean why wouldn't I be okay?"

"I see," Mark said, although he wasn't sure he did. It was hardly an open-and-shut case of Tom trying to make a move on his wife. But at least now he knew the whole story, or more of it, anyway, from Ingrid's perspective. He thought perhaps it chimed with what Aida had said to him about Tom keeping her company.

"I suppose I can't complain too much about Tom, though, after what I did to you," Ingrid said with a troubled look.

"I suppose you can't. Why did you have the affair, Ingrid? I thought our marriage was a good one, at least until then."

"I wish I knew. Like I said last time we met. I was deeply dissatisfied with myself."

"You did, but why didn't you tell me then?" Mark wanted to know, although after what she had done, could he trust what she said?

"I think the main reason, as embarrassing as it is to admit, is that I didn't want to disappoint you. So perhaps I pre-empted the hurt I would feel by having an affair before you became disappointed in me. I know that sounds stupid, but I think that had a lot to do with it," Ingrid looked down at her plate as she spoke.

"But you know I was always there to support you. Why would you think I wouldn't be there for you?"

"I don't know," Ingrid said, looking at him sadly. "I wish I could explain."

"Well, I suppose I was in my own world a lot back then. Everything was coming together with the water project, and that was consuming much of my time. Not that I'm saying that justified you having an affair, but I guess it makes it more understandable from my end."

"Mark, you have this noble side to you, which I've always loved, even when I teased you for it." Ingrid's tone became softer and more reassuring, "But it's certainly not right to let you blame yourself for my mistake. I'm a big girl. I should have told you how I felt rather than running behind your back."

After some further talk about their shared past, they headed back to the hotel, where they had agreed to meet at the bar for a nightcap. After a few drinks, Mark again pressed Ingrid on her reason for being in Washington.

"Okay, tell me the truth, why are you really in DC? Are you here to spy on me?"

"You think very highly of yourself, don't you, Wells?" Ingrid said. "Either that or you've become paranoid now that you're spending all your time meeting with the President and her advisors."

"Not paranoid, but I'm certainly curious why you suddenly show up out of the blue. Not that I'm not glad to see you, of course."

"Are you really," Ingrid said, challenging him, "or are you just saying that so I'll tell you what you want to know?"

"A little of both, I suppose," Mark said, thinking that two could play at being ambiguous.

"I see. Well, if you want to hear the full story of why I'm here, I suggest we take this back to my suite. It's getting late, and if we stay in the bar much longer, I'm worried I'm not going to be able to walk in these heels."

Mark knew where this could lead but believed himself to be in control and agreed with her suggestion. They left the bar and made their way back to room 602, where she was staying. Somewhere in the back of his mind, he knew that he had drunk enough that he would feel the pain tomorrow. But he felt good for the moment and being in Ingrid's presence was intoxicating. He was still attracted to her after all these years. It also felt good to know that she still desired him, assuming he was reading the signs right. While he was tipsy, to be sure, he hadn't drunk any more than he could handle. He continued to be confident he could control himself.

"Okay, let me hear your story of how you came to be in DC at the same time as your husband," he said as they sat next to each other on the sofa in her suite. He could feel her thigh against his own as they talked.

"Well," she said, "Dad has tasked me with finding companies to acquire in the silver mining sector. He thinks the continuing adoption of electric vehicles will send silver prices soaring further. Now, as you may or may not know, if you are mining for zinc, you will often produce a significant amount of silver as a byproduct. And it just so happens that a major zinc mining firm is headquartered not too far from here in Alexandria, Virginia."

"Then why aren't you in Alexandria?" Mark asked.

"Think about it. Why would a company want to meet the representatives of a potential acquirer at their headquarters?" Ingrid's voice was slightly slurred from all the drinking they had done.

"To keep it secret."

"Good boy," she said.

"But how did you know I was in town?"

"Wow, so many questions. I'll tell you what you want to know, but first, I need to get out of these heels. They are killing me. Wait right there."

Mark considered leaving the room before things moved in a direction that he would regret, but whether it was the drink or the desire to remain in Ingrid's presence, he found himself still sitting on the sofa when Ingrid returned. She had done more than take off her heels; she had changed clothes that did nothing to hide her shapely figure.

"So, where were we?" she asked, resuming her seat beside him and placing her hand on his leg.

"Well, you were going to get out of those heels, and you were going to tell me how you knew I was in DC. But it seems you have other ideas."

Ingrid blithely ignored his insinuation, at least for the moment. "Hmm. I don't think it would be wise to give away all my secrets, would it? But I don't want to leave you with nothing since I've enjoyed your company so much tonight. I think you can probably figure out how it happened if I tell you that I have a good friend who is friendly with someone who works in the Poulter Administration."

"And that friend knew you were in town, and I was flying to DC."

Ingrid smiled at him and stood up. With obvious vulnerability on her face, she climbed onto his lap, straddling him, her face inches from his.

Mark believed that he could stop himself at any moment. Choosing not to stop himself, he leaned forward and kissed his wife..

CHAPTER 12

"Hello, Mr. Van Heusen," Temir said as Tom's face appeared on the video conference link from his lodgings in Ethiopia.

"Tom, please, Deputy National Security Adviser Bousson. I'm not used to being called anything else these days."

"Of course, Tom, and please call me Temir."

"Will do, Temir. I must admit I was surprised that someone of your stature would want to talk to us on the ground here in Ethiopia. I'm not sure exactly what I can tell you that Mark can't. I assume you've already talked to him."

"Yes, Mr....Tom. But things can change fast on the ground these days, so we thought it important to reach out and get an up-to-the-minute report on the pipeline. Mark has provided us with a wealth of information about the project along with his SMM model, but I'm sure you can understand the value of having another source of information and analysis given the importance of the issues involved."

"I can," Tom said. "So, what do you want from me?"

"Can you give me your analysis of where the project is now and when it will likely go live?"

Tom provided a brief account of where the project was, which largely parallelled what Mark had said. Temir asked a few questions designed to demonstrate his sincere interest in the project to Tom. He knew it was important to convince Tom that learning about the project's status was his primary objective. In truth, of course, he had ulterior motives. After they had talked about the details of the pipeline project for a time, Temir changed the subject.

"Mark mentioned some trouble with a local terrorist group just after he left. Have there been any further incidents?"

"None at all. I imagine Mark told you about the UN guards at the hospital here."

"He did. He also mentioned that the leader of this group, Kamal, I think it was—"

"Jemal," Tom interrupted to correct him.

"I understand Jemal is related to Mark's partner in some way?" Temir said

"He's her uncle."

"We did some research on this group that…Jemal is allegedly linked to Al-Haqa. It would be unwise to presume that they can't be a real threat to the project or Mark's partner, Aida, I believe her name is."

"That's right," Tom said.

"So, I'm interested in your assessment as someone on the ground as to how real a threat the group is to the project and the people involved."

"Well, Temir, you understand that I'm an engineer by trade and not a security analyst."

"Of course, but my understanding is that you are keeping an eye on Aida while Mark is away, so I thought you would be well-positioned to provide an opinion, albeit not one of a security professional."

"Fair enough. I've had a chance to speak with Aida about her uncle, and I think as long as the UN continues to provide security at the hospital where she works, she should be safe. As for the pipeline and the associated water tanks, I'm unsure how much of a threat Jemal and his cohorts are. From what Aida said, even before the tragic loss of his family, he was always a big talker but with no hint of violence. Apparently, he never even owned a gun, never mind an AK47, until a couple of days ago. Aida said he never had more than one or two friends again until this week."

"Thank you for that analysis. If you remember anything else or hear anything at all, we would certainly be interested in hearing about it."

"Happy to help, Temir. I'll get in touch if I hear anything about Jemal or Al-Haqa."

"Much appreciated, Tom. I'd like to set up a follow-up call in the next few days if you are amenable. The President is very close to deciding on our policy regarding these SMMs in light of Mark's report, and I want to make sure I can present my boss and the President with as complete a picture as possible before a decision is made."

"I'm willing to do anything I can to help, although I'm not sure what more I can tell you."

"I want to discuss what I've learned from you with the team, and that process will likely generate some follow-up questions. It shouldn't be a long call, but I want to make sure to leave no stone unturned in helping prepare the President to decide on this matter."

CHAPTER 13

Mark turned the television channel in his hotel room to the news. The correspondent was outside the US Navy Yard in San Diego, reporting on the latest developments in the investigation into the explosion there. As far as he could tell, there had been little progress. The program shifted to two terrorism experts, one with experience in the intelligence community and the other in counterterrorism operations. The intelligence expert addressed the likelihood of the new LSF being linked to other extremist groups. The other commentator talked about how weak the President looked without progress being made in the investigation, adding to that the approaching SMM on the southern border. Both commentators made reference to polls putting her approval ratings in the low 40s.

Mark only half listened to the TV. His head was still spinning from the events of last night. In the morning, he kissed Ingrid and told her he had enjoyed the night but had to leave to prepare for a lunch meeting. In truth, the meeting was a lunch with an old colleague from his days working with the Macmillan administration, but he hadn't told Ingrid that. He had promised to call her before leaving.

He was still figuring out how he felt about what happened last night, although he was consumed by an overarching sense of guilt. *Why on earth did I do that? I love Aida more than anything.*

On television, the commentators continued to analyze the terrorist attack in San Diego. The cruiser listed heavily to port, where a gaping hole in the vessel's hull could be seen. As he watched, Mark wanted to call Aida but decided against it. He would call later. He had to get to lunch with his former colleague, Rex Talbertson. He and Rex, who had been Deputy Director of International Development at the State Department during the Macmillan administration, had always got along well. He had jumped at the chance to see him again when they met in the hotel lobby a couple days back. He opened the door to find Gortsky, punctual as ever, there to accompany him on the drive to La Cubano, a favorite eatery of Talbertson's.

After all these years, spending time with Rex again was a pleasure. Mark had always appreciated the man's affability and generally optimistic outlook. He also was an inveterate gossip, which Mark appreciated could be a valuable survival skill in the world of DC power politics. The first part of the lunch was spent catching up on each other's lives and careers since they had worked together. Rex was working with an NGO focused on delivering aid to impoverished communities in South America.

"We could use something like that where I'm at," Rex said after Mark had explained how the system of pipelines and water tanks would be used to move water to where it was needed in Uganda and nearby countries. "South America has areas with an abundance of water as well as areas where it is quite sparse."

"If the President agrees with my suggestion for the US to designate a certain amount of water for each person daily, it could help with funding to get such a project off the ground. If my meeting with the Deputy National Security Adviser on the topic went as well as I think it did, the chances of positive policy decisions is very good."

"Who is that?" Rex asked. "I know the National Security Adviser is Lorraine Betts, but I'm not as up on some of the smaller players in the Administration these days."

"Temir Bousson," Mark said.

"Temir." Rex looked thoughtful. "I remember him from our days in the Macmillan Administration. He was the Undersecretary for Security in the State Department. He always struck me as a slippery type."

"What do you mean?"

"I had to connect with him on a humanitarian project in the Middle East in terms of the security situation. Anyway, I always found it hard to get a straight answer from him. One day, he seemed to be challenging everything we said. The next, he would signal understanding and agreement with what was needed, even if it was at odds with what he had said the previous day. Very slippery."

"Maybe he was just making sure that he didn't promise more than he could deliver, given the security challenges? Or he needed to test what you were saying?"

"That could be, although I think it was more than that. I think he didn't want to look bad if something went wrong, so he talked out of both sides of his mouth to ensure that he was covered, whatever happened." Rex's tone grew more aggrieved as he recounted his experience with Temir.

"That type of strategic ambiguity in the service of a cover-your-ass mentality is certainly not uncommon in DC," Mark said.

"Granted," said Rex. "But there's definitely more to it. Now, the caveat is that this is just a rumor, but from what I heard, there was something nepotistic about how Temir gained his position in the Poulter Administration."

"Isn't it all about who you know for any of us," said Mark. "But I'm all ears," eager to learn more about the Deputy NSA.

"My understanding is that he was forced out of the State Department maybe five or six years ago, although I'm not sure if that was simply due to personality conflict or something more. But the rumor about how he acquired his recent position is that he gained the support of some influential figures on the far right of the Republican party who put pressure on the Administration to get him a job. These guys were not her supporters when she won the nomination, but she wanted them on board for the sake of funding her campaign, so she agreed."

"Poulter seems to be an old-fashioned moderate, so I'm not sure that the right would have all that much influence over her.

But it's certainly not unusual for people to get jobs in Washington due to the influence of their supporters."

"That is true, although I do think that people like Manuel, Gregg, and Guttenberg have some influence on the Administration, in terms of appointees, even if their politics are further to the right than that of the President."

Mark was not surprised to hear his father-in-law's name mentioned. "You know Guttenberg is my father-in-law, at least for now?"

"I do. Look, Bousson sits in a nice job in the White House, and the rumors are...well, I just explained..."

"Whatever the truth of it, I'll be sure to be cautious about what I say around him going forward. Thanks for the warning bro."

"I think that would be wise," Rex said.

Mark was left with an underlying anxiety about Temir.

CHAPTER 14

Tom was right on time for the follow-up meeting with Temir a few days after their first call. After they exchanged pleasantries, Temir got down to business right away.

"I've spoken with my staff, and they tell me that after thoroughly analyzing Mark's program, there is a real chance that the President may ask to provide US commitment to many more initiatives."

"That's great news," Tom said.

"From a humanitarian standpoint, I entirely agree. From a national security standpoint, it is a more complicated issue, but after speaking with Mark, I think that if anyone's plan can significantly improve access to water around the world, it's his. We continue to have security concerns, but we can manage those."

"Working with him on this project inspired me to put my regular work on hiatus, so I completely agree with you," Tom said.

"I can see why. The progress Mark, you, and everyone else working on the project has made is impressive indeed. I do have a few more questions about the security situation there. Is that okay with you?"

"It's fine."

"First, has there been any sign of Mark's partner's uncle in the time since we talked or of anyone associated with this Al-Haqa terrorist group?"

"None at all."

"Thank you, Tom." Temir had given a fair amount of thought to how he should phrase the request he was about to make.

"While it's too soon to say what the President will do, I think it's prudent to prepare for all eventualities. One of those possibilities is that Mark is asked to stay in Washington to develop a set of global initiatives and to be her adviser."

Tom didn't look too surprised. "It has occurred to me that might happen. However, I'm not sure he would agree to accept the role with Aida based here in Ethiopia."

"Couldn't she go to Washington to be with him?" Temir asked

Tom looked dubious at the idea. "I suppose she could, but I doubt she would. She feels that others can't easily leave 'this parched earth,' as she puts it, and her job at the hospital is vital to her."

"Understood," Temir said. "If, however, Mark did decide to take the job, someone would need to take over his role on the ground in Ethiopia. Would you be willing to do that?"

"Me?" Tom looked surprised at the suggestion. "I do not have the relationships with the leaders in this part of the world that Mark has built up over time."

"I understand it would be difficult, but I know Mark is highly confident in your abilities. You taking over while he is in Washington would, I believe, significantly improve the chances that he would accept the role."

"Maybe. But Aida's not going to like it," Tom said.

"From the sound of it," Temir responded, "she is a woman dedicated to doing good for others. If that is true, I think she would understand that Mark would be needed in Washington, at least for a time, to make sure this program brings water to the people who need it globally is a success."

Tom hesitated, and the holographic video-link went silent for a few moments while he thought about what Temir had just said. "What you've said makes sense. But I need to think about it."

"Yes," Temir agreed with Tom. "There is no guarantee about the President's ultimate decision. However, it pays to be ready for any eventuality, so I thought it would be wise to bring this subject up with you before making any decision."

"Understood. I'll think it over," Tom said. "I certainly wouldn't want the project to languish if Mark were to be offered and accept the job in Washington, and neither would he, I'm sure."

Temir felt confident that he had built some trust into the relationship with Tom by pampering him with fake sincerity. This was the real sole purpose of the meeting. He intuited Tom was now suggestable when needed in the future. He would keep up a line of communication through texts and recorded messages that could be played back holographically.

CHAPTER 15

Mark gazed around the room at the assembled advisors and presidential staff. It was indeed a gathering of some of the highest and mightiest in the land, as far as he was concerned. He knew that this was likely to be the final meeting of the President and her advisors before she decided on the Administration's policy on SMMs. A few minutes after the last of the advisors had entered the room, the conference room door opened, and the President, followed by her aides Brian and Rachel, entered.

Once seated, the President wasted no time in getting things started. One of her aides pressed a button, and detailed and real-time holographic images of the SMMs around the world were displayed for everyone to see.

"Ladies and gentlemen, we face a series of crises around the world triggered by spontaneous mass migrations. These SMMs pose a threat not only to global stability but also to the national security of the United States of America. We have previously discussed this issue with Mr. Mark Wells, who co-authored a report on what causes these events, as well as a model that can help predict their occurrence. Mr. Wells is here with us today to answer questions and share any further thoughts he may have on this topic. Let me start by saying the United States has the biggest economic and military lead over the rest of the world since World War II. Our enemies are responding with asymmetric warfare, disinformation at a level and sophistication well beyond what we have seen in the past, including fake but compelling video imagery of the United States storing giant underground containers that are miles in every direction." The President paused and looked around the room as if to let the seriousness of their situation sink in.

"General Rutherford," she continued after a few moments, "would you start by providing an analysis from the Joint Chiefs on their estimation of the approach we should take to these SMMs?"

Every head turned to General Rutherford, who cleared his throat before speaking. "Thank you, Madam President, I will be happy to do so. The danger posed by SMMs to international security is undeniable. We've seen kinetic military action and terrorism on the borders of countries in Africa, Europe, and Asia. We've seen increased terrorist action in our country, including a recent bombing at our naval base in San Diego."

"General Rutherford, if I may," the National Security Adviser waited until he nodded to continue. "Correct me if I'm wrong, but there have been intelligence suggestions that the San Diego bombing is likely to be domestic terrorism, possibly linked to the flow of migrants across the southern border. Therefore, shouldn't we be concentrating on our border security rather than SMMs in other parts of the world?"

"Point taken, Ms. Betts. Whether the event in San Diego was directly inspired by, for example, by this latest SMM in Mexico approaching the US border or not, the point stands. SMMs are the cause of increased acts of terror. The Southern border is already at a breaking point and has been so for the past two decades. This large SMM could have unimaginable catastrophic consequences if it reaches the border. But let me be clear. We can't hope to remain untouched here in the United States from the chaos and terrorism around the world engendered by SMMs. I agree with Mr Wells. SMMs are far less likely to happen if people have a reason to remain in their regions and countries. We do not view SMMs as anything remotely the same as large scale migration. The phenomena of SMMs are a first in human history."

The general was silent momentarily to let his statement sink in before continuing. "And we at the Joint Chiefs believe that these

SMMs pose a considerable threat to our interests. Several of our allies are requesting military aid to help handle the population dislocation and disruption SMMs cause. Moreover, if we can predict where these events will occur, we can take proactive measures to reduce or prevent them. All these actions serve to improve the security of this nation and position us to meet the challenges posed by SMMs. My staff has prepared an analysis, after consultation with Mr. Wells, that presents the projected fallout from future SMMs as predicted by the model he helped create. This serves as the blueprint for where our interventions would take place."

A young man sitting with the other aides in the chairs behind the main table stepped forward. He walked around the room, handing out the brief report mentioned by the general. "Madam President, I'm happy to answer any questions about this report or my comments."

"Thank you, General Rutherford. Director Betts, would you like to speak next?"

"I would, thank you, Madam President." Lorraine Betts paused a moment before continuing, looking around the room to ensure she had everyone's attention. "I appreciate General Rutherford's analysis and concur with him and his colleagues that we must strongly support our allies abroad who face military threats, whether from SMMs or any other source. However, I know I speak for many on the NSC when I say I don't believe the US could guarantee the security of these projects around the world. And we should not send our own military on a security and humanitarian mission. As we have seen in recent decades, in countries where our fighting men and women have been called to engage in so-called nation-building exercises, the results have been suboptimal, and that is the polite way of putting it."

The National Security Adviser paused for a moment to look around the room and let the import of her remarks sink in, as a nod to General Rutherford who had deployed the same technique moments earlier. "As for the issue of the US funding efforts to ameliorate SMMs around the world, I don't believe that it would be in our interest to do so outside of the efforts already being undertaken by the UN and other aid organizations around the world. Our resources are not unlimited. While the nation has taken the right steps to regain our financial footing in recent years, the cost of trying to curtail these SMMs on our own would be astronomical. It is not my place to comment on non-security matters but my colleagues on the NSC have asked me to make the connection between us returning to our debt crises of 15 years ago and our ability to guarantee our security. Our lead in military uses of AI, which puts us at a clear and sustained advantage, was possible only through our massive expenditure in these technologies. As those around the table know, some years back, the US military characterized the potential of a debt crisis and the associated financial and social instability that would present as a potential threat to national security. Having averted such a scenario in the past, we should not become complacent. There is no new Bitcoin strategy to bail us out this time."

Lorraine paused again as Mark reflected on Temir's assertion that they were inclined to support Mark's position at their last meeting. Clearly, that had been an outright lie, although this was not something he could mention right now.

"Finally," Lorraine resumed her presentation, "I will mention perhaps the chief reason I would advise against the US taking unilateral action to attempt to stem SMMs: the issue of futility. As I alluded to earlier, in recent decades, we have engaged in so-called nation-building and other humanitarian efforts overseas to little effect. One might even conclude that, in some cases, these efforts have harmed our reputation internationally by somehow causing the enmity of the countries we were attempting to assist. Our country simply can't afford the costs, financially and to our international standing, to intervene in every crisis unilaterally. It harms our long-term security. This is especially the case where, as with these SMMs, it is far from clear that we can meaningfully impact their frequency or scope. Therefore, Madam President,

I will close by stating that it is my belief that we should not alter our current policy of working through the UN and other international bodies in addressing SMMs."

A hush fell over the room at the conclusion of Lorraine's presentation. Even though he strongly disagreed with her position, Mark acknowledged to himself that she had presented her case well. After a few moments, the President spoke.

"Thank you for that, NSA Betts. Now, I'd like to hear from Mr. Wells, the man behind the report which has brought us all where we are today, to consider a change in our policy toward SMMs. Mr. Wells, the floor is yours."

"Thank you, Madam President." Mark looked around the room as he spoke. "First, I'd like to acknowledge that there is much wisdom in NSA Betts' point of view. In advocating a more interventionist approach to preventing or minimizing SMMs, I'm not saying that she is wrong in stating that there are times that such an approach can be fruitless or even counterproductive, just that there are times when unilateral leadership is, in fact, the optimal strategy. We can look to history to support this idea. For instance, our involvement in World War II or our support of the post-war Marshall Plan helped the nations of Europe get back on their feet after the devastation caused by that war, not to mention the aid we sent to Japan for the same purpose. Can we imagine a world where Europe and even Japan had submitted to Russian communism at that time? It doesn't bear thinking about. I thank God that America had the resolve, foresight, and self-interest to help Europe and Japan get back on their feet. Only the United States could have done this at that time. And only the US has the financial and military strength to lead now."

Mark continued, "The report on SMMs I co-authored provides evidence that this is one of those times where intervention is called for. The additional SMMs predicted by the report will stretch the international system of peaceful cooperation and aid beyond breaking point. As countries, some of them allied to us, descend into chaos due to SMMs, this, in turn, will threaten our ability to work in concert with other nations and undermine our economic strength, which is the foundation of our military strength."

"If I may, Mr. Wells," Lorraine interrupted.

"Of course," Mark said, gesturing with an open palm to suggest that the floor was hers.

"You seem to assume first that these SMMs will continue to occur and second that we can stop them. Reading your report, I would say that the first claim is dubious, though certainly possible. However, your report does not demonstrate the second claim that we can stop them."

Mark waited a moment to make sure she was done speaking before answering. "While I wouldn't use your terminology to refer to the report's conclusions, I certainly don't claim that they are by any means infallible. However, much of what we predicted has passed thus far, so I contend that the report provides reasonable grounds for believing these SMMs will continue. As to our ability to impact SMMs favorably, I agree that this is a more speculative claim. However, I think we can already observe the cost of doing nothing. As the US military has stated, the threat to international security and our ability to maintain our advantage is undermined by inaction. Sooner or later this comes to our borders."

Unfazed by Mark's response, Lorraine Betts continued, "A further difficulty is the issue of cost. Even if your position on this matter were plausible, the resources it would take to have an impact could well bankrupt this nation."

This was simply a scare tactic, Mark thought, but he tried to keep his tone of voice level to avoid sounding acrimonious. "To the contrary, not addressing SMMs will be the thing that becomes financially ruinous to us. The exact thing that you are trying to preserve will in fact be undermined by your preferred policy."

"But your project is not yet complete, is it, Mr. Wells? And it is only the first of its kind. It seems to me we don't yet have enough data on the effectiveness of what you suggest to devote significant funds to such a program in good conscience."

"All the independent evidence points to the problems of SMMs landing at our door, and losing ground to China in particular, as they step in to provide aid," replied Mark, as he tried to focus on her objections rather than the humanitarian points that he thought would fall on deaf ears.

Lorraine didn't look convinced, but she didn't respond to Mark's reply to her objection.

"Thank you, everybody, this has been a very illuminating discussion," the President said after a moment. "Let's take a 15-minute break to allow everyone to absorb what we have just heard."

After the break, the President started things off by quizzing General Rutherford about the SMMs projected using the model described in the report by Mark and his colleagues at Stanford.

"General Rutherford, I've had a chance to thumb through these graphics, and I must say, they are alarming. How confident are you that the number of SMMs predicted in this document will, in fact, occur?"

"We have high confidence, although, of course, there is always a degree of uncertainty when predicting events of this nature. That said, Mr. Wells' model has proven its worth by predicting all of the SMMs with a high level of accuracy, so there is every reason to believe that our report, compiled with his input, will produce accurate results within a reasonable margin of error."

"You are aware that this updated analysis of Mr. Wells' model predicts a number of SMMs in developed nations, as well as developing nations, are you not?"

"Yes, Madam President."

"Does this account, at least partly, for the Joint Chiefs recommending we intervene to attempt to prevent these SMMs to the degree possible?"

"It does. With Russia actively working against our interests and China stepping in to help in Mexico and South America, it is critical that we strive to help our allies combat any threat to their stability, including the threat posed by SMMs. We need to provide assistance in Mexico and Latin America. Russia is more likely than not to use SMMs as a cover to re-invade Ukraine and in Europe, including Poland and Finland. And it's an open secret that China will take Taiwan in a matter of hours without American assistance. If our southern border becomes overwhelmed with millions of migrants amassed at the same time, China will likely see its opportunity at this point. The world map could look very different twelve months from now."

"If I may, Madam President," Lorraine said, looking at the President for permission before speaking further.

"Please," the President said, indicating with an open palm that she wanted her NSA director to proceed.

"General Rutherford, while I'm not interested in quibbling over the minutiae of this updated forecast of Mr. Wells' model, I wonder if you and your fellow officers have considered the expense of this 'intervention' you propose? Are the Joint Chiefs prepared to reduce the Armed Forces budget in order to support this effort?"

"Our analysis did not encompass where the funds would come from, Director Betts. We responded to the President's request that we conduct this review with respect to what would be the most prudent action to take about national security. I believe no mention was made of budgetary considerations. In addition, we were not required to make a financial or budget assessment of taking no action."

"Even so, General, I'm confident that nobody in this administration wants to return to the dark days of the past decade when the specter of a debt crisis hung over our nation, potentially impacting our national security."

"Well stated, Ms. Betts," the President said. "While General Rutherford is correct that I did not request that the Joint Chiefs consider the budgetary impact of any action we might take to stem SMMs, it certainly would be a salient factor in drawing up any such plan. My administration has been working with the Democratic leadership in the House, as well as with our people, and they have agreed to support a policy that addresses these SMMs. I am inclined to support the Joint Chiefs and Mr. Wells' recommendation that we take action to prevent SMMs globally. More specifically, I want the US and American companies to support his suggestion to establish a global standard, a guarantee, of a minimum 15 liters of water per person per day. These aid projects will become the Marshall Plan of this century and the next."

There was a silence around the room as the assembled attendees considered the magnitude of the commitment the President was prepared to make.

"NSA Betts, as you know, I always appreciate your finely honed sense of realism of what can be accomplished both on the global stage and domestically. Before I appoint a team to finalize an operational plan to put this measure into effect, are there any suggestions you would like to make as to how we can optimize its chances of success?"

"Thank you, Madam President. I will leave the operational specifics to those better versed in the logistical requirements of moving the required amounts of water to where it is needed most. One suggestion I would make, however, is to appoint Mr. Wells to run the program. With his invaluable knowledge and experience with these issues, I think doing so is the best way to ensure the program will be as successful as possible."

Mark was surprised at Lorraine's suggestion. He had the feeling that, even if she didn't actively dislike him, she wasn't all that impressed with him or his recommendations. He had misjudged her, at least to some degree.

"Is that a position you would be likely to accept if offered, Mr. Wells?" the President asked, turning to him.

Mark hesitated for a moment.

"You have told us that this is the most important thing facing humanity, perhaps in our history." President Poulter did not miss a second before she pressed again.

Realizing that this was a yes or no moment, instinctively, Mark replied yes.

"Excellent. I certainly will second Director Betts' suggestion that Mr. Wells would be a good fit for the job if the operational planning team agrees. So, Mr. Wells, consider yourself appointed."

"Thank you, Madam President," Mark said.

The President gave him a brief smile before turning to her aides.

"Brian and Rachel, please draw up a list of personnel from relevant departments who could be expected to productively serve on an operational planning team for this program. And let us reach out to Democrats and Republicans to participate jointly, please. We Americans achieve great things when we come together. I have every reason to believe that the Democrats will support us."

"Yes, Madam President," her aides said as they typed notes into their personal communication devices. The President turned back to the table. "In the next day or two, I want meetings scheduled with all the departments involved in rolling this program out. This includes the public relations people, as this will need to be communicated to the American people. I doubt it will come as a surprise to the nation as I know the nature of these meetings seemed to have been leaked, and my people tell me that the numbers for support of these initiatives look extremely good."

Temir listened as the President described the next steps in the rollout of the SMM remediation program, or whatever they would call it. Guttenberg would not be happy. He now doubted that Guttenberg's plan that the Democrats would impeach the President could work, given that they were wholeheartedly supporting this proposal. This was a policy line that they would have introduced themselves were they in power. He didn't know the entirety of Guttenberg's game, but he believed that it just couldn't succeed under these conditions. The leaking of the report had backfired. The President seemed to have risen to the challenge.

At least his discussion with Lorraine had borne fruit. Temir had emphasized to her that having Wells close at hand would give them a better chance to influence him. But his real purpose of this was so that when Wells' appointment would be publicly announced, if he could be undermined with the terrorist link, the fall from grace would be pronounced. At least, felt Temir, he was being successful in what he had to do, even if Guttenberg was miscalculating the larger play.

CHAPTER 16

Temir slipped into the front passenger seat of Guttenberg's car. The President's Global Water Availability Initiative (GWAI) program was gaining momentum as if it were some modern-day Marshall Plan.

"What do you hear about the reception of the President's water availability program?" Guttenberg asked.

"As I told you on our last call, it is definitely going to pass in the House," Temir answered. "The Democrats will support this, and the Republicans dare not support it. The President seems to be a very deft operator."

Guttenberg's response continued to surprise Temir.

"We have her where we want her. She does not know what is coming. This is the beginning of the end of her. When I signal, you will deliver the message to the President that Wells needs to be sent back to Ethiopia," Guttenberg said. He continued, "If there is resistance because of Wells' safety fears, you will remind her that the Russians now have no need for Wells, as his SMM prediction super-computer is now in the public domain."

"Of course," Temir said. "But about the impeachment? Can that still work?"

"All in time. First, let President and Wells have their moment of glory. When it all comes crashing down, let that Kentucky redneck son-in-law of mine feel the full force of media and public antipathy. The impeachment is a few steps further away."

In his experience with the man, that was as close as Guttenberg had come to gloating. It must mean, Temir thought, that Guttenberg was highly confident that their plan would work, even though he wasn't sharing all the details of it with Temir. Temir had doubts, however.

"What if Mark's downfall doesn't derail the GWAI or force the President out of office?" Temir asked.

Guttenberg was unruffled by the question. "Don't be an idiot, Temir. But if you really think it will not work, then why don't you work on a backup plan B."

"Do you still want me to meet with Ingrid to see what she has learned from Wells?"

"Why wouldn't you?" Guttenberg asked.

"Well, we've learned everything we need to know about what he is up to already. I'm not sure what she could add at this point."

"If nothing else, it will make her feel useful."

"Okay, I will find out what she learned," he said.

"Good. Anything else?" Guttenberg was as businesslike as ever.

"I can provide an update on the investigation into the San Diego bombing if you like."

"Please do," Guttenberg said.

"The investigation initially revealed that the perpetrators likely escaped via below water surface level speedboats to a waiting ocean-going vessel. We now believe that they may have used a very sophisticated radar and satellite image interference AI, forcing us down a rabbit hole in terms of investigation. The AI created fake images which laid false clues for investigators who wasted a ton of time on the wrong paths. Because only we in the US possess this level of sophistication with this technology, we believe that the culprits have deep connections with our own military. Worse still, they may be our military."

"As interesting as all that is, it doesn't make me think that the investigators are all that close to finding the culprits," Guttenberg said.

"They are not."

"Keep me informed either way."

Temir could tell from Guttenberg's tone that it was time to end the meeting. He agreed to keep an eye on the search for the San Diego bombers and exited Guttenberg's vehicle.

CHAPTER 17

Mark stood at the window of his hotel room, gazing out at the Washington DC tableau spread out before him. He could make out the White House in the distance, with the Washington Monument nearby. In one direction, the National Mall led to the Lincoln Memorial; the Capitol Hill and the Capitol building that housed the US Senate and House of Representatives lay on the other. It was an impressive sight, but he turned away after a moment, distracted by his thoughts.

It had been a whirlwind three days since the meeting with the President. He had attended meeting after meeting with White House staffers as they hammered together a plan to present to Congress. The amount of money being agreed to was astronomical. The rest of the world put together could not raise this amount. His thoughts were interrupted by his phone ringing. Seeing it was Aida, he immediately answered it.

"It's nice to hear your voice," Aida said.

"It's nice to hear yours," Mark responded. "Sorry I've been hard to reach lately; ever since the President approved the project, I've been tied up in meetings just about around the clock."

"I understand, Mark; you know I believe in you and what you are doing," Aida said.

"I know, babe. I just wish I could be there with you to celebrate."

"I'm sure we will get a chance to do so when the time is right." Aida was more stoic about it than Mark. He loved her for that. She was committed to this vision and to do something so much bigger than the two of them.

"I'm counting on it. In the meantime, wish me luck. I have a meeting later today with General Endicott, who has been tasked with leading the initiative, and the leaders of Congress. We're going to discuss the Global Water Availability Initiative, GWAI for short, proposed by the President."

"Do you think they'll agree to establish this…GWAI?"

"I really do believe it will pass. But babe, if the legislation to enable the GWAI passes, it may be a while before I can get to Ethiopia to see you. But I will make sure to get there as soon as humanly possible, I promise you."

"I know you will, darling. This is more important that any of us."

"In the meantime, Tom has agreed to take over the project administration duties there on my behalf if this goes through, so I expect everything will proceed as usual."

After the call with Aida, Mark silently rehearsed what he planned to say at the upcoming meeting on the GWAI. The meeting would be crucial to getting the program off the ground. It was clear to him that US leadership was critical to stemming the spread of SMMs, and this initiative was the best way to channel that leadership into a program with global reach.

Mark thumbed through the GWAI report they would present at the meeting later in the day while keeping an eye on the TV news. The giant SMM in Mexico loomed ever closer to the border. The march had only seemed to gain in numbers, with well over a million people said to be part of it. On route many were dying. The cameras caught large numbers who lay motionless along the well-trodden path, who could walk no further, seemingly resigned to their fate of certain death. After a minute or so of coverage, the scene shifted to San Diego, where the FBI's investigation into the cruiser bombing was said to continue without result. The continued trouble at the southern border, which the public characterized as terrorism, and lack of progress on finding the domestic terrorists led to public sentiment against the President continuing to decline rapidly, at the same time as Mark Wells approval ratings were higher than any President.

As he watched the news, Mark's thoughts wandered to a more personal issue. Ingrid had left a message on his phone earlier in the day. She was leaving DC in two days and wanted to know if they could meet for dinner again before she left. He hadn't contacted her after their last meeting, mainly because he didn't know what to say. Perhaps it was because he was so consumed by guilt that by not contacting her, he could somehow pretend it did not happen. As much as he thought they had both enjoyed their previous encounter, it hadn't changed anything for him. He was in love with Aida, and even if he wasn't with someone else now, the truth was that what he and Ingrid once had was gone.

I need to level with her. She may feel the same way as I do, even after our last encounter. Either way, I need to tell her how I feel.

From the investigation into the bombing in San Diego, the news had shifted to DC, where the station's political correspondent covered the President's GWAI and its chances of getting passed by Congress. A quick video clip showing the impact of the devastating droughts afflicting a number of nations around the world brought home the immediacy of the crisis the GWAI was intended to address – 2037 was breaking records for being the driest year on record, beating the previous record of 2036, which in turn had beaten the previous record of 2034. With its images of desolate landscapes of arid plains, fallow fields where crops had once grown, and desperate masses of people crossing long distances in search of sustenance, Mark thought the video effectively made the case for providing the type of assistance envisioned by the GWAI.

A picture of General Endicott, the President's chosen program director, appeared. Still, no mention of Mark or his role as executive director of the proposed program was made. That pleased Mark, as he wasn't interested in the publicity associated with the job but rather the results the program could bring to those suffering from water insecurity around the world.

His thoughts turned back to Ingrid's request for a meeting. Given the affair, he supposed he could make a reasonably good case that he didn't owe her anything. All the same, he messaged her a proposed day and time for dinner at a Mediterranean restaurant on K Street.

CHAPTER 18

Satisfied that his snazzy tux and bow tie were in order, Temir left his residence in Georgetown and hailed a taxi. He was headed to a reception at the home of the President's National Economic Advisor. He was less interested in the subject of the soiree, "American Businesses Abroad: International Success Stories," than who would be there.

Eventually, Ingrid arrived, unfashionably late, he thought to himself. Guttenberg's daughter was attractive, without a doubt. Her blond hair had a gentle wave that ran from her shoulders front and back.

She noticed him as she walked by on her way to the bar, and they acknowledged one another with a smile and slight nod of the head. An hour or so later, with the party in full swing, Ingrid stepped onto the terrace on the second floor of the residence. Temir followed and then stood beside her, taking care not to stand too close. They both appeared to be enjoying the view of the Washington Monument from the terrace, making small talk, their body language indicating that they were acquaintances rather than friends.

"What did you find out?" Temir eventually got to the point, asking in a quiet unassuming tone, not looking at her as he spoke.

"He's speaking with the President and her advisors about starting a program to provide water to all those who need it around the world."

"Did you find out anything personal?" Temir continued to speak softly while looking at the view rather than Ingrid.

"Like what?"

"I don't know. Anything."

"Nothing at all, Temir. He doesn't talk about anything except for water. He's obsessed with water."

"Okay, thank you, Ingrid," Temir said before turning to walk away.

"Did you really need me for this?" Ingrid asked before he could walk away. "Surely you could have learned this yourself?"

Temir smiled at her and thought about telling her that his father wanted him to meet her but instead stayed silent. He walked back inside the residence. He headed to the bar for a drink. By the time the bartender had poured him a scotch, he saw Ingrid entering the room from the terrace. She didn't look at him as she joined the throng of people in the foyer and began to mingle. Why would Guttenberg want him to meet Ingrid in person, he thought. Surely, a call would have sufficed. He didn't think about it much longer as he sipped his drink.

CHAPTER 19

Mark took his seat in the Roosevelt Room at the White House, where leaders from both parties were in attendance. It had been great to get a chance to speak with Aida earlier that day, after the craziness of the past couple of days, he thought, as he and the others in the room waited for Representative Ross Talmadge, the Democrat Speaker of the House, to arrive and start the meeting. Mark was glad that Aida approved of Tom as his choice to run the project in his absence if necessary. Tom was very familiar with Mark's approach to running things and represented continuity for Aida and the people working on the project.

Mark leafed through the freshly prepared report on the Global Water Availability Initiative each participant in the meeting had been provided with as he waited for the meeting to start. He helped prepare the report, which explained the why and how of the GWAI, along with proposals for initial projects in some of the most water-insecure areas of the world that are projected to be included in the program. After another minute or so, Talmadge arrived to start the meeting by giving the President the floor. The President kicked things off by thanking the assembled leaders and staffers for their attendance before getting serious about what the GWAI was about.

"I believe that we face a historic choice, one that will have significant repercussions on the security and prosperity of our country and the world. All over this parched earth, people plead for succor, for aid from those who have the resources and ability to assist them. This presents us with what I believe is the defining question of our age: shall we offer them a caring hand of friendship, or shall we turn away from those in need and leave them to their fate? And if we leave them to their fate, how will be explain this to our children and their children?"

The President then continued to talk about how their own long-term security made it imperative that they provide the leadership needed.

She continued, "Many will say that we can't afford to take such action or that it will somehow harm American interests or create additional security risks. To those voices, I say, what is the alternative? Can we, in good conscience, stand back and let people suffer from water insecurity when we have the means to help them? And that help is not only justified from a humanitarian standpoint but also from what is in our nation's best interests. As these SMMs proliferate, we have seen, and will continue to see, conflicts spread around the globe, imperiling the security of our allies and our own. The chaos created by such a scenario harms our economy."

The President paused for the briefest of moments to look around the room, before continuing. "That is why I have brought you here today to propose a program to help combat the proliferation of SMMs. This initiative, a Marshall Plan for our age, is designed to use America's ability to get things done, our can-do spirit, as well as our soft power, our ability to form productive alliances with countries around the world, and our resources to stop this crisis in its tracks. In the aftermath of the Second World War, the United States saved the world from communism and disaster. The United States itself provided the resources for the reconstruction of Europe and Japan. That prevented another war and kept the communism of the then-Soviet Union from being an attractive option for some European Nations. The United States is rising to the challenge again as this country has always done, providing leadership, resolve, and resources. We have always overcome, and we will overcome again."

Looking ahead at General Endicott, she said, "I have appointed General Endicott to help shepherd the Global Water

Availability Initiative into existence and, once approved by Congress, make sure it functions as effectively as possible. He is here with us today. I'd like to let him take the floor now to explain how the GWAI will work and, along with the program's executive director, Mark Wells, answer any questions you may have about it."

Looking around the room, Mark thought the President's speech had made a huge impact. The publicity the proposed GWAI received had been favorable, and the President was betting that this, combined with the chaos SMMs were causing worldwide, would provide the impetus for Congress to pass enabling legislation. General Endicott was by no means an inspirational speaker, but his matter-of-fact tone exuded confidence that he could get the job done. They outlined the main planks of the GWAI, including its financial requirements, initial projected project locations, and the planned security arrangements associated with the program.

As the general presented the broad outlines of the proposed GWAI action plan, Mark's thoughts wandered to the part Temir had played in all this. He had led Mark to believe that the NSA would be behind the GWAI, only to have his boss speak out against it. Of course, Temir had not explicitly said he could get his boss behind the program, so maybe Mark was judging the man too harshly. And Betts had ended up supporting his appointment as the program's executive director. All seemed well.

CHAPTER 20

In his hotel room after the meeting with the congressional leaders, Mark idly flipped through the TV channels. He thought yesterday's meeting had gone well and felt confident that Congress would almost unanimously pass the proposal.

He turned the TV to a news channel, which featured drone footage of the massive SMM in Mexico marching ever closer to the US border. The number of people in the migration dwarfed those seen in past so-called caravans of migrants that had made their way to the border. The newscasters spoke of hundreds of thousands, perhaps nearing 2 million people on the move in this SMM. What would happen when the largest mass reached the US border, Mark could only guess.

The following day, Mark's phone rang shortly after he awoke. Coffee in hand, he answered the call.

"Wells," General Endicott said in his customarily gruff voice, "I hope you're ready to get to work."

"I am, General," Mark replied.

"Good, because the Congressional leaders are ready to move on the enabling legislation. The President wants us to pad the action plan so the International Affairs committee can use it to write the final chapters of the GWAI legislation."

"How long do we have to get it ready?" Mark asked.

"Two days," the general said.

"Two days!" Mark exclaimed. "I'm not sure that's enough time."

"With the extra staff you'll have to support you, it will have to be. The President has given me full authority to bring in all the personnel we need to get this thing off the ground in a hurry," the general said confidently.

"It's still a tall order."

"Get it done, Wells."

Mark wasn't sure if he shared the general's confidence in his abilities. Still, he thought he understood the reason for the haste—Congress had a notoriously short attention span, so the quicker they could turn the momentum from today's meeting into legislation, the better.

***

Mark had always enjoyed the décor at Kefi. He also appreciated the kebabs and gyros the eatery specialized in. He and Ingrid had ordered and were waiting for their food to arrive. He had considered begging off her request to meet, given the time constraints he was under in trying to meet the GWAI action item report deadline. But he calculated that he had to eat anyway and getting away from report preparation for a couple of hours was probably help clear his mind. His vision was getting bleary from reading the mass of information he had collected on areas of water shortage around the globe. He needed some time away from the holographic displays, if only to give his eyes and body posture time to recuperate.

After he and Ingrid had made small talk for a few minutes, Mark decided there was no time like the present to say what was on his mind.

"Ingrid, look, I'd like to talk about what happened."

"Me too," she said in a matter-of-fact tone.

Sticking to his intention to be direct but considerate, he said, "Actually, it's more the future I'd like to discuss."

"Would it upset you if I told you I already know what you'll say? And that I feel the same way?"

"No, not at all. Although I'd certainly be interested in hearing how you know."

"You're going to tell me you don't think we should see each other again, at least not romantically. As to how I know, I think the fact that you didn't call or text me after our night together was a pretty strong clue. And I feel the same way too, Mark."

Not even sending a text had been cold of him, but he hadn't known how to tell her what had to be said.

"I guess that was a good indicator," he said. "But honestly, I've been thinking it over, and it doesn't surprise me if you feel the same way. We had some great times together, but those times are gone, and I don't think there's anything we can do to bring them back, as enjoyable as the other night was."

"I appreciate your candor, Mark. I always admired that about you—the fact that you're such a straight shooter. And yes, while I would have appreciated a phone call or even a text after the other night, I do agree with you. While I hope you will always be part of my life, I think you are right—what we used to have has gone."

Mark was almost surprised to hear her echo his thoughts, but he knew Ingrid well enough to know she was a keen reader of a room.

Wanting to change the subject, he asked her how her business dealings had progressed.

"They've gone well," she said. "I expect we'll be adding another division to Guttenberg Mining in the not-too-distant future."

"Your father must be pleased with your work."

"I suppose. You know…Dad. He can be hard to read at times."

"I always found him to be polite but inscrutable, which I imagine serves him well in business dealings."

"No doubt, but it can make it hard to know what he thinks on any given subject," Ingrid said.

They chatted for another hour, Ingrid picked up the check and they left separately.

CHAPTER 21

"Where are you?" Temir asked his daughter as he tried to guess her location from the slopes of the mountain range he could see outside the window of wherever she was staying.

"Don't you remember, Dad? I told you I was going to Tucson for the conference on SMMs. It's focused on teaching how to provide aid to those taking part in them. Using drones to carry water, food and medicine. How do you think two million people spread out over hundreds of miles are being fed and watered?"

Temir did remember her telling him that, but he was so busy these days that he had promptly forgotten.

"Yes, I remember now; how is the accommodation?" Given that she seemed to spend half her time sleeping in tents at one protest site or another, he had a feeling that even a second-rate hotel would represent an improvement in that regard.

"It's fine, Dad. I'm used to much worse. If you're trying to hint that I'm spending too much money, Roman and I can just camp outside."

"That's not what I'm saying, darling," Temir said. "Your college fund can be used to fund your expenses even when you're not in school. But law school is expensive these days, so you should keep that in mind as you're flying around the country for these protests." Temir ignored her mention of her new boyfriend. As far as he could tell, Roman was yet another of the big-talking, unemployed, perpetual student type she seemed to be partial to.

"Dad, we don't fly, we drive, and Roman's car is all electric, so our transportation costs are minimal."

Temir didn't doubt that, and he further wondered if she was eating much these days, given how skinny, almost emaciated, she looked. But he knew better than to broach that subject with his daughter.

"Okay, well, I would prefer you stay in hotels rather than sleep outside in a tent. What are your plans after this…conference is over?" He hoped she would return home and get ready to attend law school in the fall, but he knew his daughter well enough to doubt that she was likely to do something so…responsible.

"Roman and I are heading to the Texas border after this. The SMM will be arriving soon, and we need to be there to help those in need." Temir recoiled inwardly at her pronouncement but tried to keep his reaction from showing on his face.

"Is that wise, Sara? That will be an extremely chaotic situation. The President has been ambivalent about her plans, but if she deploys the National Guard as many are urging, it could be dangerous for anyone in the area. And although the border is closed, there are so many people that it seems likely that…"

"Don't be a worrywart, Dad. I've been in tough situations before, and nothing has happened. Besides, Roman will be there with me," Sara's tone wasn't annoying so much as it was patronizing, which irked Temir.

Only the young could so blithely dismiss any thought of danger, not because it wasn't there but because they were too young and lacked experience. As for Roman protecting her, Temir thought that to be quite unlikely. The young man was tall but waif thin; from what Temir gathered, disputes over which issues were most likely to require the attention of his group of social justice warriors were the closest the kid had ever been to getting in a fight. For a moment, he considered hiring a private security firm to watch over Sara at the border, but he dismissed the idea as too dangerous for his relationship with his daughter. She would likely never forgive him if she found out about it.

"Okay, Sara, but please be careful," he said. "Attending a conference on SMMs will not necessarily prepare you for the dangers of being in or near two million people – that's unimaginably large, Sara."

"Dad, they won't be able to cross the border. It's probably exaggerated anyway." Sara agreed that she would be careful while she was there.

CHAPTER 22

Mark looked at the time on his phone as he finished typing up the action item list in his office in the Eisenhower Executive Office Building near the White House. He had just put the finishing touches on the program's expanded action plan as General Endicott requested. He would present the plan to the International Relations Committee of the House of Representatives later that afternoon, but he already had feedback that this would be well received. As the proposed Executive Director of the program, Mark would be responsible for preparing operational plans for any number of water transmission projects around the world. The action plan contained a summary of the plans for the first ten projects around the world.

He was about to leave for the meeting when his phone rang. It was Tom.

"Tom, how is it?" Mark asked.

"Mark, please don't be alarmed by what I'm about to say," Tom's voice was calm but tinged with intensity.

"That's probably the worst way to keep me from worrying about what you're going to say," Mark said.

"Okay, I deserve that. I'll just say it. Jemal's men staged another demonstration outside the hospital, although Jemal himself wasn't there. The UN guards drove them off, but there was some gunfire, mostly just shooting in the air. A bullet must have ricocheted and struck Aida in the shoulder. It was only a flesh wound, although it bled quite a bit, but she has been bandaged up and is resting comfortably at home. Apparently, it was not a bullet from an AK47 but a rifle that a sniper might use. One of Jemal's men must have been carrying a rifle."

"I knew I never should have left. Why the hell did you tell me to leave, Tom!" Mark was distraught at the news, and his tone of voice showed it.

"I don't think that's fair, Mark. I thought, and still think, that you going to DC was the best thing to do in the circumstances. What could you have done if you were here to stop Aida from being injured?"

"I wouldn't have left her alone at the hospital like you did," Mark snarled, realizing as he said it that he wasn't being fair. He had often left Aida by herself at the hospital to work on the water project.

"You know that's not true, Mark." Tom refrained from matching Mark's anger. "I was only doing what you yourself would be doing to keep the project on track. The UN guards there did their job and defused the situation. It was probably just an unlucky break that Aida got hurt. But she will recover fully, as I'm sure she'll tell you when you talk to her."

"I'm sorry, Tom. That was unkind of me. You're right. I'm just worried about Aida and frustrated I can't do anything to help her from where I am. When can I talk to her?"

"She's sleeping now—they gave her tranquilizers to dull the pain. She told me to tell you she will call you tomorrow as soon as she wakes up. Until then, please don't worry."

"I'm still a bit shocked that Jemal would allow random gunfire with his niece in the area," Mark said. "Aida has always said that her mother was Jemal's favorite sister. The hospital seems like a strange place for him to escalate like this."

"I admit that I didn't think he had it in him, having talked with Aida about him quite a bit recently."

"If anything, I would have expected him to conduct a demonstration in front of the UN headquarters building or something like that." Mark was trying to work out in his mind what had driven Jemal to act so recklessly around his niece.

"As I said, Jemal himself wasn't even there this time," Tom said.

"So how we do know it Jemal's men?" There was a moment of silence as Mark thought things through. "Maybe his men are getting restless for some action, and he may be unable to control them. He didn't have any men just a few days ago, so...yeah, maybe that makes sense. I still think their choice of location was strange, though."

"Especially considering the risk of getting in a gunfight with UN troops," Tom said.

"Yeah, but did a sniper target her? Let me sign off now to finish up this action list for the GWAI I'm working on, as I want to call Aida as soon as she is awake. I'll talk to you later, Tom."

"Goodbye, Mark."

Back at the hotel that night, Mark tuned into the latest news on the TV. A short piece on the passage of the GWAI was followed by a report on the aftermath of the attack on the cruiser in San Diego. The screen showed tugboats directing the damaged cruiser toward the drydock where it would be repaired.

Before he could turn the TV off and head down to the hotel bar for dinner, the scene shifted to the Statue of Liberty. Breaking news was reporting a bomb had been detonated outside the structure, slightly damaging it and killing more than twenty tourists. The video showed a scene of chaos, with sirens wailing and police hastily setting up a perimeter as tourists milled around, asking for news or loved ones or just gawking at the terrible scene. While there had been no claims of responsibility yet, the newscaster talked about the Statue of Liberty and San Diego bombings as the same group. Commentators on all channels as well as on social media persistently criticized the Poulter Administration for not making progress on these acts of terrorism. The country was in a downward spiral of fear from these terror acts as well as the skirmishes that were not developing on the southern border.

CHAPTER 23

"Does this latest attack affect our plans at all?" Temir asked Guttenberg. He was calling on a new burner phone from one of his usual locations. He changed his phone intermittently but always connected every phone to a multi-bounce VPN device.

"Not that I can tell," Guttenberg replied. "From what you told me last time we talked, if it is, in fact, the same group, they don't seem to have any precisely defined aims other than sowing chaos."

"But we can't be sure of that. It could be a ruse to disguise their true purpose."

"It could, but should we disrupt our plans due to mere speculation? You are the intelligence expert, Temir. How do you think we should respond?"

Temir agreed that what Guttenberg said made sense, but he remained hyper vigilant at how things could unravel, and how he might be exposed. Whatever this group was up to, they needn't let it disrupt their plans for no good reason.

"I agree with what you are saying about sticking to the plan. It just makes me nervous. Whoever is behind this campaign seems to have significant resources at their disposal if they can pull off a direct attack like the one in San Diego and remain undetected."

"I agree. But now is not the time to take our eyes off the ball. Can I trust you to do your part when the time comes?"

"Of course you can. Nothing has changed in that regard. Once you give me the signal, I will do my best to have the President send Wells back to Ethiopia."

CHAPTER 24

"How are you feeling today, babe?" Mark asked Aida. It had been four days since her injury, and she had spoken of feeling a bit better the last time they had talked.

"It's nothing to worry about. There's no pain and no permanent damage. I was shot in the shoulder, not the heart or the stomach. The UN doctor says it is a flesh wound but hit in the right place for it to bleed. As I've told you, it's not that big a deal," Aida said.

"You are truly a stoic, babe, but I wouldn't say that it was nothing."

"He is almost as worried about it as you are. The couple of you are like a pair of old men with time on your hands. Let's talk about water."

Mark laughed at her description of Tom and him. "You must be fine as you haven't lost your sense of humor, Aida."

"Apparently, my uncle came to try and see me, but he was turned away. He was shouting that it wasn't his men that caused the injury. I was too groggy for that after all the drugs they gave me. But I insist you don't worry about me, especially with the important work you do in Washington. Speaking of which, how are things going there?"

"I don't think you should see Jemal again. Any idea why he wasn't arrested?

Aida ignored him and said, 'Oh Mark, just please just tell me how it is going?"

"Well, I have some news. It's amazing news. Congress passed the legislation to fund the GWAI. It is the largest dollar amount in Congress' history. I've been made executive director of the program as well as advisor to the President," Mark said. "The bad news is it means I won't get to see you for a while, at least not until things are up and running smoothly here. But you knew that already."

"Congratulations, my love, this is a tremendous achievement." Mark could tell Aida was truly happy for him. "Of course, I would like to see you as soon as possible, you know that. But this program is important for so many people suffering from this global drought that it would be selfish of me to try to drag you away from it. I know you will come back to me when the time is right for you to do so."

"Why don't you come join me, darling?"

"Come on, Mark. You know I won't leave my mother and everyone else."

Mark so respected Aida's concern for those in need around the world, even if it meant that they faced an extended time apart. "I knew you would say that, babe, but I hope the right time will come sooner than we might think. I'll have to get out and visit some of the sites we are proposing for the program, and as several of them are in Africa, we might see each other sooner than you might think."

"I'm glad to hear that."

"If you could take a leave of absence or at least a break from the hospital, I might be able to find a way to take you along with me on some of my trips." Aside from their personal connection, Mark valued Aida's insight in general. He was confident having her alongside him to help evaluate prospective projects would benefit the program.

"Once I can get rid of this annoying sling I have to wear, that might be possible," Aida said. "Maybe. We'll see. No promises."

CHAPTER 25

The GWAI had been operating for a week, and Mark was exhausted. He was spending long hours working on finalizing the plans for the program's initial projects, and it was taking a toll on him. He was now in the public eye more than ever and had to give television interviews. Some of the journalists were openly hostile to him, but his popularity as an honest straight-talking guy continued to climb. One of the journalists was taken off-air as result of the public pushback. He resolved to try to take some time away from the office to de-stress in the next day or two if possible. He had finished the updated action item list and was just about to exit his office to make his way across the street to the White House for a staff meeting when his phone buzzed.

"Hey Tom, I'm just heading to a meeting; can I call you later?" Mark said as he walked out of his office, PCD in hand.

"Mark, I have some bad news. Jemal and Al-Haqa have blown up a large number of the tanks for the water project. There just aren't enough Kenyan troops to watch all of it."

"What? I thought you said he was under control. Are you sure it was him?"

"I thought so too, Mark. But Al-Haqa claimed responsibility this morning. So, there's no doubt. Although it wasn't Jemal himself claiming responsibility, it is clearly his group."

Mark was speechless. All that work rendered fruitless by one extremist and his cohorts. Then, his thoughts turned to Aida.

"What about Aida? Is she okay? Has there been another attack on the hospital?"

"She is fine, Mark. Her recovery is continuing, as I'm sure she's told you. There was no other attack. Just the bombing of these water tanks."

"This will set us back months, Tom, if not a year, but we can't let this stop us." Mark's tone was determined. He was resolute that this setback was not going to derail either the project in Ethiopia and the region or the GWAI as a whole. But he worried about American resolve. One of the major questions that the Administration and Congress had was about security. And with the skirmishes at the southern border and the domestic terror incidents, the American public was vitriolically anti anything related to terrorism.

"I hear you. The Ethiopian government has sent a team of investigators out here to bring Jemal to justice. I've spoken with the team that worked on the tanks already, and they have pledged to get back to work as soon as the site is declared clear of any explosives. We won't let this stop us."

At the review meeting called by General Endicott, Mark and the other attendees watched coverage of the bombing of the water tanks in Ethiopia while they waited for the general to arrive. He had sent Mark a text informing him that he would be delayed as he gathered information about the attack. On the TV, a picture of Jemal was displayed next to the ruins of the water towers. The pundits wasted no time discussing the potential ramifications for the President's Global Water Availability Initiative, with one opining that it should be halted until security concerns could be dealt with. Others disagreed saying that the policy and a single project were not the same thing, although most questioned whether adequate security could be provided anywhere in the world.

CHAPTER 26

Temir discreetly scanned the walls of Lorraine's office as he waited for the NSA director to turn her attention to him. They held only her diploma from Harvard and a picture of her with her husband and two children. They were meeting to discuss the fallout from the Al-Haqa attack on the water project in Ethiopia. Lorraine had asked if he minded if she took a couple of minutes to finish answering emails before they started the meeting. While he was awaiting word from Guttenberg to make his move to send Mark back to Ethiopia, he thought it prudent to see where his boss was on the topic of the GWAI. He knew she disapproved of it, but he wasn't sure if she had any plans to try to stop or slow it now that it had been established by Congress.

"So, tell me again why we're meeting," Lorraine asked, turning from her computer to look at Temir.

"It's about the destruction of the water tanks for Wells' project in Ethiopia. I know we opposed establishing the GWAI, so I wondered if this might provide an opening to renew our opposition to it."

"Once the President has decided, her position becomes ours, wouldn't you agree?"

"Of course, but as her chief advisor on national security matters, if you feel her position is wrong, wouldn't letting her know be the right thing to do?" Temir said carefully. Lorraine expected her subordinates to speak bluntly, but there were limits to that privilege, and he had no wish to anger her.

"And haven't I already done that, Temir?"

"Absolutely. I thought you countered Wells' arguments superbly at the meetings called by the President," Temir said.

"Quite frankly, I think her sagging polls may have played a part in her enthusiasm for Wells."

"Perhaps. Or perhaps the polls were sagging because she hadn't acted. Who knows. You and I are not polling experts."

"Of course. Purely from a security standpoint, I wonder if we should speak to the President again in light of this new development and let her know there is still time to change course." Temir held his breath as he finished speaking. "She could easily let it go without even making an announcement. It could get bogged down in an additional fact gathering exercise on security issues. She would not be abandoning the GWAI. It would just be on hold, but never to be resumed."

"You know, that may not be a bad idea," she said, and Temir breathed a sigh of relief. "Not in the way you have just articulated. But just a recommendation to put a hold on spending billions of dollars until the security situation can be guaranteed. But I wonder if I should be the one to approach her."

"I'm happy to raise the issue with her myself if you think that would be the best approach for us to take." Temir believed that Lorraine valued her relationship with the President. Having said her piece in opposition to the GWAI, she would not want to appear opportunistic by using the bombing in Ethiopia to renew her opposition. Instead, he surmised that she would instead use Temir to see which way the wind blew before deciding whether to renew her open opposition to the program.

"Yes, I think that would be best," Lorraine said.

Temir was very happy with the way the conversation had gone. It had provided him with cover with his boss for approaching the President about Mark Wells needing to be sent back to Ethiopia, when Guttenberg gave him the word.

"I also wanted to ask about one item that stood out at the last intelligence briefing. Have we heard anything more about the assessment that there will be a Russia-sponsored attack in the US?"

"Hmmm, I found that very odd. I'd never heard of him before...what was the name of the supposed leader of the operation?"

"Kraskolnikov, I think it was," Temir said.

"That's it. I don't believe that Russians would allow their proxies to attack the US directly. It feels like this is one that the intelligence guys have got wrong."

"I agree. Their smart move is to continue to do low-cost, low-risk disinformation about the US storing water," Temir responded.

"Definitely. The intelligence guys are using that new behavioral evaluative AI tool which brings together infinite pieces of data and photographs to predict what might be being said and planned, and by whom. Chatter alone is now meaningless as the Russians, the Chinese, and us...we are all putting millions of artificially generated conversations into the ether...so we need to figure what is being said in a different way.... You get the picture."

Temir wondered what would be discovered about him if the intelligence services ever turned their super-computer on his behaviors. "Yeah, should we recommend higher alert readiness to the President?"

"No, at that moment. Let's wait and see. Just mention it to her when you next see her."

"Got it," Temir said as he rose to his feet to leave, hearing the note of dismissal in the NSA's voice.

CHAPTER 27

"Hey Rex, what's up?" Mark said, surprised to hear from his friend so soon after their lunch. He enjoyed Talbertson's company whenever he met him, but his reputation as one of the hardest-working people in Washington DC was well deserved. Getting a chance to meet or even speak with the man could be difficult.

"Mark, I'm calling to warn you of what's coming. One of my sources in the administration said that the Washington Post is planning a major expose on the terror connections of the President's water expert. It will be added to their website as soon as today."

"That's crazy; I don't have any terrorist connections. Unless . . ."

"What is it?" Rex asked.

"I think I know what they will say. My partner's uncle is the one who blew up the water tanks in Ethiopia a couple days ago."

"What. Your partner's…" said Rex with incredulity. "That must be it. That's shit man. I am so sorry. I just wanted to let you know what was coming. Prepare yourself. You are going to be 24/7 news for a while now. Public opinion is likely to become negative against you."

"Thanks, Rex. I will do my best. Fuck."

After the call with Rex, Mark kept refreshing the Post's webpage until the article dropped at three in the afternoon. The title said it all: "Terrorism is a family affair for Poulter Water Czar." Soon after it appeared, he got a call from General Endicott. He denied any interaction at all with Jemal and his group. The General told him not to come to work for the day. He promised to get back to him after he had spoken to the President about the matter.

A few hours later, the general called him in for a meeting. To avoid the press outside the White House, they met at a military office on J Street. After they were both sitting in a conference room in the facility, the general spoke.

"Mark, I'm sorry to be the one to have to say this, but it would be best for the program and the President if you were to resign and return to Africa. On the back of the San Diego and Statue of Liberty bombings, the public is in no mood to tolerate any connection to terrorism. The President has told me she will make SpaceForce One available to fly you there as early as tomorrow. The intelligence guys don't believe you will be in any danger now as you have no value to the Russians. The information you had is in the public domain." The general's tone was kind but firm.

"Is this what the President wants, General Endicott?"

"I'm afraid it is. She became convinced by the advice from some. The program is still in a tenuous state, given that it is just getting off the ground. I'm sure you wouldn't want to be responsible for hurting its chances of success by remaining in your position after the revelation of your linkage to terrorists."

"But that's just not true. First, he's my girlfriend's uncle, not mine. And second, I have nothing to do with his actions." Mark couldn't help being aggrieved by the injustice of it all.

"I understand. And you can explain that, and stress your innocence, in your resignation letter. But do you really want to be responsible for the failure of a program that represents everything you've worked for throughout your career?"

"No, I don't," Mark said without hesitation. He was still stunned by the rapidity of his downfall, but he felt that the general was right. His presence now as executive director of the GWAI would be a distraction at best and ruinous for the program at worst. There was nothing for it but to resign and return to working on rebuilding the Ethiopian project.

"Please have your resignation letter prepared and sent to me within the next hour," the general said while patting Mark on the back. "I'm sorry it had to end this way, Wells. I've enjoyed working with you, and I hope that you will bounce back from this quickly."

"Yeah." Mark quietly spoke as he got up to leave. "One quick question before I go, if you don't mind?"

"Go right ahead," the general said.

"You said the President was convinced by the advice from some. Did you all advise that I should resign or be fired?"

The general looked at him keenly for a few moments before speaking. "This is between you and me, Wells, which is to say that you didn't hear it from me."

"My lips are sealed on the subject now and forever, General."

"Well, most of us advised that we put off any decision for twenty-four hours. The President's spokesman could say that we are looking into this. The Deputy National Adviser, Bousson, put forward a really strong case that you should be fired and sent back to Ethiopia…on SpaceForce One. So that you couldn't cause more trouble in D.C."

"Temir. Temir Bousson recommended that I should be…. Thanks for letting me know, General. I really appreciate that. And you can trust my discretion."

CHAPTER 28

"Hello, Temir." Tom addressed Temir using the holographic video link they had established.

"Mr. Van Heusen, there have been some troubling developments here that I thought I should update you on," Temir said.

"It is the middle of the night in Ethiopia. Is it urgent?"

"I'll get right to the point, as it's late. Mark Wells has resigned as executive director of the GWAI due to press reports of terrorist links between his partner and Al-Haqa."

Tom sat up, energized and animated. "That's ridiculous. Jemal is Aida's uncle, not Mark's. And Mark...a terrorist link... give me a break!" Tom's tone expressed increasing incredulity at the news he was hearing.

"I don't disagree with anything you have said. But negative publicity could halt or even terminate the program at this early point in its development, as I'm sure you can understand."

"That's total crap," said Tom.

"But there is something else that I need to talk to you about." Temir paused for a moment, but Tom said nothing, so he continued. "It's not my place to judge morality, of course. However, we have been given a recording of his...anonymously... of a highly graphic sexual indiscretion with a woman who is not his partner. In fact, it appears to be his ex-wife. Eventually, these things inevitably become public; it is just a matter of time. We want to ensure that the water project is not further undermined by any fall out between Aida and Mark. Is it worth you getting ahead of the story to save both of your friends from the surprise of public humiliation?"

There was silence for a moment, and then Tom spoke. "Are you saying you want me to determine whether Aida is told about this sex tape before Mark returns to Ethiopia?"

"It will likely come out, and that is exactly what I'm saying. We have no interest in this coming out. But if this video was sent to us, it is simply a matter of time before it becomes public. You need to make the decision in the best interests of the project, a project that is so important to all of us, including the President. You will receive a link to the video from an anonymous email in the next minute or so. Please make your decision in the best interests of the project and not in the interests of any one person. You and I have developed a good relationship, and I thought you would be best person to make this decision." Temir spoke in a neutral tone, hoping to convey to Tom that President Poulter's administration was not incentivized either way.

"Wow. I am shocked. The poor guy. Poor Aida. When is Mark scheduled to return to Ethiopia?"

"I believe he will be flying in on SpaceForce One sometime within the next twelve hours. Perhaps sooner."

After half of minute of silence between the two, Tom, barely audibly said, "Okay. Goodbye, Temir."

After the call, Temir could hardly move. He was shocked that Guttenberg had made a recording of his daughter having sex with Wells. True, it was for the purpose of creating even more difficulty for Wells rather than for his daughter, but it took a steely will to do something like that. At that very moment, as he thought through Guttenberg's immorality, Temir realized why Guttenberg had wanted him to meet his daughter to ask about Mark, at the recent black-tie event. If the recording is ever made public, Ingrid would recall her meeting with Temir, and she would conclude that he, Temir, was responsible for the recording and released the video. It would not occur to her that it was her own father who instigated the plot. As he thought through how Guttenberg operated, Temir was filled with a loathing admiration. It rapidly became equally clear why

Guttenberg wanted him to speak with Tom. By releasing it to Tom only, perhaps the audience could be controlled, thereby saving his daughter from public humiliation.

Temir couldn't say what Tom would do with the video he had sent him. But it made no difference. If Tom didn't reveal the video, he would reveal it anonymously, per Guttenberg's instructions. Wells would now be off guard and perhaps more easily taken out in Ethiopia, and they could intensify their efforts to remove the President from power. Anger and admiration gave way to anxiety and fear as Guttenberg's chess moves came sharply into view. Temir realized that what he could see was just the tip of the iceberg. Anxiety and fear subsided to give way to a feeling that verged on panic; it seemed to him all too likely that Guttenberg might remove him one day to cover his tracks.

CHAPTER 29

SpaceForce One was decelerating as it began its descent toward the landing site outside Aida's village. Mark watched outside his cabin window as the bleak arid landscape rushed by as the jet flew ever lower. Finally, they had landed, and he gathered his belongings and headed to the exit. Tom was waiting for him as he disembarked, jeep at the ready.

"You heard why I had to leave the States?" Mark asked as they headed to Aida's village.

"I did. And I know it's bullshit," Tom said. "I'm not sure why the press thinks you are somehow linked to Jemal because he is Aida's uncle."

"There's a lot of fear about terrorism in the States right now. But there also are those in DC who oppose the GWAI, and I suspect they may have had something to do with convincing the President that this link would damage her."

They drove in silence until they were almost at Aida's village.

"Mark, Aida has moved back to her mom's house," Tom said.

"That makes sense. She can help her recover from her injury."

"I'm sorry to be the bearer of bad news, but there's more to it." Tom's tone was somber.

"What is it? I'm not sure how much more bad news I can take," Mark said.

"I don't think you should see Aida right away," Tom said as they drove up to his home in the village.

"Why is that, Tom? Stop speaking in riddles and get to the point." Mark was getting perturbed by his friend's evasiveness.

"She told me that she had received a video from an anonymous sender that showed you having sex with some woman while you

163

were in Washington." Tom glanced at him quickly, then looked away as he spoke.

Mark was stunned and speechless for a moment. "Fuck," he said. "I...oh, crap." He laughed bitterly. "I should have known."

"You should have known what?" Tom asked.

"I slept with my wife," Mark said, getting out of the car. Tom exited the vehicle and stood in front of Mark, who started walking to Aida's parents' house.

"I would give her some time, Mark. She was very upset the last time I talked to her. Why don't you let her settle down before you talk to her?"

"Get out of my way, Tom," Mark said in a level tone. "I appreciate you looking out for Aida, but this is something I need to talk to her about."

"As you wish," Tom said, stepping out of Mark's way.

It didn't take long to walk half a kilometer to the house where Aida was staying now on the other side of the village. When he knocked on the door, Aida's mother answered.

"She doesn't want to talk to you," she said in a disapproving tone. "You hurt her."

"I can handle this, mama," Aida said, putting her hands on her mom's shoulders and guiding her out of the way.

"Didn't Tom tell you I didn't want to see you?" she said when she reached the door.

"He did, but you know me, Aida, I'm not always good at following instructions," Mark said in what he hoped was a suitably humble tone of voice.

"Just like you're not good at staying faithful to the person you supposedly love?" Aida's expressions were full of hurt rather than anger.

"Aida, I really messed up. I am so, so sorry. I told Ingrid before and afterward that I love you, and we can't see each other again. And she said she felt the same way. Please forgive me, babe."

"That only makes it worse. You told me it was over with her, in no small part, because she cheated on you. And now you go and cheat on me with her!"

"I'm sorry. I could say she seduced me, but even if that was the case, it's still my fault."

"Yes, it is," Aida said, her tone becoming even angrier.

"It is, and I take full responsibility for being a fool and an idiot. All I can do is hope that you will forgive me someday, if not now." Mark's tone was apologetic. "Can you find it in your heart to do that?"

"I don't think I can, Mark. In fact, I don't think I ever want to see you again."

"I don't think you mean that. We still have the project in common, so we have to see each other."

"You don't know me at all, it seems, if you think you can treat me this way and then try to get me to forgive you just like that," Aida said. "I don't think you should be part of this anymore. I think you should introduce Tom to Mikeo and everyone else and leave this place."

Mark's whole world was crashing around him, and he couldn't speak.

"I haven't spoken to ministers in Addis yet, but I will speak to them and request that you be asked to leave."

Mark was glad she hadn't spoken to them and in his heart believed she would ultimately decide against this course of action. This was an understandable emotional outburst. As well the project being the most important thing in her life, Mark believed the Ethiopian government would stand by him.

"I wish you wouldn't do that," he said, quickly recovering from the shock that she even threatened to do this.

"Right now, I want you to leave," Aida said.

"Okay, Aida. I'll go. But I still love you, and I know you still love me. Please find it in your heart to think about forgiving me in the future. Don't decide now, please."

"Just go, please."

Mark turned and walked away. Though it wasn't a long walk back to the house where Aida and he had lived, it felt like a million miles. He had been looking forward to his reunion with Aida after the GWAI fiasco, and now even that was denied to him. He wondered how she had found out about his fling with Ingrid. As he walked away, he asked Tom, who had told him it was an anonymously posted video but that he didn't want to go into more detail than that.

Mark was no conspiracy theorist, but he could only conclude that someone wanted to cause him problems to create distractions and upheaval so the water project might fail. As he reached his house and opened the front door, he thought it was most likely Temir. He could see the Deputy NSA's fingerprints all over everything that had happened to him. Why did the man have it out for him? Whatever he had told Mark, he and his boss were clearly opposed to the GWAI. What am I missing about why this is happening, he thought to himself.

The more he thought about it, the more tired he became and his half-asleep state, did not doubt that there was some plot against him. He thought about Jemal suddenly possessing weapons and being the leader of a gang of violent men. That had never made sense to him. Despite the adrenaline rush and the anxiety ripping through his veins, as soon as his head hit the pillow, he fell fast asleep.

CHAPTER 30

The following day, Mark made himself breakfast and sat on his porch, thinking. It was far from clear to him what he should do next. Aida clearly didn't want anything to do with him, and he couldn't say he blamed her. He hoped she would come around eventually and forgive him, but even if that happened, it wasn't clear how long that might take. She could be stubborn; he knew that from experience. And it would be uncomfortable for both of them if he just sat around in the house they shared, while she was at her mom's.

His thoughts turned to the GWAI. Despite his unceremonious exit, he hoped the project was a success. President Poulter had seemed to be highly invested in getting it started. He wasn't sure what effect his departure would have on its chances. Perhaps there was no plot against him. Perhaps the plot was against the GWAI and the project. And discrediting him was the way to achieve that. His mind continued to run wild with theories, ideas and plots, consuming his energy and the mental and physical exhaustion resulted in him becoming ill with a head cold.

Mark's thoughts on the future were interrupted by the buzzing of his phone. He answered immediately.

"Mikeo, it's good to hear from you."

"So you say now, my friend, but you might not say the same after you hear what I have to say." Instead of his usual jocular self, President Thundilayskila sounded serious.

"Well, everyone else in the world seems to be mad at me for some reason, so it won't surprise me too much if you are as well," Mark said.

"I'm not upset at you, but disappointed. We were making such good progress on the project, and then you go off to Washington, and everything falls apart."

"Surely, you're not blaming the actions of Al-Haqa on me?" Mark said, his tone defensive.

"Not that. It's getting yourself fired from the GWAI program. What hope does it have without you to run it, my friend?"

"While I'm flattered you think so highly of my abilities, Mikeo, I assure you that they will find someone just as competent as me to take my position."

"That is horseshit, my friend. It will die slowly as people become more and more exhausted by the endless and pointless talk. How could you let them remove you from the position just when the program was getting started?"

"I wish I knew, Mr. President. I suspect powerful forces in DC do not like me or, more likely, did not want the program to succeed and therefore conspired against me." There was a pause on the line as Mikeo digested what Mark had just said.

"I believe that is very probably true, Mark. I have faced many plots of this type myself, and your situation feels similar. You needed to be more careful."

"You're right, Mikeo. The plot to get me out of the GWAI program was well-planned, as far as I can tell. I believe it likely involved coordination with the press and possibly even collaboration with my wife."

"It seems you have somehow amassed enemies without knowing you had done so. Again, I can empathize. I have an ex-wife who I would not care to meet in a dark alley, especially given her skills with a machete," Mikeo said.

"Was she a former soldier?" Mark asked, curious to hear where Mikeo's ex-wife had developed her weapons skills.

"No. A chef. But that is another story, my friend. You have been outmaneuvered in Washington."

"I can't dispute that," Mark said. "But if the goal was to, ultimately, destroy the GWAI, why go to so much trouble to remove me from my post, even to the point of enlisting my wife in the operation? Will getting me out of the picture really kill the program?"

"If you are not driving the program, my friend, it will likely kill the program. Don't assume these plotters have exhausted their ammunition just yet. They may have further tricks up their sleeve. And you do not even know who they are. One thing is for sure; there are no coincidences here."

"There's not much I can do about it now. I guess I could tell the President of the plot against me, possibly led by her Deputy National Security Adviser, but given that I don't have any proof to speak of, it would probably just sound like sour grapes on my part."

"It would be fruitless to make accusations at this point. You and I do not know who they are. You may point fingers in the obvious place, and it could be that you are pointing at a friend rather than a foe. This is a time for you to think more carefully. To think several chess moves ahead."

"You are not as shocked as I thought you might be by these assertions, Mikeo. As a veteran political operator, you would be accustomed to this type of thing. I'm an academic, born and raised in rural Kentucky. My mother had to work three jobs to get by and obviously didn't teach me how to operate in the shadows."

"When you swim with the sharks, you must take precautions, my friend. You must be better prepared for these plotters in the next round."

"The next round? In case you didn't know, Mr. President, I had to resign my position in disgrace and return to Africa, which suits me better than America right now, that's for sure. Anyway, I'm no longer on the playing field."

"So you say, my friend," Mikeo said, scoffing, "but I know you to be a fighter and a man with big dreams—a man who does not give up easily. I don't know about your American politicians, but here in Africa, our politicians may be up one year and down the next, so they know that the winds that blow against them today may fill their sails tomorrow. I myself was defeated at the ballot box at one point and worked as a chef for years before I returned to office."

"I appreciate your optimism, Mikeo, but I don't see any way to resolve the situation. I lack the ability and resources it would take to mount a comeback. And you were not a chef, Mikeo. You're making that up. I know you cannot cook."

Mikeo laughed so loudly that Mark started laughing, too, before Mikeo became serious again. "Your battle is my battle, my friend. These SMMs threaten the security of nations around the world, especially here in Africa. Why don't you come to see me in Kenya? I will fly you out here, and we can discuss our strategy for your glorious return to the fight against spontaneous mass migrations."

Mark had to smile at the Kenyan President's infectious optimism. "While I don't think anything I've done or might do is likely to be all that glorious, I'll accept your offer and come to Nairobi. It will be so good to see you again."

It was Mikeo's turn to chuckle. "Your humility does you credit, my friend. And it also makes it clear why you are so unsuited for politics. But never fear; we will work with the tools we have to help those in need. My assistant will contact you later today to arrange your journey to Nairobi."

CHAPTER 31

Temir watched the reports of Russian and Ukrainian civilians fighting in hand-to-hand combat across northeast Ukraine. He turned to the footage of the latest developments at the Mexican-American border with concern. The first part of the SMM had reached the border a few days ago, and people were finding ways to cross at many different locations. Some were equipped with tools to cut down metal fencing. The governor of Texas had called out the National Guard to prevent people from crossing. The chaos of the scene was worrying to him, given that Sara was likely to be somewhere in the thick of it. And he sincerely doubted the ability of her latest boyfriend, Romeo, or Roman, or whatever his name was, to protect her. He had called her several times today, but she hadn't gotten back to him as of yet.

As worried as he was about his daughter, he had an important meeting to attend. Half an hour later, he slipped into Guttenberg's car at the customary meeting spot at the billionaire's compound near the State Park. Guttenberg wasted no time in congratulating him on his recent work.

"I appreciate the kudos," Temir said, "but I'm worried we could lose the momentum we've gained by discrediting Wells. If we're going to get rid of Poulter, now is the time."

"Everything is proceeding according to plan, Temir; there is no need to speed anything up. With the GWAI likely unworkable without that fucking redneck Wells, who is regrettably still my son-in-law, at least for the moment, the SMM at the Mexican border spreading chaos, and this string of deadly terrorist attacks on the homeland unsolved, it should be clear to everyone this

171

president is unfit to govern. Even those fucking idiot Democrats won't lose this opportunity."

Temir wished he could be as confident as Guttenberg that everything was going to plan. "Then why not act now? The longer we wait, the more time she has to be able to remedy the situation."

Guttenberg glanced at Temir before speaking. "If you are so impatient for action, why don't you work on that plan B you've been advocating for? I presume you've spent some time thinking about it since we last talked?"

"I have. It's occurred to me that the 25th amendment might provide an opportunity to remove the President due to her delusional policies that are putting American security and prosperity at risk."

"While I agree with your characterization of the President, the 25th amendment would temporarily assign her duties to the Vice President, whereas our goal is to remove her from office permanently and for the Vice President to take over permanently. He is our hope. In any case, I doubt the Cabinet will go for it. I am confident that her power and credibility is rapidly eroding so there is nothing to be concerned about," Guttenberg said.

Guttenberg's tone made it clear that he didn't want anything done that would detract from his current plan.

"Understood," Temir said.

As he walked back to his car, he wondered, not for the first time, who else in the administration Guttenberg had working for him. Unbelievable as it sounded, from what Guttenberg had said, the Vice President seemed to be involved. He was certain he himself wasn't the industrialist's only ally in the government. With all that had transpired with how Mark Wells had been removed, Temir now feared Guttenberg more than ever, for his own safety.

CHAPTER 32

Mark took in the view from the third floor of the Presidential Palace in Nairobi, Kenya. The city was teeming with people in motion. The portion of the city he could see from the palace was just a tiny part of what was one of Africa's major cities. He had ventured out into the city several times in the week or so that he had been in the city as a guest of President Thundilayskila. It had been a heady experience, full of colorful sights and the sounds of throngs of people and vehicles rushing to get from one place to another.

Mikeo had left the same day Mark arrived, convinced by his advisors of the necessity of undertaking a last-minute diplomatic mission to Uganda. There would now always going to be minor tensions between that country and its neighbors over water sharing. But the leaders were adept at ensuring that their minor tensions did not become major headaches. Before he left, he had promised Mark they would discuss the East African water project's prospects and how to get it back on track when he returned.

Mark had followed the news in the States during his stay at the Presidential Palace. The reports about Congressional anger over security for the GWAI projects and his resignation were not the only bad news. The investigation into the latest bombing, which the mysterious Liberty Salvation Front had also taken responsibility for, was so far no more successful than the search for the culprits behind the San Diego bombing. Mark and Mikeo spoke by holographic video phone and agreed that President Poulter's presidency might end in the next few weeks. The Democrats sensed that this was their moment to strike.

Mark had called Aida to apologize once more for his actions, but she wasn't returning his calls. He had spoken with Tom briefly after he first arrived in Nairobi, and Tom had agreed to keep an eye on her in case Jemal and his crew were to make another appearance. He supposed the best thing to do was to give Aida time to cool off. He believed, or rather, hoped, that she would eventually forgive him, but bugging her about it was likely counterproductive. He had good reason to believe that she had not yet spoken to any government officials in Ethiopia to have him removed. He thought that she would put the project before her own feelings.

After a hearty lunch served by the palace staff, Mark returned to his room. After taking in the view once more, he turned on his computer and scanned the latest news. He had been doing that a lot to kill time while waiting for Mikeo to return from his state visit. The news from the US was disturbing, as it so often seemed to be these days. There had been another terrorist attack, this time at the Lincoln Memorial in Washington, DC. There had been damage to the structure of the building housing Lincoln's statue, and over a hundred people had been killed. No formal claim of credit had been issued, but the Liberty Salvation Front was named as the only suspect. At the border, the SMM had turned violent, as thousands of migrants had burst through various points at the border. Border patrol agents lined up to stop them from entering the country. Many had died on each side. President Poulter was being slated on all sides, and her approval ratings were the lowest recorded for any President.

Mark turned from his computer as the sound of vehicles approaching the palace caught his attention. He walked to his window, where he saw a convoy of SUVs approaching the gates of the palace grounds. If he was not mistaken, Mikeo had returned.

CHAPTER 33

"Are you on a secure line?" Guttenberg asked.

"I am," Temir replied. He had left the office and driven to one of the customary locations, from which he called again with a different number and burner phone.

"Why the sudden Mexican accent?"

"Oh, sorry, I just turned on the voice disguiser by mistake," said Temir, switching it back off.

"Why are you calling?" Temir sensed a bit of impatience in Guttenberg's tone.

"You asked me to tell you if I learned anything interesting about Wells' activities back in Africa," Temir said.

"I did. What's going on with him? I would have expected him to hang his head and lay low after his ignominious exit from the GWAI."

"Well, he's certainly having troubles in his love life, thanks to us. But that was to be expected. The more salient fact is that our sources tell us that he's flown to Kenya and is staying in the Presidential Palace as a guest of President Thundilayskila."

"Any intelligence about what he's up to there?"

"Nothing concrete yet. But clearly, he is being supported by the President."

"That's a reasonable assumption." Having had time to process the news about Wells, Guttenberg's voice was calmer now. "Given the damage to his reputation, it doesn't seem like Wells is in a position to do much that can hurt us. But there's no reason to underestimate him, even in his current circumstances. Have your sources keep an eye on him and let me know if you learn anything substantive."

"I don't have too many sources on the ground," Temir said.

"The next part of the plan is taking shape," said Guttenberg, cryptically.

"What...which plan?" replied a befuddled Temir.

"I have it on very good authority that the Democrats will launch an impeachment investigation within hours. They are seeking revenge for what we did to their President last time, and this is their chance. This will conclude very quickly in the House. At first, they won't believe they can be successful in the Senate, but there are enough Republicans who will support it. Our allies in the Senate will remain silent until the last possible moment and then vote with the Democrats on the basis of putting the country's interests first. Then the Vice President will be sworn in." Guttenberg's tone was one of confidence and authority.

"You seem confident. Is there anything I will need to do?"

Guttenberg explained, "Once the impeachment process starts, there may need to be a leak about how much Poulter knew about Wells' terror connections before she sent for him. To give it the final momentum."

"That won't stick. It will be exposed as a lie." said Temir.

"It won't need to stick. It just needs to cause enough damage for a short window."

And with that, the call abruptly ended.

CHAPTER 34

Mark sat in a plush, comfortably appointed chair in the palace's conference room, facing Mikeo and his chief political advisor, Konigwe Kaskanda, who sat across from him. The President of Kenya had been as good as his word and scheduled this meeting with Mark just two hours after his return from his state visit to Uganda.

"So, tell me, my friend, how will the EAWTP, the East African Water Transfer Project, regain the momentum it has lost due to this bombing by Al-Haqa?" Mikeo said.

"I have some thoughts on the subject, but I must warn you that they require strong action from a leader in the region who is determined not to back down and let these terrorists ruin things for everyone," Mark said.

"My friend, if you are suggesting that I reiterate my support for the project, I am happy to do so. Besides the utility it provides for countries in the region, I and my advisors," he turned to look at Konigwe, who nodded to indicate his support, "believe it is perhaps our best chance to put an end to, or at least reduce the scope of, these SMMs. The only other solution will be hundreds of years of conflict in East Africa. Our people deserve better."

"I agree with you, Mikeo," Mark said, "but I think even stronger action on your part would go a long way towards enabling the EAWTP to regain its momentum and achieve long-term success."

"Mark, I appreciate that you like to prepare your friends by warning them that you are about to say something of significance before saying it. So, consider me warned. What is on your mind, my friend?"

"Mikeo, I believe that if you were to announce that Kenyan troops, in conjunction with the UN, were prepared to provide a massive increase in security for the EAWTP throughout Ethiopia, and not just at the storage section and intersection of pipes, it would take away many of the security objections that have become the narrative in the US. President Poulter had skillfully ensured that there was bipartisan support for the GWAI initially, but with the terror attack, both parties now have security and cost concerns. If Kenya provided the security..." Mark left his sentence unfinished and looked for Mikeo's reaction.

Mikeo looked at him thoughtfully for a moment. "My friend, I have always appreciated your bold thinking. That might be helpful, as you say, but how will it go down in Ethiopia? And what about the UN?"

"Ethiopia needs to stem these SMMs more than anywhere else in East Africa and they have Gudonov to deal with. The Ethiopians will make the request for more security from Kenya..." Again, Mark left his sentence unfinished.

"Mark," said Konigwe, choosing his words carefully," I believe, as does the President, that you are an honorable man despite the troubles you are currently experiencing. But there are those who might view your recent history with...distaste. Are you sure you can be successful in encouraging these 'old friends' you speak of to support our cause?"

"I understand your skepticism, Konigwe," Mark said. "The people I speak to understand that the stakes here are much higher than any distaste they may feel. The UN and Ethiopia are desperate to do something to try and stem the dislocation caused by SMMs. I know the US. They will want security guarantees and because of you, Mikeo, Kenya has built a formidable military and intelligence reputation in this last 15 years. Your security infrastructure is trusted in the US."

Konigwe nodded his head to indicate he was reassured by Mark's statement. After a moment, Mikeo said that he liked the idea but would need to discuss it with Konigwe and his other advisors before agreeing. Mark was happy that at least Mikeo hadn't dismissed it out of hand. If he could get the Kenyan President's support, it could provide a real boost to the chances of completing the EAWTP. The Ethiopian government was hugely destabilized by the presence of Gudonov in their country and unable to provide sufficient resources for protecting the pipeline infrastructure.

CHAPTER 35

Temir looked around the Situation Room at the assembled bigwigs of the intelligence profession. The backdrop to the meeting created an intense atmosphere. Democrats had quickly instigated an investigation to impeach President Poulter and quickly geared to a vote. In addition to Temir's boss, NSA Betts, the CIA and FBI directors were in attendance, as were the head of Homeland Security and the Director of National Intelligence (DNI). The Deputy Director of the FBI in charge of counter-terrorism investigations, along with the Vice President and President were also there. In a sign of the seriousness with which the formation of the counter-terrorism task force was being taken, General Johnson, Chairman of the Joint Chiefs of Staff, was also present. The President was under extreme pressure, with multiple crises swarming her leadership. Even some of her supporters were talking about replacing her with the Vice President. However, any trial in the Senate seemed likely to fail—with a 51/49 Democratic Senate. The Democrats just didn't have the numbers.

President Poulter seemed confident as she began to speak with no sign of weakness in her voice. She started the meeting by stressing the vital nature of the task force under discussion. Its goal was to increase the resources available to solve the series of bombings that were killing Americans and making its national law enforcement agencies look bad.

"We have encountered what we believe is an AI-driven screen of social media-driven allegations and claims of culpability for these events. This leads us to believe that a very sophisticated group or state actor is behind these attacks," the FBI director said in response to a question from the Vice President, who Temir knew fancied himself an expert in matters of national security.

"Director Baden," the VP directed his next question at the CIA Director, "have there been any signs of foreign involvement in these events?"

"There are no signs of any foreign involvement." Baden's tone was dry. "The Russians are active with the use of proxies for such exploits, but I don't see that random terrorist attacks in the US would serve their purposes, as they are more vulnerable than us to the same if we were to reciprocate. Let us be clear Mr. Vice President. We could bomb Russia into the Stone Age in terms of their conventional weapons. Aside from that, their main effort for actions abroad recently has involved the mercenary group linked to the Kremlin, the Gudonov group. But having said that, there are some unsubstantiated highly speculative intelligence reports that there is a Russian plot on US soil. Picking up chatter has been rendered meaningless because of AI, so we are experimenting with AI-augmented behavioral intelligence, as this has come up with a theory that there is a Russian bomb plot being considered on the US mainland, and—"

"I don't buy that behavioral shit," Vice President Hugh Degrasso said with a sharp interruption. "Aren't Gudonov mostly active in Africa?" the VP asked.

"Our behavioral intelligence is a trial, so…none of us are convinced by it at the moment. And you are correct, Mr. Vice President, about Gudonov in eastern Africa," the CIA Director confirmed. "The outbreak of these SMMs has provided them with cover to increase their attempts to destabilize a number of our allies in the region and to potentially invade Belarus and reinvade Ukraine."

"That is a conversation for a different day, I believe," the President said. "Director Betts, besides the added resources the task force can provide, are there any avenues of investigation that, in your opinion, we should prioritize as we look to assist the FBI in solving these cases?"

"Madam President," Lorraine said, "I strongly believe that whatever their inspiration or funding, the culprits behind these attacks are likely residents of this country, and with connections to our military. They have AI-augmented cyber capability to constantly throw us off the track. I've spoken with Director Gupta about extending the scope of the search to a wider range of radicalized groups and individuals in the country, and he supports taking this step. I'm confident that doing so will provide this task force and existing assets on the case with a wealth of relevant leads to pursue."

"The AI propaganda and the terror attacks are obviously the same people," said Hugh Degrasso.

"That is our working assumption, Mr. Vice President," FBI Assistant Director of Counter-Intelligence, Voorhees, said, speaking for the first time at the meeting, "but the AI is being propagated via a web of proxy servers, and this is where Russia may be indirectly aiding these terrorists. Piercing these layers takes time and is ultimately likely to prove fruitless."

"Why would that be?" the Vice President asked. "Once you have the location of the servers, I presume you could then approach whoever is operating them to provide you with whatever information they have about the identity of the individual or group behind these algorithms."

"While that is true in the US, Mr. Vice President, it becomes much more difficult abroad. This is especially the case when, as I suspect is likely with these AI programs, as I said, the servers used are thought, without direct evidence at this point in time, to be located in Russia."

"Which doesn't necessarily mean that the Russian government is behind these programs," NSA Betts cut in, "but it does make it extremely difficult to trace who is responsible for them."

The Vice President nodded to indicate that he understood the point the National Security Adviser was making. He turned to look at General Johnson.

"General Johnson, does the Joint Chiefs share NSA Betts' analysis of the situation with regard to propagation of propaganda via Russian servers?"

"Mr. Vice President," the general said in his characteristically deep, authoritative tone, "while we wait for more data on the potential use of such servers for this purpose, I can say that we are in alignment with her assessment. Our position is that Russia does not seek a kinetic confrontation with the United States. Instead, we see them, in addition to supporting disinformation campaigns against us, supporting proxy movements that harm our allies abroad, including their use of the Gudonov mercenary group. But not on US soil. Although that cannot be discounted. The behavioral AI has had success in other spheres."

"Okay, anything to add, Director Gupta?" The President said, "What further action can the Bureau take?"

"Madam President, I think both the Vice President and NSA Betts have made salient points today about how we can use the task force's resources to conduct this investigation in a way that will, I hope to quickly generate results. I have nothing further at this point in time."

"Thank you, Director Gupta and everyone," the President said. The FBI Director nodded his head to indicate agreement. The President then turned to logistical issues and asked Temir to close the meeting by summarizing action items for the group's members to undertake and, if there was no disagreement on those items, write up a memo listing them.

Temir was impressed that President Poulter continued to project an air of confidence and business as usual, even though the political pressure she was under was enormous.

***

Temir was busy working on the memo of the goals of the recently formed counter-terrorism task force when news of a surprise Congressional press conference caught his attention. The press conference was being held by the Democratic leadership in the House, and Temir immediately guessed what the subject might be. As Guttenberg had assured him, the legislative side of their plot was taking shape. Given the cascading crises the President was facing, if there was ever a time to launch the next step in removing Poulter from office, it was now. The public had the impression that the President was impotent in the face of these crises.

Temir realized how insignificant a figure he was and that Guttenberg was just one part of a wider conspiracy. He wasn't even sure if it was Guttenberg or someone else was pulling the strings. *Were Guttenberg and his connections in government responsible for the terror attacks as well as being involved in spreading the disinformation that was allowing the SMM to swell?*

Temir turned up the volume on the TV as the Democratic Majority House Leader, Ross Talmadge, began speaking. As Temir had anticipated, he announced that at the conclusion of the press conference, articles of impeachment would be filed against President Poulter.

"First," Leader Talmadge said, "this President has failed the country by allowing terrorist groups to commit crimes against US interests with abandon. The most egregious example of this is the recent spate of terrorist attacks in the homeland, all of which remain unsolved to this day. By failing to secure the nation against such attacks, President Poulter has abrogated her duty under the Constitution as our country's Commander in Chief."

Talmadge continued, "Second, the President has failed at another crucial task of her office: securing the nation's borders. When a spontaneous mass migration from Mexico brought hordes of refugees to our nation's border, she forbade them entry but failed to mobilize the necessary forces to prevent them from swarming the Border Patrol officers on site. The result was a catastrophic failure of national security that left hundreds of innocent people dead and saw hundreds of thousands of criminals swarm into our country illegally. Given President

Poulter's ineptitude, more SMMs are now beginning to march toward the US.

"Third, the President has mismanaged her own program designed to deal with SMMs, the GWAI. We supported her in this program, and while our intent was noble, the design of this program is likely to be successful only in enriching those well-connected consulting and construction firms that secure contracts from it. Moreover, her initial choice for executive director of the GWAI was forced to resign in disgrace almost immediately after the program's formation due to his close connections to the brutal Al-Haqa terrorist group in Ethiopia. That same group, by the way, was responsible for blowing up the water tanks on the project the disgraced executive director had been working on before he joined the GWAI. We demand to know how much President Poulter knew about Wells' terrorist links before she summoned him to the White House. And if she didn't know, why didn't she? As with the other points mentioned, one wonders where simple incompetence ends and malignant conspiracy begins. In either case, the charges of criminal malfeasance against the President are validated.

"Given these high crimes and misdemeanors against America's citizens and the country's ability to secure itself against terrorism and invasion, I am confident that these articles of impeachment will win approval, not only in the House but also in the US Senate." While sounding confident, Leader Talmadge did not believe that the impeachment would succeed in the Senate, but he had the numbers in the House.

Temir allowed himself a brief smile of contentment. After all the work they had put into maneuvering Poulter into a situation where her removal was feasible, it felt good to finally reach the endgame. He didn't know how it would happen, but Guttenberg's confidence gave him confidence. But at the same time, the feeling that he himself might at some point become expendable caused him a permanent underlying anxiety.

CHAPTER 36

Mark scanned the surrounding Ethiopian landscape with interest as the driver navigated along the dirt road with considerable skill. Rolling hills dotted with trees and long grasses marked this as prime savanna territory. Mikeo had agreed to provide Kenyan troops to help secure the EAWTP, and he was on a trip to view the progress made so far on rebuilding the storage sections and pipelines to deliver water from place to place. The Ethiopian government welcomed the support from the Kenyan leader, as did the Ethiopian public who were supportive of having Kenyan troops to provide improved security against the Gudonov group.

Mark could make out an open trench maybe 300 feet ahead. The pipeline would continue underground over the next few miles to avoid damage caused by the frequent mudslides in the area. The vehicle crested a ridge overlooking the trench system and pulled to a halt. The driver signaled it was time for lunch, which reminded Mark of how hungry he was, now that the bumping and jostling that had been a constant feature of the ride thus far was over, at least temporarily.

As he chewed on the beef sandwiches prepared for them, his thought turned back to the States. The satellite service in the region allowed him to read the news from back home, and things seemed to be going from bad to worse. The Liberty Salvation Front was still at large, with apparently no progress in bringing the group to justice. At the border, the SMM had continued to be violent, as every now and then thousands of migrants and water refugees had burst through the border patrol agents lined up to stop them from entering the country. The most startling news, to Mark at any rate, was that the Democrats had begun impeachment proceedings against President Poulter. He couldn't see how it could succeed as the Democrats didn't have the votes in the Senate. This just seemed to have become a tit-for-tat norm in the US now.

Even though he had been in DC not long ago, it seemed far away from him now. He wasn't sure how realistic the chances of her being impeached were. He doubted that the Vice President, who would replace her in the unlikely event the impeachment was successful, would be sympathetic to the goals of the GWAI. Mark hoped she could beat the charges and stay in office, but he concluded that the GWAI might be dead either way. His plan was to make the EAWTP become an example of success that could be followed elsewhere.

After lunch, he walked with Harake and the other two guards to inspect the trench system. It was an impressive system, and more impressive still was the underground storage tank system they would see being re-built on their next stop. These tanks would hold a vast amount of water that could be transported to areas in need in times of extreme drought.

CHAPTER 37

Temir mulled over the latest news as he waited in a comfortable lounge chair outside the Oval Office. Betts had sent him to deliver the weekly intelligence briefing to the President while she was busy in meetings relating to the attempt to get to the bottom of this latest string of terrorist bombings. In addition to her daily intelligence assessment and situation room meetings with the CIA and FBI higher-ups, the President relied on Betts to provide her analysis of recent events in these weekly meetings. With the National Security Adviser's schedule taken up by important meetings today, Temir hoped he would suffice.

The news was all bad for the country and the President, with a third unsolved terrorist attack, chaos at the border, and a loss of support for the GWAI program, until security could be guaranteed. Temir did not know the names of the Republican Senators who Guttenberg had assured him would betray the President at the last minute. However, given that everything Guttenberg had predicted had come to pass, he now had no doubts about the outcome. He believed the President was finished.

An hour later, Temir exited the Oval Office, having delivered the weekly intelligence summary to the President. He trusted he had done an adequate job at the task. There had been no discussion of the impeachment proceedings. President Poulter had communicated to her staff that she expected them to continue to conduct business as usual in the wake of the announcement of the charges. Whether or not she was truly as confident of defeating them as she appeared, she had made it clear that she viewed the charges mainly as a political stunt and didn't want the situation to impede the administration's priorities.

He was about to head for the exit when he noticed a hubbub coming from one of the meeting rooms. Turning the corner, he saw several intelligence community luminaries, including the Director of the CIA and the Assistant Director of the FBI, milling about outside the room. A briefing must have just concluded, he surmised, likely on the anti-terrorism task force that had recently been formed.

"Is NSA Betts here?" he asked the Secret Service agent on duty at the entrance to the Situation Room. If she was, he could report to her that after successfully delivering the briefing to the President, there were no follow up questions.

"Yes, she is, sir," the agent replied.

He was a familiar face in the White House, so the agent nodded his okay when Temir asked if he could enter the room. When he did, he was surprised to see Lorraine and Vice President Hugh Degrasso deep in conversation in a corner of the room. All the other attendees had left the room, which was otherwise empty except for an attendant fiddling with the video display equipment. As far as he knew, Lorraine and Degrasso weren't all that close. Degrasso was known to be a national security hawk, so Temir supposed it was no surprise to see them talking after a meeting on the subject. When Poulter had beaten Degrasso in the most closely fought primaries in living memory, there was intense pressure on her to put Degrasso on the ticket.

He hesitated at the doorway momentarily, then decided not to bother Lorraine with his report. It wasn't so important that he should interrupt her. Telling the agent at the doorway that he didn't want to interrupt her conversation, he headed for the White House exit.

CHAPTER 38

At the site of the underground water storage tanks on the Kenya side, Mark stared in amazement at the size of the craters created in the ground. In addition to his chief guide, Harake, two security guards accompanied them on the trip. After the attack on the water tanks in Ethiopia, Mikeo had felt it necessary to insist that Mark travels with enough security to scare off potential attackers.

After he had had a chance to circle the entire site of the tanks with Harake and the two guards by his side, Harake pointed out a rocky hilltop not far from their vehicle as a good spot for lunch. As they walked up the slope, with all three Kenyans carrying guns, the sound of approaching vehicles caused the four of them to stop and look behind them. Three SUVs were approaching them, their windows heavily tinted.

"I don't like the look of this," Harake said. "Let's get to the high ground." He waved upwards at the rocks above them. His instinct was proven correct a few moments later. After the SUVs stopped in front of their vehicle, a dozen men leapt from the SUVs, automatic rifles in hand. Gunfire rippled from below them as they raced for cover behind the rocks. One of the guards, Katembe, stopped to fire off a burst from his AK-47 at the top of the hill, and a scream from one of the men below showed he had hit the mark. A second later, Mark heard the sickening sound of bullet hitting flesh as Katembe fell to ground beside a large rock.

Harake kept up a steady series of bursts of fire from behind the rock where Katembe had fallen, and the other guard, Martin, with Mark's help, quickly pulled his comrade to safety behind the covering rocks. Glancing out from his position behind another large rock, Mark saw that the group of men, about half of them black and half of them white, had retreated to their SUVs for cover. Mark had little doubt that this was the Gudonov group. Whether they were here to kill him or kidnap him, he wasn't sure. Looking at the ground behind the rock outcropping, he was dismayed to see it was a flat, mostly treeless tundra. A few moments later, one of the SUVs drove into position behind them, clearly intended to prevent any escape. Even with one of the attackers down, Mark estimated there were ten or eleven still standing.

"Mark Wells," a voice shouted from below, with what Mark thought was a slight Russian accent.

"Yes," he said, figuring that any delay caused by talking should be grasped.

"If you agree to come with us, you, the men with you, will not be harmed."

"Who are you?" he asked, feeling it was worthwhile to try and buy time.

"You will learn that once you surrender. If you do not surrender, we can't guarantee your safety."

"Give me a couple minutes to talk to my friends here."

"Two minutes, no more."

While Mark had been talking, Harake and Martin had used Katembe's shirt to make a tourniquet to stop the bleeding from his upper arm, where the bullet had struck him. His rifle lay on the rocks beside him; it was clear he couldn't use both arms to wield it.

"Have you ever shot a gun?" Harake asked Mark.

"It's been 25 years or more, but I used to do some hunting in Kentucky when I lived there as a boy," Mark said.

Harake handed him the AK-47. "We don't have much time. I will show you how to fire and reload. Switch off the AI guide like this. We don't have time to show you how it works."

"I can handle it," replied Mark. "But I will surrender to these men to spare your lives."

"Do you trust them to spare you or us? I think not," Harake said.

"I don't see how we can survive otherwise. Even with the high ground, they can use their numbers to get among the rocks before we can shoot them all."

"Then we will shoot the remainder among the rocks," Harake said.

"Why are they here? How do they know we are here? The information about SMMs from my model is in the public domain." Mark couldn't think straight.

"It is clear they want you dead or captured, Mark," Harake said with a smile. "With you gone, the success of this project becomes much more difficult. That is all I can think of. You have made too much of a name for yourself as the leader of all water initiatives. And perhaps you are too popular everywhere." Harake's laughter put Mark and the others at a little more ease.

Mark shared Harake's assessment that they would not spare any of them. But that still didn't explain how they knew he was back in Ethiopia. However, it would not take a genius to track his flight details.

"Time's up, Mr. Wells, what have you decided?" came the voice from one of the mercenaries.

"I've decided to have lunch first. I'll get back to you once I'm done," Mark said. "If you want to join me to continue the conversation, put your gun down and come up alone."

There was no response from the leader. Instead, crouching behind their SUVs, the mercenaries unleashed a barrage of semiautomatic rifle fire in the direction of the rock outcropping. Harake had assigned Martin to guard their rear, and as Mark took cover behind a large rock, he could see Martin popping up from behind cover to return fire from the SUV behind them. Katembe, who was crouched down next to Mark, held a large knife in his left hand.

"Hold your fire," Harake said in a voice just loud enough to be heard over the din of gunfire. "Conserve ammunition. Don't shoot unless you have a good chance of hitting your target. Let them waste their ammunition."

After another minute or so of firing, the mercenaries seemed to have reached the same conclusion. Peeking out at them, Mark saw that they had started up the SUVs. He aimed a shot at the driver's side windshield, but the sound of ricocheting ammunition led him to believe the glass was bulletproof.

"They are up to something," Harake said intently.

"Maybe they will pull back and wait for darkness to fall," Mark said, doubting the thought even as he expressed it.

"I do not think so," Harake said.

A moment later, the two SUVs in front of them slowly started to move up the slope towards them. Mark thought he could make out at least one mercenary following behind one of the SUVs. He fired at an SUV's tire, but the shot had no effect. As the SUVs reached the first ring of rocks, the four men trailing behind them dived for cover. Mark and Harake fired, and one man cried in pain as he fell just short of cover. Shortly thereafter, the front and rear doors of the SUVs opened, and two more men ran for cover in the first row of rocks.

"Spread out; they are trying to flank us," Harake said to Mark, who made a dash for cover behind a rock thirty feet to his left. Sure enough, bullets from behind two smaller rock formations directly in front of him whizzed by him.

If any of those bullets had hit, there wouldn't have been much left of him to kidnap, Mark thought. There were two mercenaries at either end of the rocks in front of him. They popped out to take a shot at him when he moved slightly to his left to look through the gap between the two large rocks he was taking cover behind. Behind him, he could hear constant firing as the rest of the mercenaries tried to pick off his comrades.

Suddenly, the firing stopped, creating an eerie silence. Mark thought it was the calm before the storm, and he focused on breathing deeply and calming himself.

194

Harake said, "I will turn on the drone jammer in case they case they launch a drone attack."

The unnatural stillness continued for a few moments longer, and then the sound of movement broke the calm. The mercenaries were scuffling into position, Mark thought. It wouldn't be long now. He glanced through the gap between the rocks just in time to see the two mercenaries opposite him break cover at either end of the rock formation they had been hiding behind. Rifles blazing, they rushed towards the rock where he was taking cover. Simultaneously, he could hear gunfire erupt behind him as the other mercenaries were undoubtedly doing the same.

CHAPTER 39

Temir turned the channel to take in the latest news. As he expected, the impeachment against President Poulter dominated the coverage. He allowed himself a small smile of triumph as he watched the commentators discuss the chances the charges would succeed. While her popularity was dwindling in the face of the chaos at the border and the recent unsolved terrorist attacks, not to mention the contention from some that she had committed to spend American dollars frivolously on the GWAI, the pundits thought that while the charges probably wouldn't succeed in the Senate, there were unattributed murmurings and briefings that some Republicans were going to join with the Democrats in Senate. But none believed that when it came down to it, fifteen or sixteen Senate Republicans would join the Democrats.

It was all speculation at this point, of course, as the House still needed to hold hearings and vote on the articles of impeachment.

The news coverage then shifted to the now ongoing chaotic scenes at the Mexican-American border. From there, the program moved to scenes of the drought-stricken Mexican interior and other parts of South America, where unrelenting heat accompanied by paltry rainfall created the conditions for the SMM. The pictures displayed a grim landscape of dusty plains and barren hills, where only skeletons of trees remained. The on-the-ground correspondents made reports of Chinese influence on easing the path from South America all the way to the US border and Russian social media disinformation about water in the US.

Temir picked up his phone to call Sara again, but before he could hit the button to ring her, he received an incoming call.

He didn't recognize the number, but the name associated with the number alarmed him: El Paso Consolidated Community General Hospital. Hoping against hope that it wasn't related to Sara, he answered the call.

"Is this Temir Bousson?"

"Yes, it is."

"This is Doctor Chadhoury. I'm an ER physician at El Paso Consolidated Community General Hospital." The man's voice was authoritative, and his tone was neutral. Temir couldn't help but fear the worst.

"Is this about Sara?"

"I'm afraid so, Mr. Bousson. She has been injured in the events at the border. She has suffered a head wound and has been placed in a medically induced coma. I am sorry it took so long for us to call, but it has been chaotic."

"Why was the coma necessary, Dr. Chadhoury?"

"We are trying to save her life. She has suffered massive swelling along with internal bleeding from a blow to the head. Putting her in a coma helps us buy time to give the swelling a chance to subside."

Dr. Chadhoury's tone was flat. Temir wanted to ask him what Sara's chances of surviving were or whether there was likely to be brain damage, but for one reason or another, he could not bring himself to do it.

"Thank you for your help, doctor. I will head to El Paso immediately." There was nothing more to say. He could find out the details of how she had been struck and ask the doctor for a detailed prognosis once he was at the hospital. He was sure her mother would want to be there. He would call her from the car on his way to the airport.

Temir left a full message for his boss, Lorraine Betts, and left for El Paso.

CHAPTER 40

As the mercenaries behind the rock ledge in front of him rushed him, Mark stood up and fired to his right, and one of the mercenaries fell to the ground. In the meantime, the other mercenary had made it to the other side of the rock he had taken cover behind. He turned his rifle to fire at the man but could sense he was too late. A fierce pain engulfed him as a bullet struck him in the side. The pain caused him to drop his rifle as he fell backward. The mercenary in front of him smiled as he raised his gun, only to scream in pain as a bullet struck him in the chest, disrupting his aim and causing his shot to miss Mark. Another bullet struck his head, and his mutilated corpse collapsed to the ground.

Harake grabbed Mark by the arm and yanked him up. Katembe was by him, knife in hand. "We're moving," he shouted. Just to their left was a small circle of rocks at the peak of the outcropping. Once there, they would be trapped, with no easy exit, but that was the only place of relative safety right now. Gunfire burst out behind them, and Mark looked back to see Martin cry out and fall beside the bodies of two mercenaries who had been shot in the assault moments earlier. Bullets collided with the rocks beside them as they ran for the circle of rocks.

"Goddamn it," Harake cried as they dived for cover behind the rock formation. Mark's wound was causing a dull pain, but he could still move. *The adrenaline must be keeping me going*, he thought. Harake helped him out of his shirt and told him to hold it to the wound to staunch the bleeding.

Looking out from behind the small circle of rocks, they could see that the remaining mercenaries had taken cover there.

Bullets continued to bounce off the stones as the mercenaries attempted to pick them off one by one.

"We are low on ammunition," Harake whispered to Mark. "We must make every shot count. Only take clear shots." Mark looked at Harake and admired the man's cool under fire. He nodded his head in agreement, barely able to remain conscious.

Once again, an eerie silence reigned as the mercenaries suddenly ceased firing. Mark knew it wouldn't be long now before they made their move. Only a minute or so later, it began. A barrage of what Mark guessed was covering fire struck the rocks around them. Through it, he could barely make out the sound of footsteps, which he guessed were some of the mercenaries using the covering fire to take their positions behind the rocks closest to their position.

Once again, the firing ceased, and Mark painfully raised his rifle to his shoulder, ready to do his best to repel the next assault. He wasn't sure how much longer he could stay conscious and believed that his end was near.

For some reason, a vision of Temir's face came to him at that moment. It all came back to Temir, somehow. He wondered what he had done to cause the man to work so hard to destroy him. Mark refused to think about Temir in what he thought were his last moments. Instead, he pictured Aida. The memory of his love for her would be a fitting last thought. He held on to that as the world seemed to spin around him. He felt thick-headed and extremely tired. If he closed his eyes, he could fall asleep instantly.

Strangely, he thought he heard a loud thumping sound as if a giant was beating a tarpaulin with its fist. The sound of bullets striking the rocks near them seemed to have ceased. Then, the sound of gunshots in rapid succession echoed in his ears. Mark flinched, but the bullets didn't sound as near to them as the recent barrage. He tried to fight off the torpor which had enveloped him and rise. Enervated to the point of immobility, he gave up the attempt, resigning himself to his fate as the loud whirring sound and the roar of bullets striking rock and earth seemed to draw nearer.

Was he dreaming, he wondered, because it seemed he was looking up at a helicopter flying directly overhead. He dreamt he saw Mikeo leaning out the side door of the helicopter, firing a fixed gun. A nice thought to pass out on.

CHAPTER 41

Temir sat in a chair opposite his daughter's hospital bed in the ICU, lost in his thoughts. He arrived in Texas as fast as possible after getting the phone call about Sara. A compression bandage was wrapped around the back portion of her head where the horse had kicked her, but other than that and some bruising on her arms from falling, she looked like her normal self. The ventilator she was hooked up to, kept her body functioning while she was in a medically induced coma. The doctor had stressed that Sara needed time for the swelling in her brain to subside, and this would help that happen.

It was possible, even likely, according to the doctor, that she had suffered some brain damage. A certain amount of amnesia, short- or long-term, was also possible. Temir remained calm while the doctor delivered his diagnosis of Sara's condition. While calm outside, Temir was in turmoil internally. While sitting in the chair opposite his daughter's bed, he was overcome with a deep sense that Sara's condition was somehow his fault. Not proximally, of course, but metaphorically, or perhaps, morally. Though he couldn't settle on the right word to explain his feelings, he was nonetheless ridden with guilt.

While he had been scheming to remove a sitting president for ideological and personal reasons, the country itself seemed to be coming apart at the seams. Unsolved domestic terror, a massive breach of its southern border. And what was he doing to stop this as the chaos mounted? Nothing. In fact, his actions and those of the people he was conspiring with were intended to stoke the flames and generate even greater amounts of chaos to achieve their political aims. Where previously he had been certain of the righteousness of his actions, now he was not so sure.

His thoughts turned to Roman. He had been wrong about the young man, who had lost his life trying to protect Sara from the frenzied horse that had kicked her in the head. Shortly after his arrival, Bethany, one of Sara's comrades in the protest movement, had stopped by for a visit and told him how Roman had thrown himself in front of Sara just before the horse struck her. He had been knocked off his feet and then trampled by two other horses that had been startled by gunfire.

Several hours later, Temir stood beside his ex-wife on a walkway outside the hospital. Diane had arrived perhaps two hours earlier and had stayed by Sara's side while he had gone to the hospital cafeteria to get some water. After returning to the room, Temir suggested they walk on the hospital grounds to get some fresh air. Despite their differences, mainly driven by his tendency to be a workaholic, they had co-parented well. Their divorce and subsequent relationship had been, if not quite amicable, at least non-contentious. They had worked out a custody schedule and tried to keep the demise of their marriage from unduly impacting their daughter.

"Diane, I have to tell you, this has been a wake-up call for me. I can't help but think if I had paid more attention to helping Sara get ready for law school, none of this would have happened."

Diane gave him a sympathetic look.

"You can't blame yourself for something you had no control over, Temir. You know as well as I do that our daughter has a mind of our own. Even if you had spent more time advising her, there's no guarantee she would have listened to you or that it would have changed anything."

"I can't deny that," Temir said. "But I guess I'm just looking at my life in more of a holistic sense and seeing things I've done wrong. Our relationship, for example. Even if it was destined to end eventually, I certainly didn't treat it with the care I should have, given its importance."

"Maybe not. But I'm sure I could have handled it better myself."

CHAPTER 42

He moved stealthily through the jungle, stalking his prey. Just ahead, he glimpsed a clearing through the dense foliage. When he reached it, he saw his quarry, a tiger, the lord of the jungle. He raised his pistol to fire, at the same time wondering why he had brought a pistol instead of a rifle on the hunt. If he didn't kill or disable the tiger with his initial shot, and the beast got him in its jaws, it would be all over for him. He needed to get closer to have a reasonable chance of hitting the tiger, so he crept through the tall grass on his belly.

Luckily, the tiger seemed to be distracted by something at the edge of the clearing, and it didn't notice him as he maneuvered himself within range. Just as he judged himself close enough to risk taking a shot, he saw what, or rather who, the tiger was stalking. It was Aida. She was picking flowers in a meadow in Kentucky, oblivious to the beast, which was within seconds of pouncing on her.

Realizing any delay would risk the tiger savaging Aida, Mark rose to his feet and fired...

Mark opened his eyes, and the image of the tiger and Aida was replaced by the surroundings of a hospital room. He was in a hospital bed, with tubes attached to his body and beeping coming from the machines behind him. Turning to his right, he saw Harake, who looked up from the holographic image he was been reading and greeted him.

"It is about time you awoke. President Thundilayskila will be glad to hear it."

"Where am I?" Mark asked.

"You are in a hospital in Nairobi." Mark had already guessed that much.

"What happened? How did we get out of that? Did I really see Mikeo....... President Thundilayskila, in a helicopter?"

"You did. My friend, did you think he is called the Lion of Kenya for nothing? The President does not take kindly to mercenaries attacking his guests."

"How long have I been here?"

"This is the second day you have been here. You lost a lot of blood from the bullet wound, and they have given you two transfusions."

"What about the bullet?"

"The doctor performed surgery to remove it. They have sewn you back up and made you as good as new."

"While I appreciate your optimism, Harake, I don't feel all that new at the moment. But there's something I have to do. Will you help me?"

"If it is your plan to escape from this hospital, I cannot agree. The President has told me that I am to guard you from any danger."

"The way I feel, I'm not sure I could walk to the bathroom, much less escape. No, that's not what I want. I need my phone; I need to make a call."

"That is a request that should not involve any danger. I will press the button to summon the nurse and see what they have done with your phone."

CHAPTER 43

Temir disinterestedly watched the latest news on TV as he sat on his sofa. He had landed at Dulles Airport mere hours ago after returning from Texas. Diane would stay with Sara for the next few days until the doctors felt she was ready to be transferred to a hospital in Arlington, Virginia, not far from where she lived and close to DC. Temir felt that everything had changed somehow. He wasn't the man he had been, but he wasn't quite sure what that meant.

He had a meeting set for tomorrow morning with Guttenberg. For some reason, he wanted to attend this meeting even though he felt Guttenberg would understand if he had to rearrange, given the situation with Sara.

A breaking news banner on the TV caught his attention. "Person of interest identified in terror incidents." Temir turned up the volume to hear the news anchor proclaim that the investigation into the Statue of Liberty bombing had led investigators to one Dalton Devereaux. A Louisiana native, he had been caught on video in the area near the time of the bombing. He was said to be sympathetic to the American Glory movement and had served two years in jail for assaulting a police officer.

He had last been spotted in upstate New York not too long after the bombing at the Statue of Liberty. A manhunt was underway. The news channel introduced two talking heads, both security specialists, who were brought on to analyze the latest developments in the case. One of the analysts mentioned that in addition to the American Glory movement, Devereaux was also thought to be linked to a militant group called the Project for Renewing America (PRA). The name struck a chord with Temir. He had heard of it before but couldn't quite recall in what context.

He supposed that naming a suspect in the bombings might help the President to some degree. But as long as the man was on the run, it wouldn't necessarily do all that much to boost her popularity. Between the stalled GWAI, the still unsolved bombings, and the chaos at the border caused by the Mexican SMM, the country was in chaos. News was also coming in of battles between migrants and Americans in several southern states. The American Glory movement was stoking the fires with talk of a civil war.

***

Temir slipped into Guttenberg's car and exchanged greetings with the mining magnate. Guttenberg was sympathetic about Sara and offered him the best treatment in the country for her. They quickly go to the topic that Guttenberg was obsessed with.

"What are you hearing about our friend with nine lives? He somehow survived an attack from Gudonov in Ethiopia."

"I thought he was no longer a threat," said Temir.

"We need him gone. He has become a figurehead for all things water. Much of the press has concluded that he had no real connection to Jemal and his public support has increased rather than waned. He needs to be taken out. We do not need any successful examples of water collaboration."

"I have been able to find out very little since I returned. My sources say that he has the ear of President Thundilayskila. And he is being protected." Temir did not believe they could easily get to him. "I had no idea you were going to be trying to take him out."

Guttenberg was impatient and frank. "I tell you what you need to know, Temir. No one should know everything, including me. It gives us a degree of protection. I need you to find me an asset in Kenya. Just get me a couple of names, and I will take care of it."

Temir knew better than to directly refuse Guttenberg's request. "I can't promise anything, but I'll see what I can do."

"Thank you, Temir. We are on the cusp of success and can't allow anything to derail our momentum. Now tell me about how Poulter intends to fight the impeachment process."

Temir relayed to Guttenberg that the President was resigned to being impeached but confident that she would survive the trial. She was more concerned with not making progress on the apprehending the terrorists, the chaos at the southern border, and the stalled GWAI.

CHAPTER 44

With his phone in hand, Mark hesitated for a moment before he pressed the button to dial Aida. He wasn't sure if she was still mad at him, but he told himself this was about her safety, not trying to rekindle their romance. It was imperative he alert her to the danger that she was in. A thought occurred to him. He should call Tom first. That would give him a chance to gather some intel on how Aida was doing these days. He rang Tom's phone but got no answer. He then rang Aida and got straight to the point.

"Aida, I'm calling to warn you that you are in serious danger. I've just been attacked by the Gudonov mercenary group. We were able to fight them off, but I'm sorry to say that just means that they may come after you next as a way to get to me."

"Oh, Mark, are you okay?"

"I was hit and lost a lot of blood, but I am going to be okay. I am back in Kenya now. But we need to get you somewhere safe, just in case."

"I truly appreciate your concern, Mark, but wouldn't they have come for me before if they had wanted me? And I have the UN guards." Aida's tone was skeptical, which Mark guessed she would be.

"Aida, I know you're upset with me, and I deserve that. But don't let your anger at me put your life in danger." Mark's mind was still cloudy from the meds they had been injecting him with, and he couldn't think of a more elegant way to get his point across.

"I'm not angry at you, Mark. At least not anymore. What happened, happened. It's over now. But since, unlike some people, I believe in truthfulness; you should know that I'm with Tom now. He has been a real rock."

The revelation that Aida and Tom were together took Mark completely by surprise. While his heart sank, he remained more concerned for her safety. "That's your choice to make, Aida. But for God's sake, listen to what I'm saying. Gudonov may come for you. It would be best if you left as soon as you possibly can. If you won't leave Ethiopia, please go to that place you know is secure. That place where they won't be able to find you."

Mark was confident Aida would know the place he was referring to. The hill country to the east of her village was laced with caves, some large enough for a person to store supplies and hide out for a lengthy period. "Take Tom with you if you like."

"If I go, how will I know when it's safe to return?"

"I'll contact you. Take the satellite phone I gave you. I'll let you know as soon as it's safe to go back home."

CHAPTER 45

Temir and several of his colleagues at the NSA gathered around the television in the lunchroom. The latest news on the investigation into the bombings in the house was not good for the President. Despite the identification of a suspect in the Statue of Liberty bombing, the FBI was having no luck in locating Devereaux. In addition to the chaos caused by the SMM, the border, and the GWAI scandal, the articles of impeachment in the House vote was expected imminently and it was a foregone conclusion that it would succeed. Knowing they had the numbers in the House, the Democrats were drip feeding the process so as to cause the maximum pain.

Temir wasn't sure how he felt about any of this anymore. Since his epiphany, he began reevaluating his view of the President. While he couldn't say he agreed with her policies, he had started to think that his previous condemnation was treacherous. Literally treacherous.

Temir's phone buzzed with a message from NSA Betts asking him to stop by her office when he had a chance. He knew that meant, unless you are engaged in a vital or time-sensitive task, drop what you are doing and see me immediately. Watching the latest news on the impeachment proceedings was not likely to qualify as critical, so he left the lunchroom and headed to her office.

Lorraine was alone in her office, and her assistant quickly ushered Temir into the room and closed the door behind him. Her first question was about his daughter. Then, quickly, she turned to the latest news on the domestic bombings. She then turned his attention to another topic.

"On another subject, Temir, I understand you were asking someone from the CIA about our assets in Kenya. May I ask why?" It hadn't taken the NSA long to get to the point.

"I wanted to get some real-time intelligence about what's going on there. Given that the Kenyans are providing troops to help protect the EAWTP in Ethiopia, I thought it would be important to be able to provide the President with up-to-date intelligence on the subject if she asked."

"You didn't think to consult with me." The National Security Adviser did not sound happy, and Temir's reply was not convincing.

"My apologies, Lorraine. I will always reach out to you first in future."

"That would be wise." Lorraine's tone had returned to normal, although he had a feeling they weren't quite done with the conversation.

"So, tell me, did this need for information have anything to do with the presence of Mark Wells in Kenya?"

Temir tried to keep his face impassive, and his tone relaxed as he answered. "In part. As you know there was an attempt on his life."

"He seems to be becoming a hero in the eyes of much of the public, doesn't he? Okay, thanks Temir. Let's move on."

Betts changed the topic back to the latest on the search for Devereaux and then briefed Temir on the latest on the possible Gudonov or Russian attack.

"I've had a chance to talk to our agency partners about the intelligence we discussed regarding the potential of an impending Russian operation domestically," she said.

"What did you find out?" Temir asked.

"The Behavioral Scenario Builder – BSB, as the intelligence analysts have started calling it now – still has a Russian attack on US soil as a central scenario. And they have found out who this Kraskolnikov is. Apparently, he is a former special forces captain in the Russian army who has recently joined the Gudonov mercenary organization. They think he has gone to East Africa. It's all very sketchy," Lorraine said.

"What do the intelligence guys think?" Temir responded.

"They don't know what to make of it. There is no evidence for a Russian plot on US soil. Just the BSB evaluation. But Kraskolnikov does exist, so...." Lorraine uncharacteristically looked into the distance as she finished speaking, before bringing her gaze back to Temir.

After a few more minutes of discussing the search for Devereaux, Lorraine ended the meeting, and Temir returned to his office. He breathed a sigh of relief as he walked. That could have gone much worse. He knew the risk he was running in contacting his source about assets in Kenya. He had been able to get the information and passed it on to Guttenberg. He needed nothing further to add to what was going to happen, although he was now directly lending a hand to the assassination of Mark Wells. He realized he might be exposed if there was a future investigation about Wells' murder. Temir felt the walls were closing in on him, and deservedly so. He tried to retrace the steps that led him to being in league with traitors to the Republic. He had no way out now. Guttenberg could well be having him watched.

CHAPTER 46

Mark gingerly took a seat in the conference room at the Presidential Palace. He could walk, but standing from a seated position was jarring to the wound on his side. A few minutes later, Mikeo and his advisor entered the room. After they exchanged greetings and questions about Mark's recuperation, Mark asked about the progress of the EAWTP.

"The re-build is slow my friend. But I am happy to report that the UN has agreed to coordinate our troops to enhance security for the program," Mikeo said. "It was possible only because Ethiopia publicly asked for support from Kenya."

"The East African nations are leading the world in their geopolitical thinking right now. That is great news," Mark said. "I hope my contacts at the UN were helpful in the process."

"My advisor tells me they were," the president added. "So, what is next for you, my friend? I hope you are not contemplating further tour of the project's facilities."

Mark chuckled at Mikeo's comment before wincing in pain. "Please, Mikeo, don't make me laugh. My doctors strictly warned me to abstain from humor in order to keep my stitches from splitting and landing me back in the ICU."

Mikeo, his aide Konigwe, and Mark all laughed.

"As for what's next, I do plan to stop by Ethiopia and try to convince Aida to go with me to the US. I don't think she's safe here, given that Gudonov knows of her links to me."

"That is chivalrous of you, my friend," Mikeo said, "although I believe you said that you and she were no longer together and that she has already declined your offer several times."

"Not only that, but she has recently taken up with a good friend of mine who is running the central storage sections in Ethiopia – in many ways the most consequential part of the EAWTP. But I care for her very deeply, so I plan to do everything I can to convince her that she needs to leave the country for her safety. Perhaps if I can say this in person, she will listen."

"Let's hope that you can get her to see reason. I know firsthand how difficult relations can be with an ex. Still, if my life can offer any guidance, there is hope. I am having dinner tonight with my ex-wife and her new husband."

"That is quite amicable of you, Mikeo. However, I would suggest that you offer to do the cooking yourself if only to keep her away from the knives. You may be the lion, but she was always the lioness." All three of them began laughing again.

"If she were going to chop me up with her knives, she would have done so long ago, my friend. However, I will make sure to keep a close eye on her husband."

"Is he good with knives also?"

"Of that, I'm not sure; however, he is lethal with his hands. He has attained the highest belt possible in the discipline of karate."

"Between her knife skills and his unarmed combat ability, they sound like a lethal couple. Have you met him before?"

"Of course I have. He was formerly my chief bodyguard."

CHAPTER 47

Temir stopped by the gaggle of employees in the lunchroom watching the news on TV. It didn't take long to see what they were watching. The House had voted to impeach the President. This was expected. The Democrats took their revenge for what had happened four years earlier, which had signaled the beginning of the end of two consecutive Presidential terms for their party. Temir was now certain that he could no longer support the plot to oust a legitimately elected President and put Vice President Hugh Degrasso in place to reverse her policies.

Back at his desk, his thoughts turned to his visit to see Sara in the hospital in Arlington the night before. The doctors said that her vital signs hadn't changed, so the move had apparently done nothing to harm her. But as to when or if she would come out of the coma, they couldn't say. The feeling that he had failed her and what she stood for was persistently gnawing at him. He had tried to be a good father but had lost touch with being close to her somewhere along the line.

He was preoccupied with regret. He wished he could start again. He wanted to be a good father, a good person, a good man, someone she could be proud of. He thought about the plotting and scheming he was involved in with Guttenberg. Yes, it had padded his pockets with the untraceable inter-generational crypto wealth. He viewed his vanity now in plain sight, realizing that he was going to somehow escape the plotting, which would put him and his family in danger.

Not for the first time, he wondered who else besides himself was involved in the plot with Guttenberg. He was convinced that

Vice President Degrasso was part of the plot, but who else? He was paranoid that Guttenberg's followers were watching his every move. There was no one he could confide in. He was on his own.

CHAPTER 48

Later that day, President Thundilayskila summoned Mark to have some tea with him on the verandah overlooking the gardens of the Presidential Palace. After some small talk, Mark asked if Mikeo's investigators had been able to identify the dead mercenaries as Gudonov.

"We weren't able to make a conclusive case. They carried no ID, whether they were white or black. But, of course, we are under no doubts as to who they worked for. I lodged a complaint with the Russian ambassador, who delivered the usual shameless denial."

"Did he deny they were Gudonov?"

"He said that Gudonov is a private company, not under the control of the Russian government, and that that government condemns any mercenary action of any kind in East Africa and anywhere in the world."

"In other words, they are independent enough to offer the government the cover of plausible deniability. Thank you for your support, Mikeo. I don't expect to be here long. I will depart for Ethiopia and then New York soon to see if I can rekindle support for the GWAI and get additional UN funding for the EAWTP."

"What will you do in Ethiopia? Has your ex agreed to go with you to the US? Will her new partner go with you as well?" Mikeo smiled mischievously.

"Thanks for reminding me of that, Mr. President," Mark said ruefully. He had known Mikeo long enough to know that the President enjoyed needling his friends now and then.

223

"I take no happiness in your romantic travails, my friend. I just hope it is not distracting you from the important work we must do for those who depend on our diligence."

"She and Tom are in hiding in a very safe place. I'm stopping by the project to check on the rebuilding progress on the interchange tanks for myself. Thank you again for your troops when I get there. No one dare take them on. I am sure they will keep me safe."

"I'm glad to hear it. I wish you the best, as always, Mark. These are trying times, and we need people of your caliber to help us deal with these SMMs. Otherwise, even a perennial optimist such as myself might get a little gloomy."

***

Later that day, Mark took in the sights and sounds of Nairobi as Harake negotiated the twists and turns of the central city carefully. The pedestrian traffic was even heavier than usual here. After another ten minutes, Harake pulled into a parking lot. They would make their way to the basket store he wanted to visit on foot. On several occasions, Aida had explained to him how she admired the beauty of Kenyan baskets. He would purchase one to give her the next time he saw her, whenever that might be.

Thirty minutes later, he exited the store carrying an intricately woven Kenyan basket. After maybe thirty meters, they turned left and headed back toward the parking lot. Then, everything seemed to happen at once.

"Get down," Harake shouted as he tackled Mark, who dropped his basket as he fell to the ground. He heard the sharp retort of a semi-automatic rifle firing and felt tremendous pain in the right side of his chest as if he had been smacked by someone wielding a baseball bat. In falling, they had tumbled into the street and were lucky to avoid being hit by an oncoming car, which stopped just behind them. In front of them, a jeep was stopped. The driver blared the horn to get the car in front of him to move, only to fall back in the seat after being struck in different parts of his body as a fusillade of bullets hit his vehicle.

"Are you okay?" Harake asked as he cautiously looked around the jeep in the direction of the firing.

"I'm alive, thanks to this vest you made me wear," Mark said. He would have quite the bruise on his chest, but the vest had protected him from serious injury or death.

"Stay here," Harake said. "I saw where he fired from; I'm going after him."

He jumped to his feet and ran to the right of the jeep across the street and straight toward a two-story building across from them, his military pistol in his hand. Another round of bullets skittered across the concrete behind Harake; a passerby picked the wrong moment to cross the street and fell to the ground after taking a bullet to the head.

Feeling that he might regret it, Mark nevertheless cautiously rose to his feet with a groan and moved along the left side of the jeep. If nothing else, his movement might cause the shooter to target him and give Harake a chance to close on him. Be careful, he told himself. Hearing no further shots for the moment, Mark found he could move mostly behind the cover of the vehicles, which were stopped along the road until he made it to the side of the two-story building Harake had headed for. He heard another rapid burst of fire and then two shots in succession, which he guessed were from Harake's pistol.

Thinking that Harake had entered the building through the front door, Mark made his way to the back of the building. Every step was an exercise in agony due to the chest contusion caused by the bullet, so he was forced to move slowly. There was a single door in the middle of the back wall. It occurred to him that if the gunman were able to flee, it wouldn't do him any good to be standing within easy firing distance of the door.

The door opened outwards, and Mark positioned himself right behind it, not sure exactly how he could help, given the difficulty he was having merely standing upright, much less moving with any speed. When the door opened with a bang, a tall, skinny man with an AK-47 slung over his shoulder exited the building and came face to face with Mark. Before the man could unsling his weapon, Mark grabbed him in a bear hug and tried to topple the man to the ground.

While the gunman was slight, he was also strong, or perhaps Mark was unable to exert enough force due to his injury. Before the man could shake him off and put his rifle to work, Mark placed his right foot behind the gunman's foot and shoved with all his remaining might. However, the gunman was able to turn and slip out of Mark's grasp and remain upright as Mark hit the ground. He raised his rifle to fire, and a shot rang out. Harake had hit the gunman.

Bleeding from where the bullet had hit his torso, the man managed to stay on his feet and turn to his left as he desperately tried to get a lead on Harake before he could fire again, but he wasn't fast enough; another shot, this one to the side of his head, caused the tall man to fall to the ground and lie there, unmoving.

"What took you so long?" Mark said.

Harake smiled and pointed at his leg, where blood was seeping from a shot to his upper thigh. "You seem to attract trouble like a magnet, my friend. He would have been able to outrun me with this leg wound, so I owe you my thanks for slowing him down."

"You're welcome," Mark replied. The sirens of Nairobi's emergency service rang. Harake holstered his pistol as two police officers ran towards them. "What will you do with yourself when you leave Kenya and you no longer have me to protect you from danger?"

The two men guffawed with laughter.

CHAPTER 49

Temir sat stoically in Guttenberg's vehicle as the man ranted. Temir had never seen Guttenberg lose control this way before.

"You told me the shooter was a trained military asset of the highest caliber. I set up a synthetic front man in Venezuela and payment, which can't possibly be traced back to you. And he let an academic with no military experience, a redneck from Kentucky, defeat him."

Temir forced himself to stay calm and respond in a measured tone.

"He was highly trained."

"What?" Guttenberg's tone was cutting. "We should have enlisted two or more shooters for the job."

"I couldn't get another one," Temir said. "Betts was asking too many questions about why I was inquiring about assets in Kenya."

"You don't need to worry about Betts."

Temir was surprised by Guttenberg's response. Perhaps Guttenberg had been careless that Betts was also one of his people, or perhaps he had wanted Temir to know.

Temir immediately thought back to when he had seen Betts and Degrasso in deep conversation. *Was she part of the plot? Why would she call him in to ask about untraceable assets in Kenya?*

Temir went back and forth in his mind and ultimately felt that she probably was part of it. *Of course, by probing me about the asset, she was subtlety and cleverly warning me to be more careful without exposing herself as part of Guttenberg's people.*

Temir was very glad that Mark had survived the latest attempt on his life, although he knew better than to even hint at that fact to Guttenberg.

Guttenberg eventually calmed down and changed the subject to domestic terror incidents.

"What do you hear about the search for Devereaux?" Guttenberg asked.

"There is not much to report thus far, other than they tracked him to a former residence in North Carolina, but he was gone by the time they searched it."

The two men went their separate ways with no further discussion about what to do about Wells.

CHAPTER 50

Mark was packed and ready for his trip to New York by way of Ethiopia. Mikeo had asked him to stop by and speak with him before departing. Harake, who was recovering well from the wound to his thigh, and a driver were waiting in the foyer to drive him to a military base, where he would be transported to a location in Ethiopia secretly by drone. The President was waiting for him on the Verandah, enjoying the view of the gardens behind the Presidential Palace.

"How are you feeling, my friend?" the President asked him.

"My side is getting better, although I've found it wise to avoid rapid movements to keep from jarring the wound. As for my chest, I have a huge bruise, which makes it somewhat painful to breathe. Other than that, I feel like I could run a marathon or two."

Mikeo smiled. "I feel your pain, Mark, in spirit if not in reality. Rest assured, I will make every effort to root out who made this attempt on your life in our very capital." The President's tone was firm, and Mark had no doubt he would do what he said.

"Was it Gudonov?" Mark asked.

"Very unlikely, according to my security people. Gudonov do not dare work in Kenya. My people tell me that there is a rat in my house. How else could Gudonov have known your exact timing and location in Ethiopia? And how was it possible to know that you were in the Nairobi market today? Only those in the Presidential household would have known your whereabouts." Mikeo spoke with a steely glare.

"I pity the guy that betrayed you, Mikeo. Before I go, do you mind if I ask how you got the nickname the Lion of Kenya?"

Mikeo smiled. "Not at all. Let me take a sip or two of my tea, and I will tell you everything you want to know about it."

CHAPTER 51

President Poulter sat at her desk in the Oval Office. Her husband, Ari Fisher, stood before the desk. She had just dismissed her assistants so she could talk with her husband alone.

"Anything new on the Devereaux incident?" she asked.

"Nothing. After killing the two park rangers, he took off a stolen vehicle he had at the ready. That car was found in the middle of a heavily forested area. They've brought out the drones, helicopters, and bloodhounds, but he has not been seen since. The FBI is leading what they call the most extensive manhunt in American history to find him, but no traces so far."

"Do they believe he is still in North Carolina?"

"They believe he could not have gone too far on foot. But the Blue Ridge Mountains provide a lot of cover for hiding out. All we can do is wait until they've combed the area as thoroughly as possible," Ari said.

"I still can't believe he pulled all these bombings off alone... the FBI has yet to find any link to other POIs."

"At least they're not blaming you for the FBI's failure to work faster."

Ari had meant it as a joke, but his partner took it seriously. "Don't be too sure they won't. The press seems to blame me for everything. They are criticizing me for moving Wells back to Africa. And if that's not enough, they are blaming me for the assassination attempts on him. Temir was so persuasive that Wells should be sent back to Ethiopia. Why is Gudonov still after him when the SMM data is out in the public domain anyway?"

"I don't know, darling. We should concentrate on the Senate trial."

President Poulter smiled, enjoying a rare moment of being with somebody close. "With the latest developments in the domestic terrorism cases occupying her time, NSA Betts has Temir providing the intelligence update this week. Do you want to hang around for it?"

"No, dear, I don't. I'll let you and your trusty assistants wade through the various threats and ominous signals from home and abroad. I have a round of golf scheduled with Senator Delacroix at two."

"Make sure he knows which way to vote, sweetheart," the President said.

"Of course, Madam President."

CHAPTER 52

Temir was ushered into the White House and made his way to the Oval Office waiting room. He was a few minutes early for the intelligence briefing, so he took a seat in one of the plush chairs. He had visited Sara last night, and the sight of her lying motionless in the hospital bed, her breathing still being controlled by a ventilator, stayed with him. She wanted a better world for those who had few opportunities in life.

Temir's thoughts were interrupted by Brian McCormick, who informed him that the President was ready to meet with him. He exchanged a quick handshake with her husband, who was just leaving the Oval Office, and then sat opposite President Poulter. After exchanging greetings and a conversation about his daughter, he launched right into the briefing. As he went over the various points in the brief, he readied himself to begin a conversation that would likely result in him being arrested and equally likely to be taken out by one of Guttenberg's people on the inside while in custody. But he didn't feel like protecting himself any longer. He was going to take the chance. He asked the President to ask her aide to leave and put his fate in her hands now.

"Madam President, would you mind if you and I spoke alone for just a few minutes? I have something of the utmost importance I need to relay to you." Temir could hardly believe the words coming out of his mouth. He felt as if some other force, or consciousness, was taking over his body and causing him to utter the words.

President Poulter didn't precisely know what Temir wanted to discuss, but she imagined he had gone through so much with his daughter possibly going to suffer from brain damage that she asked McCormick to leave.

"Very well, Temir. I'm extremely busy, as you can well imagine, but I know you have been through a lot. Is it about your daughter?"

Ignoring her question, he said, "President Poulter, I have information relating to a plot against you and your administration. A plot that amounts to a coup. One that, sadly, I have been a part of until just today."

There was stunned silence. And Temir did not fill the silence. They stared at one another; she with disbelief, and he with a mix of fear that he might spend the rest of his life behind bars but with a certain relief that he had let it go. President Poulter considered ushering in security but calculated that if Temir had started to give up this information, she could let him spill the beans. Very consciously she decided to remain calm and elicit more information.

"I take it you are not the leader of this plot," the President said.

"No. I am not. I will tell you everything I know about it," Temir said. "I only ask that you let me tell you the whole story before you decide whether to have me arrested or use me to help you stop the plotters." Temir's well-prepared statement caught the president's attention.

"I'm listening." The President leaned forward at her desk. Temir could see one hand on her lap, doubtless cupping the emergency beacon she could press to summon the Secret Service if necessary.

"This plot is led by the mining magnate and the main donor to the Republican party, Fred Guttenberg, who is in concert with some in our government, in our Secret Service, the FBI, the cabinet, and with Gudonov, and therefore Russia as well. His connections in our government ensure that he and his associates are never suspected or detected. He is not alone, but I do not know everyone involved. He, or I should say we, manipulated

Congress to bring impeachment charges against you, set up Mark Wells to take the fall for a terrorist incident that was committed very probably by the Gudonov mercenary group to discredit the GWAI and you, and who knows what else. Guttenberg does not tell me everything he does, but I have suspicions about his involvement in the bombings…"

President Poulter interrupted him. "You said he has high contacts in our government. I assume this includes other officials besides yourself."

"Yes. I don't know all of them. But I am almost completely certain one of them is the Vice President. And since yesterday, I have also suspected my boss, Lorraine Betts, of being in league with him."

"Do you have proof against Betts and Degrasso?" President Poulter seemed to taking the information in her stride, showing no sign of shock or disbelief.

"Less so for Betts. But Guttenberg himself has mentioned that the Vice President is sympathetic to our cause and will help us achieve our goals once he is President after your impeachment. I also suspect that the domestic terror incidents are manufactured to undermine you, but I am guessing about this point."

"But they do not have the numbers in the Senate to impeach me. It will all be for nothing. Isn't that too big a risk to run and potentially be charged for treason?"

"Madam President, according to Guttenberg, they have the numbers. At least sixteen Republican Senators are staying silent, but as the terrorist and SMM situations worsen, which they will, with the help of Russian disinformation, these Republicans will *reluctantly* vote with the Democrats to have you removed. They will not expose themselves until just before the vote."

"If all of this is true, why are you telling me now and potentially putting yourself in danger?"

"My daughter." Temir brushed away a tear from his eye.

Calmly, President Poulter asked, "Tell me why I shouldn't just have you arrested, as well as the other plotters."

"I don't think that would be wise, Madam President. I have no hard and fast proof that ties them to the impeachment charges or even to Gudonov's activities in Ethiopia. Most of the plotters will be able to melt away to regroup and take you down another day. However, if you are willing to let me pretend to continue working with them, we can get the proof."

"Why don't I just arrest you, then? You could testify against your co-conspirators to get a reduced sentence."

"It won't work, Madam President. They can deny everything. And it will look bad for you in the Senate, where it will seem like you have become paranoid due to the impeachment charges. Having me arrested will not result in you avoiding being impeached. If I am arrested, I guess that my life expectancy won't run to me being able to testify. Madam President, the Democrats don't realize it, but they have the numbers. You *will* be impeached."

There was a pause as the President thought about what he had just said. "So, why are some in my own party secretly turning against me and going to these treasonous lengths to get rid of men? What is the point?" she asked.

"We all had a suspicion since before you became President that you would give away and commit US resources, technology, and know-how to fight climate change. Water has been huge business for a decade. And you said you would work with the Democrats. None of us shared any of those policy positions with you. Large numbers of people sympathetic to the American Glory movement were secretly put in positions of influence and power many years ago. If a Republican president went down certain policy routes, she or he would be removed. It takes only a small number of people in certain positions to protect someone like Guttenberg. The whole of government doesn't need to be infiltrated."

The President was silent again for a moment, and Temir held his breath, knowing that his fate hung in the balance. Whatever decision Poulter made in the next few moments would likely

236

mean the difference between a long jail sentence or worse, or an opportunity to try and undo at least some of the wrong he had done.

"How can I trust you won't change sides again if it seems convenient? Or that you aren't trying to manipulate me right now, either for this plot or for purposes of your own?"

"Madam President, my fate is in your hands. If you say the word, I will be tried for treason. Not to mention, Guttenberg and his group are powerful, ruthless, and extremely vindictive people. If they learn what I am doing, I believe they will not hesitate to take me out. And they have the reach to do that. Once I start working for you against them, I am bound to your side."

The President was testing Temir but in essence believed that he was truly changing sides.

Temir continued, "Also, consider your current predicament. Much of the public has turned on you, and the chances of the impeachment charges succeeding are much higher than you believe. As I said Guttenberg's allies will not break cover before the vote. If I were thinking of myself, I would continue supporting the plotters and look forward to the opportunity to ascend to a higher office once the Vice President took your place."

"I see your point." There followed a long silence as President Poulter looked at Temir. "I won't arrest you, at least for the time being. But you will need to demonstrate by your actions that you are committed to helping bring these plotters to justice, and quickly. There will be some personal risk to you."

"I intend to. Another reason not to move against them is that it would alert the Russians to warn Gudonov to curb their actions in Ethiopia. Ideally, we can take down both the plotters and their Russian mercenary group at the same time."

"We are from being in an ideal position at the moment, Temir, even after what you have told me today. Now, we need to end this conversation before the length of our conversation arouses suspicion. If what you say is true, these plotters have tentacles everywhere."

"Agreed. I recommend that you and I not talk alone again, Madam President, for that reason. I would suggest you send someone to talk to me on your behalf. It must be someone you have trusted completely for decades. We can communicate through them without attracting undue attention. And Madam President, other than your husband and that aide, please tell no one else what I have just told you unless you are absolutely sure of their loyalty to you and the Constitution. We don't know who we can trust, and until you devise a plan to deal with Guttenberg and the VP, we must not arouse suspicion."

"Understood, Mr. Bousson. Heaven knows I've sat through enough intelligence briefings in my time to know how the game is played. Someone will be in touch shortly."

With that, the President reluctantly ushered him out of the Oval Office, thanking him for sharing an update about his daughter so that those in the anteroom could hear. As Temir left the White House, he was partly in disbelief that President Poulter had allowed him to leave.

Later when the President relayed all of this to her husband, he was his usual supportive self. "You see, darling," Ari said, "only you have that quick thinking and assured judgment to instantly know this was the best option. Anyone else would have called security, and I believe, as you do, that you would have been worse off. Your course of action leaves us with a chance."

CHAPTER 53

"When I was in my youth," Mikeo said, "I helped escort wealthy foreigners on safaris. I was a decent shot with a rifle, so they had me guard the tourists who came to see the big five."

"I had the feeling the other day at the reservoirs that it was not your first time firing a weapon," Mark said.

"No, indeed. Anyway, I grew disenchanted with the safari business, so I used the money I had made and trained to be a chef. I was young and did not have political ambitions."

"What, you really were a chef? Is that where you met your first wife?"

"Yes, I was. And no, I met my wife later. In any case, as I was new to the profession, and it was hard at first to find a job as a cook. I answered an advertisement from the government who needed to identify and kill a pride of lions who were causing havoc."

"You are a brave man, indeed, Mikeo."

"The money was the main motivation at the time; if I had fully understood the danger, I might not have taken the job."

"Were they endangering human life?"

"Yes. The lions and lionesses. Generally, they were attacking herd animals, but in some cases, they were maneaters or at least mankillers."

"Wow. That must have been a nerve-wracking job."

"Truthfully, I was still young and convinced of my own immortality, as the young often are. I generally worked with a tracker and at least one game warden, so that reduced the danger somewhat."

"But not entirely."

Mikeo smiled at this. "No, my friend, not entirely. That brings me to how I got my nickname. We had cornered one lioness in a stand of brush, and I was perhaps twenty meters from her while the two wardens flanked the area, one to the right, one to the left. Suddenly, I heard a roar from behind me and saw a male lion rush from behind us and leap on the tracker before I could get off a shot. I carefully fired at the lion and scored a hit, but this was a massive beast, and it kept savaging the tracker."

"I'm getting nervous just hearing about this, my friend," Mark said. "Thankfully, you didn't wait until we were on a hike through the savanna before telling me this story."

Mikeo chuckled. "I sometimes wake up in a sweat myself when I dream about this event. To continue, I reloaded and was preparing to take another shot at the lion when the wardens, who had rushed toward me, shouted a warning. Another lioness burst from the brush and charged directly at me. I got a shot off before it knocked me over, as did the wardens. Even though the lion was hit, it still retained the power to slash at me with its claws. Would you like to see the result?"

Mark said that he would, and Mikeo pulled up his shirt to show a series of long, deep scares that extended from his stomach all the way up to his chest just below the neck. "My rifle was knocked from my hands by the lioness, so I yanked my knife from the sheath and stabbed the lioness in the side. Then, another shot from a warden finished the beast off."

"What about the other lion?"

"The fight was not yet over. Just as the lioness on top of me expired, I heard a scream from my side as the other lion, having killed the tracker, leaped onto the other warden. I picked up my rifle but found it was damaged in the lion's charge and was unusable. So I leaped onto the lion and stabbed it through the throat. Still, that did not kill the beast. It threw me off its back and was about to leap on me when the remaining warden shot it in the head, killing it instantly."

"Wow. Remind me not to sneak up behind you, Mikeo; with reflexes like yours, I'd be afraid of what could happen."

Mikeo smiled at Mark's levity. "I am old and broken down these days, my friend. And most of what I did then was prompted by the adrenaline that drives the urge to fight or flee that we all share in such situations."

"Perhaps, but I think many would have fled in such a case rather than fighting as you did."

"Well, it was my job, after all, and I've never been one to shirk my duties. In any case, when the two of us survivors made it back to the ranger's station and told the head warden our story, he said that it takes a lion to kill a lion. And so, the nickname was born."

"What a story, Mikeo. Amazing. I am glad you told me that story before I leave."

"Be careful, my friend. We have taken precautions, but at some point, Gudonov will become aware that you are back in Ethiopia. Someone wants you taken out, and I do not believe that it is just the Russians. You have become a bit of a cult hero in parts of the media and public in your country, a water-for-all hero, and someone does not like that, my friend. You will travel by drone to the location you want. It cannot fly further as there will be some danger that it could crash in the mountains. This will be a very, very uncomfortable and cramped journey, my friend. There will be a car waiting for you where you land. Remember, you must release the chemical to dissolve the drone after you land. Goodbye, and be safe."

CHAPTER 54

Temir walked down a corridor in the West Wing of the White House. After attending an intelligence briefing on the hunt for the domestic terrorists, including Devereaux, he was due to meet with Brian McCormick at the White House. He knocked on a door and the President's Deputy Chief of Staff, was waiting for him.

Brian McCormick had contacted Temir at the behest of the President, and they had scheduled this first meeting to discuss forming a plan to deal about the plot against the President. To ensure they did not arouse suspicion, no attempt was made to hide the meeting, but they agreed to keep it to 30 minutes. If they needed a cover story it would be that McCormick was supportive about Temir's daughter. He had been with the President since her time as governor, and she clearly trusted him.

"We have a lot of ground to cover, and we don't have much time," Brian said after locking the door behind them and taking his seat across the table from Temir. "Why don't you take five minutes and give me the background on this plot and your place in it? Of course, the President has filled me in, but I'd like to hear it straight from the horse's mouth if you don't mind."

Temir proceeded to outline the plot he and Guttenberg had devised to bring down the President. Sadly, it seemed to have every chance of success. Once he had finished, he offered to fill McCormick in on the additional information he had acquired after doing some intensive digging over the past couple of days. It had occupied so much of his time that he had been glad Lorraine had been out of her office attending various meetings, giving her little time to monitor what he had been doing. McCormick responded that he was very much interested in hearing whatever Temir had learned that might help them in their planning.

"My first insight is that digging into Devereaux's record, his history with the special forces made me wonder if he's a lone operator," Temir said.

"Is there any evidence he is working with other dissatisfied ex-military personnel?"

"Well, let me say this. The purpose of these domestic bombings, in my opinion, is part of the strategy to make President Poulter unpopular and pave the way for her impeachment. I don't know this for a fact, and I cannot put my finger on it, but Guttenberg is always very interested in how the investigation is going."

"So, you think Guttenberg is behind it?"

"I believe he is. As I say I cannot be certain, I have no proof, and he hasn't said as much. But there is something about the way he asks questions about the investigation and what we have unearthed. It just doesn't make sense that he would want so much information about the investigation."

McCormick asked, "But don't Guttenberg's tentacles extend into the FBI and the Secret Service at the highest levels? So why would he need to ask you about it?"

Temir looked puzzled for a second. Then both of them raised their eyebrows at the same time, and in unison, using almost the exact words, "Yes, why would he bother asking you if he already knew? He is testing you, testing his other sources, and triangulating."

"Shit," said Brian.

"Anyway, it gets even worse. You might ask, how has Guttenberg gotten away with pulling all these strings without detection? As I said, partly it's his contacts in the government, such as the FBI or Secret Service. But it's also because he is supported by plans hatched years ago, not by him, to be used against any President who did not support the American Glory movement's agenda. Whether it is by frustrating a President or removing a President, they will do what is necessary and most practical at the time. I have already told President Poulter all of this."

"I know you have. But you will need to repeat this a few times. The stakes could not be higher."

While he believed Temir, Brian wanted to test him further about the extent of the plot. "I hear what you're saying people being placed in position. But isn't that something many administrations now try to do when a President from another party is about to take over? Make changes that will be hard to undo. Seed the bureaucracy with their loyalists, that type of thing. As well as try to find reasons to impeach a President, or at least go through the motions of an inquiry?"

"That is true. But this is different. We were orchestrating trying to bring her down from the outside and from within. Guttenberg doesn't even appear as a player in intelligence circles. How could that be possible?"

"I see that. Guttenberg is like a spider at the center of a web, spinning his threads around everyone and everything," McCormick said. "He is not on my radar, and neither the President's; nor I have heard anything remotely negative about him. He is the top donor to the Republican party."

"You can see why I counseled the President to be extremely cautious of telling anyone about what we are doing. If he even suspects I'm working against him, I am not exaggerating when I say I will be taken out." Temir knew it sounded dramatic, but he had no doubt that Guttenberg would try to do the same thing to him that he had attempted to do to Mark in such a case.

"It will be difficult for us to get to the bottom of this conspiracy if we are constrained from using the full power of the Presidency for fear of alerting them that we know what they're up to," McCormick said.

"True. But if we use that power carelessly and do something prematurely, I fear the result will be the impeachment of President Poulter. Any move to arrest the Vice President and NSA Betts without sufficient evidence would make her seem like a paranoid tyrant and cause senators who are currently sitting on the fence to vote against her. And it would tip off Guttenberg and Gudonov."

"I understand that. I'm just frustrated that Guttenberg's position is so strong that it's hard to see how we win this fight when we have just a few weeks to stop him." Temir could understand McCormick's frustration. Guttenberg had designed the situation like a chess game, with his moves already calculated ahead. The thought of the formidable resources available to Guttenberg was indeed chilling.

"We will likely lose if we do nothing, just as we will lose if we act too hastily. We need to devise a plan that draws the conspirators out into the open," Temir said.

"That makes sense to me. What do you propose?"

"I think our best bet is to try and arrange a reason for Betts and the VP to meet in such a way that they say or do something to incriminate themselves."

"I'll run it by the President, but it sounds like a good idea to me."

CHAPTER 55

On the ground in Ethiopia, Mark planned to move fast while he was in the country to reduce the chances of Gudonov's operatives intercepting him. The barren plains of the region would make it hard for anyone to tail him. He used AI to create a plausible but fake schedule for these movements before he left Nairobi to throw off anyone who might try further. While Mikeo had made closely guarded arrangements to land him by a small self-navigating drone, a fake journey on a commercial airline was arranged. To the rest of the world, he was on a plane to Addis Ababa. And if anyone was listening, AI-generated fake conversations were made with Aida at a false location near Addis. He had decided not to use his satellite phone for any real contact with Aida to avoid any chance of the call being used to find her real location.

The Drone set down when it ran out of power and a car was waiting for him. The rest of the journey was long. He had driven half the night to reach the hill country before pitching his tent and getting some sleep. Now, he had to drive the winding dirt roads, which he hoped would lead him to where Aida and Tom were hiding. She had once taken him to what was called the "sanctuary" cave, a remote spot deep in the hills that few outside her people knew about.

Hours later, he turned a sharp corner and pulled to a stop on a flat strip of ground below an imposing series of hills. Thankfully, he remembered going to the sanctuary where he dearly hoped to find Aida and Tom. He honked the horn a few times and then got out of the car to wait. If he recalled it correctly, this spot could be viewed from the cave. He thought it would be better to let them know he was here this way than to surprise them by walking up to the cave. Maybe ten minutes later, Tom walked out from behind the rock formation that had hidden the path up the cave.

"I presume you didn't think it was safe to call on the sat phone," Tom said after they had exchanged greetings.

"Yep. Where is she?"

"Look, Mark." Tom's tone was apologetic. "I don't know how to say this after the driving you've done to get here, but Aida doesn't want to see you. You can leave your message with me, and I'll make sure to give it to her."

"Thanks for the kind offer, old friend, but after driving all this way, I'm sure you can understand that I'd like to deliver the message personally."

"Sorry, buddy, but that would only upset her, and I'm not going to let you do that." Mark ignored his words and started to walk around Tom to get to the path to the cave, but Tom stepped in front of him. "I don't think you're hearing me, Mark, so I'll repeat myself: she doesn't want to talk to you."

"She doesn't," Mark said harshly, "or you've convinced her not to?"

"You know, Mark, maybe that's why she's not with you anymore because you don't seem to listen to what other people want instead of always thinking of yourself."

Mark laughed at the comment. "Oh, please, Dr. Freud, spare me your expert behavioral analysis. I'm not here to try and get her to dump you or to take me back; I'm here because I care about her safety."

"Great," Tom said. "Why don't you tell me what you need to know, and I can relay it to her? You can wait right here while I do."

"Thanks for the helpful suggestion, but as I said I've come a long way to talk to Aida, and that's what I'm going to do."

Mark once more tried to walk around Tom, who once again stepped in his way. Mark could feel his temper rising, and his fatigue made it harder for him to control his anger. "If I can't walk around you, buddy, I'm going to have to walk over you," he said.

"You're welcome to try," Tom answered.

CHAPTER 56

Temir walked to the end of the row of retail stores and entered the bookstore, which was the last shop in the row. He knew the proprietor, who allowed him to exit through the emergency exit in the back of the store when he needed to conduct a private meeting. After glancing around him to make sure nobody was watching, he typed the code to deactivate the alarm for thirty seconds and exited the building, closing the door behind him. It was a short walk from the alley to Rock Creek Park. Once there, he made his way to an isolated strand of trees deep in the park. Mendez was waiting for him.

McCormick had relayed approval for his plan to see if they could capture evidence of Betts meeting with Guttenberg or Vice President Degrasso outside of her customary interactions with him. To encourage her to reach out to one of them, at Temir's suggestion, the President's Chief of Staff would ask Betts to meet with the President, who would say that she didn't trust the judgment or motive of her deputy, Temir Bousson. She recalled that she sent Mark Wells back to Ethiopia on his advice, only to find that Wells' popularity became even greater than it had been and that the link to the terror group was false. The President would ask Lorraine to keep the matter between just the two of them. Hopefully, this would cause Betts to either speak with Degrasso or contact Guttenberg. McCormick had been able to gain approval to give Temir access to an off-book slush fund for the purpose.

Mendez was just the man for the job of following Betts. He had been useful in following Guttenberg's man Carruthers and Temir's daughter (his own niece) Sara.

"I was surprised to hear from you again so soon," Mendez said. "I didn't know government salaries had become so high."

Temir allowed himself a slight grin at Mendez's humor. "Look, there is a certain degree of danger involved in this," Temir admitted without going into details.

"That's obviously why you are paying through the nose."

Temir continued, "The person I'd like you to tail is protected by her own security detail and has the best security resources to hand."

"Okay. In other words, no tracking device on her car, or disabling her home security system and sneaking into her pad for a look around. Just like before."

"Exactly. I would like to know who she meets, where she goes, and any unusual activities, like secret phones, she undertakes. It sounds obvious but you must not expose yourself," Temir said.

"Roger that. Who is this person?"

"My boss. The President's National Security Adviser."

"Wow. Do I really want to be involved in this?"

"Is this enough money for you?" Temir held up his phone with an enormous Bitcoin amount typed in.

"Yes. Half now, half at the end?" said Mendez as his eyes lit up.

And with a flash, Temir transferred the crypto to Mendez, the entire transaction untraceable.

As they parted, Temir's last words were, "As always Rob....if you get caught...the buck stops with you."

Mendez nodded his head and said, "You have said that every time you paid me to do something."

Later that day, Temir drove to Arlington to visit Sara at the hospital. There was no change in her condition, nor did her attending physician have any updates to her prognosis. They just had to wait and hope for the best. Temir found the sense of powerlessness that caused him to be unnerving. However, it seemed to completely diminish his fear of what he was now embarked on.

Temir could only hope Mendez would come up with something to tie Betts to the conspiracy before the trial started. The more he thought about it, the more he believed his hunch that she was involved. But they would need more than a hunch to find a way to definitively connect her to Guttenberg.

CHAPTER 57

Enraged at the thought that Tom had the nerve to try to prevent him from speaking to Aida, Mark shoved his former friend backward, causing Tom to trip and fall to the ground.

"You're a total asshole. You were after my wife, and now you're after my partner. Can't you find your own woman, Tom?"

He started to walk by him, but Tom rose to his knees and grabbed him by the leg, causing them both to tumble to the ground. He was much heavier than Tom, but with his multiple injuries and fatigue, he knew he was in no condition for a fight.

"You're a self-centered prick, Mark. That's why women don't want to stay with you."

Mark managed to break free from Tom's grasp and rise to his feet. He ran for the path to the cave entrance only to be tackled by Tom as he turned the corner.

Once more, he scrambled out of Tom's grasp and swung at the man, striking Tom in the chest. Tom shrugged off the blow and stepped toward him, his fists raised. Mark struck another blow, and while it connected, Tom managed to move to one side at the last moment, causing Mark to hit the side of his head rather than his face.

Mark tried again but could not restrain Tom. Both men were on their feet, and they circled each other again. Mark could feel the adrenaline that had kept him going until now despite his recent injuries, beginning to fade. Tom lashed out with a right cross, which he barely blocked. Mark retreated a few steps, breathing heavily, while Tom watched him, sensing that he was holding the upper hand. "You need to leave, Mark," as he stepped forward to build on his perceived advantage.

Mark, unable to continue, fell to the ground.

CHAPTER 58

President Poulter swiveled her chair to look out from the Oval Office at the beautifully manicured White House lawn and garden. Her mood was morose, so the view did not inspire her as it usually did. She turned to face Ari as he opened the doors and walked into the office. She had a meeting in fifteen minutes with the Chairman of the Joint Chiefs of Staff and his intelligence expert to discuss the problems SMMs were creating around the world. The latest episode had seen up to 50,000 people lose their lives in Spain. As they traveled from the drought of the interior of Spain to the coast, without warning two years of rainfall fell in a single day in south-east Spain, which had trapped tens of thousands of people. She was given a briefing that Chinese officials had offered massive aid and practical support, which was already on its way to Spain.

"You don't look happy," Ari said, good as ever at reading her mood.

"I'm not. You should know that I've written a letter of resignation. I've been thinking about the situation, and I'm beginning to think about the best thing to do for me and the country is just to quit."

"I don't agree, honey. You've never been a quitter. Look at the Republican primaries. The press thought you were down for the count, but you came back to win the nomination. You weren't favored to win the Presidency either, yet here you are."

"It just seems so hopeless. Every time I turn around, something else seems to be going wrong. Wells, the GWAI, the crisis at the border, domestic terrorism incidents, the plotters..."

"I know it seems gloomy. But if you beat the impeachment charges, that gives us time to turn things around. You know how fast things can change in politics."

"Yes, but beating the impeachment seems highly unlikely, especially after Davenport just announced he finds the charges against me convincing. Temir said that Guttenberg already had the votes. I have to hand it to them. This is a well-constructed plan. I don't even know who the plotters are. And if I move against Guttenberg now, I will be made to feel paranoid against the one person who keeps the Republican party so well-funded, and I will still be removed. I can't trust anyone."

Ari pondered and replied, "There are certain people we can trust. If you hope to defeat this conspiracy, you have to take a chance and confide in them."

"Who? Other than McCormick and a few others we have known for years, none of whom have the power we need. Who can we trust, and how do you know we can trust them?"

"I think you can trust General Johnson. He is a straight shooter. I believe he is a patriot who will not be happy with what Guttenberg and his cronies are trying to do."

President Poulter thought about her husband's statement for a moment. "You know, darling Ari, I believe you may be right. General Johnson."

"Even Machiavelli said you must trust someone to be a successful leader. I'm not sure how much he can help us, but in my view, he is highly unlikely to be part of this plot. There is another reason why should not quit; if these people take over, they will form an unholy alliance with Russia."

"I'm meeting Johnson in five minutes anyway. Let me think about how I sound him out."

"Yes. But I believe he will be accompanied by his intelligence chief."

"McCormick is scheduled to be in the meeting. Please ask him to join me right away, darling. I'll tell him to pull Johnson's assistant out of the meeting to go over some data, which will give me a chance to speak alone with the Chairman for a few minutes."

"Brilliant, Madam President. I believe the people of this country should be proud to have such a—"

"Devious—" the President interrupted him.

"Skillful chief executive."

With that, Ari left the Oval Office to ask McCormick to join the President before the Chairman and his intelligence chief arrived.

CHAPTER 59

Temir had taken the usual route to meet Mendez at one of their usual spots in Rock Creek Park. Looking through the trees at their customary meeting place, he noticed a hiker walking near-by. The man didn't seem inclined to move fast, as he seemed to be intent on snapping pictures of the surrounding foliage. He didn't look all that suspicious to Temir, dressed as he was in typical tourist attire—tennis shoes, shorts, and a t-shirt, but his presence in the area meant it was time to hike to the backup meeting spot.

Mendez was waiting for him in a stand of trees at the southern edge of the park. The spot was on a small incline, allowing them to look out at the trail below while remaining hidden from sight. Temir got right to the point after walking over to stand beside the detective.

"Anything interesting turn up?"

"Nothing so far. Just a few shopping trips and lunch meetings. I took some photos just in case she met with anyone you find interesting."

Mendez, having been told to keep everything non-digital, handed him a manila folder. "I'll look at these later," Temir said before putting the folder inside his button-up shirt. "Keep the surveillance going."

"Roger that," Mendez said before they each left the meeting spot in separate directions.

***

Later that day, Temir traveled his customary path through the national park to meet with Guttenberg. His earlier discussion with Mendez had made him even more concerned about being followed. As he got closer to the meeting spot, he varied his path even more than usual. He doubled back several times to reassure himself that nobody was tracking him. As he walked, he steeled himself to maintain his composure with Guttenberg. He needed to behave in the way the billionaire expected to avoid giving the man any reason for suspecting his loyalties had changed.

Temir revealed that he had nothing new on Wells. As far as he knew, he told Guttenberg that Wells was in Ethiopia or Kenya, but they had lost track of his precise whereabouts. Guttenberg seemed agitated. He had expected to have Wells beaten by now.

Temir tried to put a positive spin on it. "When Poulter is removed, Wells won't matter. How far are we from the President being impeached?"

"It is already a done deal. I told you. The American public will understand that the party had no choice. Country before party is what they will assume. But we need Wells taken out."

"When do you think the Senate will hold the trial?" Temir asked. "Do you think Talmadge will wait until after the summer recess to start the hearings?"

"If he is smart, he will hold it before the recess. He has Poulter on the rocks. The only question is whether the majority leader has advisors smart enough to tell him this and is wise enough to listen to them."

On his way back, Temir thought about how convenient the timing of the domestic terror plot had been in terms of undermining the President. As he had told McCormick, it was just a hunch that Guttenberg had been orchestrating this. Now, feeling under constant threat, his mind was hyper-vigilant, resulting in him being alert to possibilities and solutions. It was in this state of mind that he recalled Mendez had given him a photo of a meeting he had observed Carruthers had with a bearded man. An old, retired FBI friend had ascertained from military records that this bearded man was Corey Stoddard and that he lived as a trapper and hunter in North Carolina. Temir had thought nothing of this at the time. But what peaked his attention suddenly was that Devereaux was believed to be hiding out in the dense forests of the Blue Ridge Mountains. Could Devereaux and Stoddard be connected? Surely that would be the case if Carruthers had met Stoddard. Which would point to Guttenberg being connected to the bombings.

It felt like a long shot, but it did also fit if Guttenberg was the orchestrator. If he was right, and the information somehow helped lead to the capture of Devereaux, it would provide a massive win for Poulter and perhaps help improve her chances of beating the impeachment charges in the Senate.

After returning home, Temir grabbed a previously unused burner phone and drove to a location where he could make an anonymous call.

As he drove, he did his best to recall all the details of the one interesting report about Carruthers' movements from Mendez. He had seen Devereaux's file, and while the fugitive had been in a different special forces unit to Stoddard, Temir had seen nothing to indicate that he was an expert backwoodsman or survivalist. It could be that he would need help staying alive off the grid. If so, who better to assist than a fellow ex-soldier whose address of record was in the mountains? It all pointed to Corey Stoddard.

Temir called Carranza, one of the agents leading the hunt for Devereaux.

"Who is this?"

For reasons he couldn't explain, Temir decided to speak using the AI voice disguiser, setting it with a Mexican accent. "You do not need to know who I am. I have information about

Devereaux. There is a man in North Carolina who I think may be linked to Devereaux. His name is Corey Stoddard." Temir followed up with an address and with that, he put the phone down, took out the SIM and battery, and got rid of everything, including the voice disguiser in different parts of the city.

CHAPTER 60

Desperate to see Aida, Mark lifted himself off the ground, jabbed at Tom with his left hand, and then followed it up with a round-house punch, hoping to stun Tom long enough to make a run for the cave entrance. But Tom blocked his punch and swung back, striking Mark in the face, who fell to the ground. As he struggled to rise to his feet, Tom moved forward, ready to land another blow.

At that moment, a shout rang out.

"Stop it, both of you. Stop it now!" It was Aida, standing on the path maybe ten meters above them. "You are pathetic...like little boys. The world burns and you..."

In response, Mark and Tom sheepishly took a step or two away from each other.

Tom spoke first. "I tried to convince him that you didn't want to speak with him, but he wouldn't listen."

"He's never been very good at that, has he?" Aida said. The anger in her voice suggested to Mark that she still had not forgiven him.

Mark struggled to find his breath, but after more than a minute, he said, "Aida, you must listen to me," he said. "Your life is in danger."

Tom moved closer to Mark as if to drag him away, but Aida held up her hand.

"Let him speak, Tom. He *has* driven an awful long way, so I suppose I owe him that much."

"Gudonov has tried to kill or capture me on two separate occasions. I strongly believe that they plan to go after you next as a way to get to me," Mark said.

"You already told me that," she said. "Why did you come all this way just to repeat yourself?"

"Because I'm going back to the USA to lobby for more assistance for the EAWTP, and I'd like to take you with me for your safety. Tom can come too if he likes." Mark didn't relish the thought of being in Tom's company for the flight home, but if that's what it took to get Aida to agree, he would have to put up with it.

"That's what you said before. My place is here, Mark, you know that," Aida said. "Once things die down, I will go back to the village and resume my work at the hospital."

"It's not clear things will quiet down anytime soon, Aida. You can't stay here forever, and if you go back to the village, you will instantly become a target. Why not spend some time in the States and keep yourself safe?" Even as he said it, he knew he wasn't making the best case for her to accompany him. He was still slightly out of breath from the fight, and fatigue clouded his mind.

"I'm sorry you came all this way just to hear me say no, Mark, but that's the truth of it. I can't take the easy way out while thousands of others can't leave."

"But Aida, I don't think that's wise—"

"Mark, leave it be, buddy," Tom broke in, "you're not going to change her mind, you know that."

Aida could be stubborn. Mark knew that she was unlikely to return with him, but thought she would realize how much he loved her.

"Fine. But at least let me leave the supplies I've brought for you. It will save the risk of you having to drive to a town to resupply for a while."

Aida nodded her head. "That would be appreciated."

Tom and Aida helped him unload the supplies from the jeep. Aida then invited Mark to stay and have some tea. He was in no fit state to leave immediately, and as soon as he lay down to rest, he fell asleep. Several hours later, Mark said goodbye to Aida. He wondered if he would see her again.

CHAPTER 61

Temir stopped outside the designated meeting room in the White House corridor to ensure he was unobserved and then slipped into the room. Along with McCormick, General Johnson's intelligence chief, General Azar, was waiting for him. The Chairman of the Joint Chiefs had needed some convincing that the plot was real, but once he realized that it was, he had reacted with shock and anger to the President's description of the efforts of Guttenberg and his group to remove her from office. McCormick had informed Temir that Johnson had characterized their scheming as a plot against the soul of the Republic. Poulter had told him she had no one else to turn to, and he responded by offering to do everything he could to prevent Guttenberg and his co-plotters from succeeding. He had sent General Azar to this meeting to learn as much as he could about the conspiracy so they could formulate a plan to thwart the plotters.

After Temir filled in Azar on the extent of Guttenberg's machinations as he understood them, the focus of the conversation turned to the next steps.

"I still think we should just have Guttenberg arrested. Maybe Betts and Degrasso, too," Brian McCormick suggested out loud.

General Azar gave his reasons for recommending a different path. "Most importantly, we need to know who else they are working with. At the moment, we have Guttenberg, maybe Betts, maybe Degrasso. That's it. We do not know who is involved in the FBI, government, or judiciary, nor do we know the names of any Senators. Even if we stopped it in its tracks, these people would simply lie low until they could strike again. Not to mention, we will have no chance of taking out the Gudonov group. All of this is unsatisfactory to the President and to the Chairman. It is high risk, but she would like to take out the conspirators and Gudonov and is willing to take the chance of being impeached."

McCormick observed that, "She has always been one hell of a risk taker."

Temir and McCormick started to talk simultaneously; McCormick stopped to let Temir speak.

"How do we draw out Gudonov?" Temir asked.

"What about Wells?" McCormick asked. "My understanding is Gudonov has been trying to capture or kill him."

Temir responded. "They have been. But after their latest assassination attempt on him in Kenya, he has been staying at the Presidential Palace in Nairobi, doubtless under heavy guard. We don't know exactly where he is right now."

Temir refrained from mentioning that he was partly responsible for the last attempt to kill Wells. He was glad it had failed, but he had no choice then at the time. If he had refused Guttenberg's request, it would have immediately made the billionaire suspect Temir. *Neither the President nor anyone else ever needs to find out I was part of the plot to kill Wells, as Guttenberg took care of payments and orders through some faceless AI-generated intermediaries.*

"If he's in Kenya, is it likely that Wells will return to Ethiopia anytime soon?" Azar asked.

"It is at least very possible. The project, his partner. He may be in Ethiopia already. We just don't know," Temir responded.

"Why would he risk his life to go see an ex-girlfriend?" General Azar said, turning to look at Temir.

"He may feel that Gudonov will target her in order to get at him," Temir said.

"If that is the case, why is he in Kenya and not Ethiopia?" McCormick cut in to ask.

"As I said, we don't know where he is exactly. We have lost track." Temir figured the less said about the second attempt on Wells' life, the better.

"Which brings us back to where we started," McCormick said, "figuring out how to finger Betts and the Degrasso and strike a significant blow against the Russians for their interference with our activities by significantly degrading Gudonov's forces in Ethiopia."

"I'll talk to General Johnson about how we put this together. In the meantime, please let us know if the surveillance of Betts reveals anything of importance, Temir."

"Of course," Temir said. "I should mention that, and I'm sure General Johnson knows, we are operating under tight time constraints. If the Senate majority leader decides to hold the impeachment trial before their summer recess, the President could be removed from office sometime in the next three weeks."

"General Johnson is aware of that," General Azar said. "I expect he will present his plan to the President for approval within the next twenty-four hours."

CHAPTER 62

After leaving Tom and Aida, Mark had driven via a circuitous route to the UN office near Aida's village. There, he discussed the UN security officers' plans for guarding the water tanks and rebuilding the project, and how they would work with the newly arrived Kenyan troops. Afterward, Mark and his two UN guards, and a dozen Kenyan troops headed to Aida's village.

He planned to spend less than an hour gathering a few things he had left at her house. After that, he would head for the main airport; at this point, Gudonov would be tipped off that he was back in town, but he would be heavily guarded. As he was leaving, he was surprised to see Fana, Aida's mother, approaching.

After greeting him, she got right to the point.

"A friend told me she saw you here. Mark, I wish to speak with you about a matter troubling me."

"Of course. I'm sorry I didn't think to stop by and say goodbye before leaving last time, but as I'm sure you know, Aida and I aren't getting along too well these days."

"She has told me, and I am sorry to hear it. My daughter is... fiery. She has a big temper, and when you betrayed her, she was so unhappy. I do not like this new man, this Tom. He is not his own man."

"I'm sorry to hear that, but you know your daughter. She can be stubborn. If you tell her that you don't like Tom, it will likely only make her more committed to the relationship."

"She has always been willful. But I don't think this man is good for her, and I think you should know that."

"I'm not thrilled that she is with Tom now, that's for sure. But he's always been a reliable friend. Why don't you trust him?"

"It is just a feeling I have. That is all. I have never liked him even before he was with Aida."

"Is this the matter troubling you?" he asked. "I need to leave soon if I'm going to make it to the airport on time."

"It is about my brother. Jemal. I want to tell you that I do not think he would do what they say he did." Fana had a serious look as she waited for his reaction.

"I understand your loyalty, Fana. But he did parade around the hospital with guns and men. And he has claimed responsibility for the attack on the water tanks."

"That is not proof that he did what they say. Anyone could have made such a claim. I know my brother, and while he is hurting still for what happened to his family, I know he would not do this."

"Why wouldn't he?" Mark asked.

"Because he is not a violent man."

"Well, I'm not saying that you are wrong. But without some evidence of his innocence, I'm not sure if anyone will believe him, given his past actions."

"That is why I am here, Mark. He came to see me not long after it happened. He couldn't stay long, as the police are hunting him."

"What did he tell you?"

"He said that on the day of the bombings, he was in a town in the far north of the country. But my brother is a smart man, Mark. He was first in his class in school. He used the most advanced agricultural methods on his farm."

"I'm sure you're right, Fana, but how does this help show he didn't blow up the water tanks?" He appreciated that she had come to him, but he needed to be on his way soon. If she didn't reach the point quickly, he would miss his flight and be forced to stay in Ethiopia longer than he had planned.

"On the same day he heard of the bombings, he immediately went to the town square and took a picture of himself in front of the clock tower, holding a newspaper with the date in his hand."

Mark paused, putting his bag to one side. "That might be useful, Fana. I can use fake image detector technology to evaluate it. Do you have a copy of this picture?"

"Yes, back at my house."

Mark thought he may not be leaving Ethiopia today after all.

CHAPTER 63

President Poulter took a moment to look around the room before speaking. Sitting across from her in the Oval Office were General Johnson, his intelligence chief General Azar, Ari, and Deputy Chief of Staff Bret McCaskill. The Chairman of the JCOS responded as she had hoped when she explained to him the threat that she and the country faced from a multitude of threats. Now that General Johnson had had time to gather as much information as possible about the situation they faced and consider potential action they could take to thwart the plotters, she was about to convene a meeting to hear his plan.

"Gentlemen, I don't need to inform you of the gravity of our situation," she began. "I speak not merely of my personal political survival but much more importantly of a threat to the nation from a sinister and secret cabal of individuals who believe that they have the right to subvert the duly elected President of the land to suit their nefarious purposes. That, in itself is bad enough, but as George Washington warned, giving a foreign nation undue consideration in the construction of our policies is an evil of quite another kind. And this is exactly what I believe will result if the plotters are successful. An unholy alliance with Russia."

She continued, "I won't labor the point other than to say I'm convinced we must act boldly to keep that from happening. General Johnson, thank you for your patriotism in stepping up to help the country overcome the danger it now faces and your insight in recognizing that this is not simply a matter of domestic political infighting. Please."

"Thank you, Madam President; I am honored that you came to me in this time of need. To recap: Guttenberg and an unidentified and unknown number of US citizens are acting in concert with Gudonov and therefore, the Russians, who are also allied to the Chinese. Together, their disinformation and hard bargaining with the Mexican government have led to the huge swelling of the SMM on our southern border and our border being breached by tens of thousands, with more to come. This is the context in which we are operating."

Pausing to cough and then taking a glass of water, he continued. "Thus, the time has come to heed the words of our commander-in-chief and implement a plan designed to thwart the machinations of these plotters. In doing so, I believe our goal should be to deal a sharp blow to the Russians by destroying the Gudonov mercenary group. We will deal with the Chinese later – their agenda is to use climate migration to distract us from their plans to invade Taiwan."

He continued, "The plan General Azar and I have devised centers on drawing a major portion of Gudonov's strength in Ethiopia into the open so we can destroy them via a secret deployment of troops to the region. We also now believe, although the evidence is circumstantial, that Gudonov either armed the Al-Haqa group or is framing them for bombing part of the infrastructure of the water flow command center in Ethiopia. As you may know, I have an excellent relationship with my opposite number in that country. I believe he will allow us to insert a sizable force into the area to deal with Gudonov. As you can imagine, Gudonov's actions in the country have not endeared them to Ethiopia's people and their leadership."

"How do you plan to draw them out, General Johnson?" the President asked.

"There are a variety of ways to do so. The most convincing thing would be to have Mark Wells travel to Ethiopia if he isn't already there. Gudonov should then learn that he is there and has minimal protection."

276

"How can we be sure they would still want Wells to be taken out?" Ari asked.

"Because they have tried to kill him already and lost a lot of men in that attempt, and in addition, Guttenberg and Temir have failed in their efforts to discredit him. They do not want this water collaboration project to succeed." Azar was clear in his assessment.

"That could work. But then, how do you plan to convince Wells to go to Ethiopia?" Ari asked.

"He may already be in Ethiopia. If he isn't, we could contact him and tell him we have intelligence that his ex-girlfriend in Ethiopia is in danger from Gudonov," General Azar said. "This plan has the advantage of likely being fairly close to the truth."

General Azar continued. "The second part of the plan is aimed at entrapping Vice President Hugh Degrasso and National Security Adviser Betts," General Azar explained. "To do this, the President would convene a meeting in the Situation Room on the pretext of a major operation in Ethiopia against Al-Haqa designed to capture or kill Jemal and the other members of his group."

"I presume the reason for the subterfuge is to keep them from warning Gudonov of what is going on," Ari said.

"Precisely," General Johnson responded. "Once they see what is happening, it will be too late, and they will be trapped in the situation room. The President can say that the true nature of the mission was concealed to prevent any leaks, given her understandable concern about security."

"They may or may not know that we are on to them by the time the mission is completed, Chairman Johnson," Ari said. "Do you advise arresting them on the spot?"

"As I mentioned, it depends on what evidence we have gleaned by then. Madam President, this, of course, will be your call."

"It's a bold plan, General Johnson. I like it," the President said. "But it involves putting Wells and whoever is with him in danger. Would they be informed of their role in this plan?"

"I would advise against that, Madam President," the general said.

"But he would be risking his life and that of his companions, will he not?"

"Madam President, everything we do from this point on is a risk to the future of everyone in this room. I am convinced these plotters will stop at nothing to achieve their objective. You have asked us to act boldly, which is what this plan is about. Mr. Wells may not come out of this alive, and if we fail, it will be the people in this room who might be arrested rather than Degrasso, Betts, and Guttenberg. At best, I estimate our odds of success to be 50/50. And if that were not enough, these people would allow SMMs and climate change to send large parts of the world into the dark ages. It seems to me that they believe that will propel the US into unimagined power."

There was silence for a moment, then the President spoke. "Thank you for your directness, General Johnson. It is what I was looking for from you."

"Ari, what do you think?" Poulter turned to face her husband.

"I'm afraid the general is correct. I fear we have no choice but to follow General Johnson's suggestion and hope Mr. Wells retains the ability to sidestep the danger that has kept him alive thus far."

"While I think the idea of using the Situation Room to neutralize Betts and Degrasso is a good one, what happens in the aftermath? Because we currently have no hard evidence against them, any move we make to arrest them or force them to resign will be questioned. With the impeachment proceedings pending, as the Chairman mentioned, this may pose a problem."

"We need to act in parallel and amass evidence against them at the same time as try to gather the identities of the co-conspirators." General Azar said.

278

"Let us hope we can accomplish that in an expeditious manner, General Azar," President Poulter said. "In the meantime, I believe this plan is likely our best chance of stopping this plot in its tracks. General Johnson…you have the green light."

CHAPTER 64

"Thanks, Rex, I'm counting on you," Mark said on the phone.

"I'll make sure it happens," Talbertson said, and they exchanged goodbyes and ended the call.

Mark looked out the window of Aida's house in Ethiopia. His UN and Kenyan guards sat on the porch, drinking the tea he had brewed for them. He had felt it was vital that the President learned that Jemal had not been involved in the bombing of the interchange water tanks, which made the Gudonov mercenary group the most likely culprit. When pondering how to get the news to the White House, he remembered Talbertson telling him he was friendly with Brian McCormick, the President's Deputy Chief of Staff.

A few minutes later, he was on the phone with Rex, who understood the importance of the revelation. He had scanned and uploaded the photo of Jemal being far from the bombing on the day it occurred and sent it to his well-connected friend. Rex had promised he would get the file with the photo and the story that went along with it to McCormick.

That done, Mark had another task on his to-do list. He picked up his phone and dialed Mikeo's number. With evidence of Jemal's innocence in the destruction of the water tanks in his possession, he had formed a new plan for speeding up the rebuilding of the water tanks in Ethiopia and the progress of the EAWTP more generally. He hoped this would ultimately pave the way for getting the GWAI back on track. If Mikeo agreed, he planned to return to DC to reveal the truth about the bombings, which he hoped would have the effect of restoring his reputation as well as helping both the EAWTP and GWAI regain their momentum. Mark was increasingly buoyed by the positive publicity he was still getting at home.

Mikeo answered, and after they exchanged greetings, Mark got right to the point.

"I've found evidence that Jemal didn't blow up the water tanks in Ethiopia, which leads me to believe that the Gudonov group was behind it but trying to frame Jemal. This information can help us speed up the rebuilding of the water tanks in Ethiopia and turbocharge the EAWTP's progress. I should have thought about it properly before; Jemal has never even owned a gun, and Al-Haqa was a protest movement against America. There were never any terrorist plans."

"I hope you are right, my friend, although I think you want something more from me than my sage advice on this matter."

"Mikeo, you are indeed astute, and I suspect that is a major reason you have risen to your current position."

"Spare me the flattery and get to the point, Mark. I know you too well not to know when you are about to make a request."

Mark chuckled at the President's words. "I can't deny it, Mr. President, so I won't even try. In short, you have committed Kenyan troops to protect the EAWTP. I need your support in something else."

"Of course. What do you need, Mark?"

"Mikeo. Your support means more to me than I can say. Thank you, my dear friend. Rather than go to the US immediately, I will first need to meet with you and other Presidents in Nairobi; I need to propose additional funding to finish the project urgently. I believe I can convince the UN to give us these funds, but we first need to present a united front. I could not convince Aida to come with me to the States, so I still fear for her safety. Hopefully, she remains in hiding for a while longer."

"I am sorry to hear that, my friend, but let us work quickly. She is not stupid. She will remain in hiding, I am sure. I will send a driverless drone for you by helicopter in the same spot you landed on. Please stay safe until it arrives. Gudonov may already know that you are back in Ethiopia so my troops will escort you. All of us will be here when you arrive."

"I will, Mikeo. On another subject, how is the hunt for my would-be assassins going?"

"We are making progress, my friend. I will tell you what we have learned when I see you in Nairobi."

CHAPTER 65

Temir peered at the small cabin, almost entirely hidden by the dense foliage surrounding it. He had somehow managed to be part of the FBI team potentially close to finding Devereaux. Temir was wearing an FBI jacket himself, supplied by Carranza, as a way to avoid questions about who exactly he was from the FBI agents involved in the raid. The tactical team had been on standby to deal with Devereaux if he was sighted. When Carranza had given the word, the team had joined them in driving deep into the Blue Ridge mountains to an access point perhaps five miles from the cabin.

Given the broken terrain and dense foliage, the hike to the cabin had taken well over an hour. No wonder, Temir thought, that Devereaux had been able to avoid detection despite the massive search for him. Carranza had been able to implant a miniature electronic tracking device on Stoddard's shoe, hoping that he would lead them to Devereaux. The tracker revealed the cabin's location, and agents spotted Devereaux yesterday.

As the tactical team closed in on the cabin, Temir suddenly wondered if finding Devereaux hadn't somehow been too easy. Could this be a setup? He dismissed the idea from his mind. Nobody knew that he was here, aside from Carranza. Still, a feeling of unease remained. If it wasn't a setup, what was bothering him?

"Why don't we get closer in case we need to provide backup," he said to Carranza.

Carranza replied, "Backup? Are you kidding? There's thirty men in the team."

Temir stood up and started to walk towards the cabin. "Humor me. I want to be there when they apprehend him."

As two agents approached the door, flanked by another agent on each side and two more, ten feet behind them, a massive explosion erupted. Four FBI agents were knocked to the ground; the two furthest from the door immediately took cover behind nearby foliage as bullets rippled from the window by the front door. An agent who had just risen to his feet after the explosion was hit and fell to the ground. Return fire from the two agents behind trees in front of the house shattered the window where the firing had emanated.

As the agents stopped to reload, there was an eerie quiet. Temir motioned for Carranza to follow him around the back of the cabin. Just as they turned the corner, another explosion sounded, blowing an FBI agent, just ahead of them, off his feet. The back door opened, and Devereaux exited the house, sprinting for the cover of a stand of trees some twenty feet from the door. An FBI agent fired at Devereaux, striking him in the side. Still, the ex-soldier, clearly wearing a tactical vest, staggered but kept going until he reached the trees.

Temir outpaced Carranza and entered the trees just behind Devereaux, desperate to reach the man before he could disappear into the trackless forests in this part of the Blue Ridge mountains. Temir took a run at Devereaux, and he used his momentum to barrel into him. Devereaux turned, gun in hand, to face Temir.

The gun discharged as Temir tackled him, but he had disrupted the fugitive's aim. They fell into the stream, and Temir grabbed the gun arm as he tried to aim it. He kept hold of the arm and moved it away, using his other arm to elbow Devereaux in the face. Carranza appeared from the decline, and Devereaux suddenly produced a knife from his jacket and threw it at the FBI agent. He then spun and punched Temir square in the face as he exited the stream, knocking him off his feet.

Devereaux was hobbling to a nearby boat to escape, but Temir and Carranza had slowed his escape sufficiently for several agents to descend and arrest him. He was caught.

CHAPTER 66

President Poulter fidgeted in her chair in the Oval Office. Ari was late for their meeting yet again.

"Did I ever tell you the story of how Ari was late for our first date?" she asked McCormick, sitting in his customary chair to the side of her desk.

"I believe you have, but I'd be happy to hear it again," he said diplomatically.

"No need for that. It doesn't get any better in the retelling. And it will only make me more cross with him than I already am."

The door opened a moment later, and Ari walked in, an abashed look on his face.

"Madam President, my apologies for my lateness. I was talking to General Azar about the capture of Devereaux in North Carolina and lost track of time."

"We got him?" confirmed President Poulter, ignoring his apology.

"Yes. He is not talking, but this is a big win," replied Ari.

"It doesn't stop the impeachment trial, but it is important to get him. He is a murderer plain and simple." The President breathed a sigh of relief.

Ari chimed in, "I think capturing Devereaux has helped us already. The bastard took three agents down before we got him. It demonstrated that this administration can bring the perpetrators of these domestic terror incidents to justice."

"I want the names of the agents, and I want to speak to their families today." President Poulter knew this was a win but wanted to acknowledge the high cost paid by some.

Ari excitedly continued, "Let us pray that the Ethiopian operation goes as planned and provides you with further ammunition, demonstrating that your administration can strike against the country's enemies both at home and abroad."

"We can only hope that the capture of Devereaux convinces the majority leader to delay the trial," the President said. "On a tangential topic. Do you think we can trust Temir?"

"Do we have a choice at this point?" Ari answered with a question.

The President looked thoughtful. "You are probably right that we don't have much choice. But he is such a devious character that I can't help but have doubts about whether he will turn again. Are we keeping him under tight surveillance?"

"Yes, we are. His knowledge has been invaluable to us. We could not have caught Devereaux without Temir asking a private detective to tail Guttenberg's bag carrier, Carruthers." McCormick gave a summary of how Temir had led them to Devereaux via Corey Stoddard. They all laughed when McCormick revealed that Temir had used a burner phone and an accent disguiser device to give an anonymous tip off, and then later revealed it was him.

"Why do you think he did that?" asked the President.

"I think he has just spent so long in the shadows that he is accustomed to covering his tracks. But his fate is tied to yours, Madam President," McCormick continued. "I think we should certainly keep an eye on him, but from what I've seen, he's been nothing but sincere in his efforts to help thwart Guttenberg's plot. And he could have been killed in capturing Devereaux."

"And what of his daughter?" asked President Poulter.

"No change," replied McCormick.

"I'll guess we'll just have to see," the President said.

"Indeed," Ari said, nodding his head in agreement.

"Your meeting with the Kenyan ambassador is scheduled to start in twenty minutes, Madam President," McCormick said, "and I'd like to bring you up to speed on the talking points before you meet him."

CHAPTER 67

Fred Guttenberg sipped his whiskey as he watched the latest news on the television in the den of his Virginia house. The house also had a concrete-lined basement, which was convenient for...other matters.

The news was all about the Senate majority leader's impending decision on when to schedule the impeachment trial.

Guttenberg was satisfied with how his plan had proceeded, but he knew that as the moment of truth got closer, it was vital not to underestimate the chances of things going wrong.

He was concerned, however, that somehow, the FBI had tracked Devereaux to his lair in the Blue Ridge Mountains and apprehended him. Guttenberg had been told Devereaux was a true believer who would never betray the cause. Besides, he did not even know that Guttenberg existed. Everything had been arranged through intermediaries. The other piece of news he had received earlier in the day had also been troubling. His security team had been monitoring a meeting between Betts and Voorhees when they noticed suspicious behavior linked to a car parked within camera range and the signature of an AI camera.

The team got a picture of the driver of the car exiting his vehicle and ran the man's photo in a database that identified him as a private detective. They had then placed a tracer on the vehicle that belonged to the private eye, a man named Mendez. The team had tracked him to Rock Creek Park the next day and apprehended him. The question they needed to know now was who had hired him. They needed to know who he worked for.

Guttenberg's phone rang. It was his assistant Carruthers. He picked it up off the end table where it lay and answered.

"He's ready."

"Perfect. I'll come down."

Guttenberg left the library and made his way down to the hidden room in the basement. A man was strapped to a chair in the corner of the basement. He was hooded, and his body was bruised and bloody.

"Has he had anything of interest to say?" Guttenberg asked Carruthers.

"He just said that he wasn't following anyone."

Ever careful, Guttenberg spoke directly to the man through an electronic voice disguiser. "Why don't you tell me what I want to know, Robert Mendez, and save yourself the trouble of doing this the hard way."

"What do you want to know?" Mendez said.

"Are you FBI?"

"I don't work with the FBI."

"Why were you taking photos of the National Security Adviser?"

"I take photos of government officials wherever I can. I may be able to sell them. Maybe they are having affairs or meeting people they shouldn't be meeting. In which case the photos become valuable."

"You're lying to me, Robert," Guttenberg responded without delay. "I fear a certain amount of persuasion will be required to get to the truth."

Guttenberg walked over to the counter and looked through the tools Carruthers had prepared for him. He picked up a scalpel and walked back over to stand before Mendez.

Guttenberg applied the scalpel to the sensitive skin under Mendez's fingernails. Mendez winced in pain.

"Unfortunately for you, although I decided not to continue with a medical career, one thing I did retain from my early training was the knowledge of the location of the major pain centers of the human body. That means your attempt to avoid telling me what I want to know will ultimately prove fruitless."

Guttenberg removed the gag. But Mendez had passed out.

"Wake him up, Carruthers."

Carruthers splashed cold water over Mendez's head.

Guttenberg ordered Carruthers to continue the questioning, stipulating that he needed to be kept alive.

CHAPTER 68

Aida carried water buckets in both hands as she walked down the twisting path that led to the natural spring. It was perhaps two kilometers away from the sanctuary cave. Its presence was a primary reason the cave made such a viable hiding spot. The combination of remoteness and accessibility to drinkable water made it suitable for a long-term stay, as long as whoever stayed there had access to food resupply.

Tom had left that morning on a resupply run, which had compelled her to make this trip to refill the water cistern. She would make another trip later to ensure they had enough water for the next few days. As she walked, she considered the question of when they should return to her hometown. She was inclined to think a month hiding out was long enough to preserve her from any immediate danger. Once Mark departed for the USA, whatever attention he drew from these mercenaries would likely go with him. Or so she conjectured.

Another thing to consider was the UN guards stationed at the hospital after her uncle's demonstrations. As long as they continued to keep watch over the area, she felt confident the Gudonov group thugs would stay away. She hoped that Mark had followed his plan to decamp for the USA. She loved him and wanted him to be safe.

Certainly, Tom would be more at ease if Mark was in the US. While he had apologized to her for fighting with Mark, she had no illusions that either of them was eager to spend much time around the other anytime soon. Maybe in time, but they weren't there yet.

Buzzing from the satellite phone receiver behind her startled her. Turning, she walked to the back of the cave and picked up the device.

"Aida," Mark said when she answered the call. "I need to talk to you again. Please don't hang up."

CHAPTER 69

"Madam President," yelled McCormick, barging into the Oval Office without the customary approval. Realizing that he had entered a private meeting between the President, the Chairman of the Joint Chiefs of Staff, General Azar, and Ari, he apologized profusely.

The President waved away the security detail and asked McCormick what was happening.

"The impeachment trial is delayed. Delay means it's over. Talmadge didn't realize he had the numbers. You have won."

A smile crossed the President's face, maybe the first genuine smile he had seen from her in weeks. "This is good news. If Talmadge didn't believe he had the numbers today, he won't know he has the numbers after the summer. You are right. We have won. We can bring back the GWAI, obtain evidence on Betts and Degrasso and any others, take out Gudonov, guard the southern border, and one of the terrorists has been caught."

"I concur, Madam President," the always supportive Ari said. "And in your capable hands, I think we can turn it around. But we need to stay alert to what Guttenberg and his cronies may do."

"What do my military advisors think?" the President said, turning to General Azar and Johnson.

General Azar spoke confidently, "I think you have hit the nail on the head, Madam President. The Democrats don't believe they have the votes. If we are to believe Bousson, and I do, the secrecy of some of the Republican Senators' positions has undermined their cause. However, we do not know the identities of most of the conspirators. But we have time to prepare. Madam President, we have much to do, but we are on the front foot."

CHAPTER 70

Guttenberg, his hands bloodied and his face with traces of blood, snarled as he watched the news. "Those fucking fossils. Why can't he and the rest of his party work out that they have the numbers? The Democrats are fucking idiots."

Carruthers, standing by his side, just shook his head. He had never seen Guttenberg in such a rage. Guttenberg looked around, his gaze fixed on the golf clubs in the corner of the room. He had played a round earlier that day. Without a further word, he walked over to the clubs and removed a 9-iron from the bag. Then he proceeded to bash the big screen TV on the wall. He struck it blow after blow until the screen lay mostly in fragments on the ground.

"Fucking assholes," he shouted. Carruthers nodded his head to indicate agreement with his boss.

"Set up a meeting with Dr. Muller," Guttenberg said, his tone now calm and cold. "I think it's time we made use of that implantable chip he has been talking about. Keep Mendez alive. We will need him."

CHAPTER 71

"What do you want, Mark?" Aida asked. "I thought you shouldn't risk calling me."

"Mikeo has got me connected to a device that disguises our locations. We are heading back to the US soon to drum up support at the UN for the EAWTP," said Mark. "I'm in Kenya, meeting with all the leaders to put together the plan for additional funding. And President Poulter has beaten the impeachment charges, and it seems the GWAI could be back on track. I may even be reinstated."

"Oh, Mark, that's wonderful news. Please get this finished. Tom means well, but he is not the leader." Realizing what she had just said, she changed the subject. "But why do you think you will be trusted with this project in the US?"

"I now have proof that your uncle is not a terrorist and that Russian-backed mercenaries tried to frame him. Your mom visited me when I was back in your village. Jemal went to her after the bombing and gave her a photo proving he wasn't even in the region when the bombing happened."

"That's great news...she must have found out after I went into hiding." Her mother had always been fierce when it came to protecting those she loved. Aida was proud of her for seeking out Mark to clear Uncle Jemal's name.

"Aida, you're not safe in Ethiopia if you return to your home, and you can't stay in hiding forever. Please come with me to America, where you will be safe with me there."

"I wish you well on your trip there, but I told you I'm not going to the US, and that hasn't changed." Aida was touched by his concern for her, but she was never going to leave Ethiopia at this moment in need. Ethiopians had suffered more than most from drought but so many of them had returned from overseas to help their country in these last two years.

"Mikeo believes that—"

"Mark, stop. I do know you care. But I would not be going back to the US with you, even if you hadn't slept with..."

She hesitated, then spoke somberly, "How can I leave when my mother, family, and thousands of others can't? I do understand what you are saying, so I will remain in the cave for a while longer."

"Babe..."

"Mark, I told you, stop. Just get the money and finish this project. People I love are dying."

"Okay, babe."

CHAPTER 72

McCormick looked up as he saw Temir. They had established a good place to meet where they could not be seen.

"Hi, Temir. It looks like Jemal had been out of the area when Ethiopia's water tanks were destroyed. That means it was obviously Gudonov had been behind the explosions. Which, in turn, means that General Johnson's plan to destroy the group's forces in that country takes on an extra dimension."

Temir looked puzzled. "What do you mean?"

"If we can expose Gudonov and the Russians, followed by a military operation to destroy Gudonov in East Africa, I don't see how the delayed impeachment can be resurrected."

Temir thought about what McCormick had said and then nodded in agreement. "That's absolutely right. Yes, that makes complete sense."

"We should get back. Separately. Before we are missed. But things look positive for us."

"Okay, I will try to call Mendez and see if he has found anything yet. I was supposed to meet him today, but I was late with everything that was going on. He was gone by the time I got there. I'll get in touch with him later today to reschedule."

"Okay, keep me updated," said McCormick.

"And I need to get in touch with Guttenberg in the next couple of hours. He will not be happy right now, I imagine, and I don't want him to suspect anything."

"I am sure he will be pissed. I am sure you heard on the news. The SMM on our southern border has ground to a halt. The torrential rain has killed thousands and no one can move. It is a humanitarian catastrophe."

CHAPTER 73

Mark had returned to Nairobi via the small single-seat drone provided by Mikeo a few days earlier. While Aida had refused to leave Ethiopia when he talked to her by satellite phone, he thought her tone had softened. Mark felt assured that she was safe for now, sheltering in the caves with Tom.

Mark looked around the palace conference room at the assembled leaders of Uganda, Kenya, Ethiopia, and others.

Mark began to speak. "We have formulated an ambitious, even audacious plan to present to the UN that will help the EAWTP regain its momentum, rebuild the destroyed water tanks in Ethiopia, and serve as a powerful example in our battle against the havoc caused by SMMs."

Mark continued, "The continent of Africa has been hardest hit by SMMs. We could use help from the rest of the world to stop their spread. Especially from the United States which has the technology, resources and know-how. But the US is skeptical, particularly about security. So, let us in East Africa lead the world in showing the United States a success story. I believe if they see a success story, they will get back on board. The military protection by Kenya to protect the physical infrastructure is vital. I believe it is in our interests that we meet at the UN in New York together to present a united front. Our success here can also serve as an inspiration for the rebooting of the GWAI, which can help deal with the problem of SMMs globally."

"So, when should we depart for New York?" Mikeo asked.

"We should all leave, on different planes of course, for security reasons, within 48 hours," said Henry.

Mikeo, with a raised voice, suggested, "Let us all make the necessary arrangements today."

Everyone joined in banging the tables, and individual conversations started.

Taking him to one side, he asked, "Mikeo, how is the search for the vipers in the palace going?"

"Quite well, my friend. We have uncovered information about the would-be assassin, as well as those who fed him information."

"That's great news. I certainly will feel better about visiting Nairobi in the future now that you have discovered the culprits behind the attempt to kill me. Who were they, if you don't my asking?"

"It is better that you don't know, my friend," Mikeo said.

"Okay, but do you know why they wanted me dead?"

"From your perspective, the more interesting question may be who wanted you dead."

"Are you saying he told you who hired him?"

"Yes. Our interrogation was very persuasive, and he spilled the beans, as they say, on the ringleader of the plot. I am afraid he will never be able to speak again, though."

"Who was this ringleader?"

"There were many layers, and the intermediary wasn't even a real person. It was an AI generated intermediary in Venezuela."

Mark was disappointed. "But this is no news at all."

"Quite the contrary, my friend. The fact that it is AI reveals a lot. AI is not all the same, I am led to believe. It can leave a signature, similar to a style of writing. This was the most advanced AI - definitely out of the US. Someone big, with massive connections, wants you dead. And it is someone in the US. No doubts."

"I think I know who it is," said Mark.

"Who?" replied Mikeo.

"The Deputy National Security Adviser, a man named Bousson."

"Once we alert his superiors of what he has done, they can make sure this Bousson can no longer trouble you."

"Mikeo, if I may, I would suggest that you don't accuse him of this crime, at least not yet."

"For what reason?" Mikeo asked.

"For one thing, I am not absolutely certain. Secondly, I think if he is identified, the bad publicity could easily impede our efforts. If a member of her administration is seen going rogue like this, it will reflect badly on the President. I think it's better to talk to my friends in DC and have them speak privately to Poulter about this man so she can handle it in the way she deems fit."

"My dear academic friend. You are becoming wise in the theater of espionage and politics," chuckled Mikeo.

"I have been shot at twice, Mikeo. I need to wise up quickly, or I won't make it to the other side of this crisis."

Mikeo thought for a moment about what Mark had said. "As much as I would like to expose this man for the crime he has commissioned in my country, what you say makes sense. I will refrain from providing the ambassador with this information."

"Thank you, Mikeo. Your assistance on this and other matters is, as always, much appreciated."

"Our fates are joined together now, my friend," Mikeo said. "Driven by natural disasters and human frailty, the world teeters on the edge of chaos. We must do all we can to pull it back from the abyss. I will see you in New York."

EPILOGUE

In the shadow of Washington's monuments, Mark gazed at the Potomac River, reflecting on its steady flow—a stark contrast to the global water crises he was fighting to resolve. In the wake of President Poulter's successful sidestep of the impeachment process, the White House meeting had galvanized bipartisan support for international water-sharing technologies and agreements. But Mark knew the path ahead was fraught with challenges, and things would get much worse over the coming years. His thoughts drifted to Aida, thousands of miles away, tending to her patients and holding the fragile hopes of her community. He smacked his hand against an imaginary solid object, saying out loud to himself: *What a fucking idiot you are, Wells.*

A couple saw him and smiled at him as though acknowledging his pain.

He immediately called Aida, and surprisingly, she answered.

"I will always love you, Aida. Nothing will change that, whatever you think of me."

***

President Poulter was standing at her desk, smiling at Ari. "I can't believe we beat the impeachment simply because the Democrats didn't realize they had the numbers. They easily had enough."

"We just need to take out Gudonov, and we are done," replied Ari.

"Yes, that should be the easy part. And keeping Betts and our dear Vice President in place for now will help set that up for us."

President Poulter looked confident as she took the whiskey to her lips. She paused and said, "We owe Temir. This could have gone very wrong."

Ari, without hesitation, added, "And Mark Wells. He's made us look competent. That fellow has got a big following."

"I know. I don't feel good that we are going to put him in danger to take out Gudonov."

***

Elsewhere, Jorge and Maria had successfully crossed into the US but were separated by US soldiers when Jorge became injured. Maria joined thousands in makeshift camps, her dreams tempered by harsh realities.

Jorge lay injured in a hospital near the Texas border, having become embroiled in fighting with local Americans. Both traumatized by the horror of the tens of thousands of deaths they witnessed by the once in a ten-thousand-year flooding.

A nurse walked in, and Jorge reached out and was able to whisper:

"Maria…"

"Your wife is alive. Rest now." she replied.

***

"Señor Baldini. I have been recalled by Beijing," said Zhang Wei.

Hector Baldini looked stunned as he noted, "But you only got here a few months ago. Why are you leaving so soon?"

"Señor, let me be blunt: I have failed. The only way that the People's Republic of China can be reunited with Taiwan without American interference is if they have an unfixable permanent problem at their southern border."

Hector Baldini looked stunned and was silent while Zhang Wei loaded encrypted data onto his forearm-embedded device.

Finally, he muttered in a tense whisper, "These floods killed perhaps 100,000 or more. We sent my countrymen to die."

"This is just the beginning," said Zhang Wei.

***

President Pavlova was aware that the failure to destabilize the US would lead to a power struggle to succeed her. She was adept at understanding the lay of the land and knew that decisive action was required. She looked at the Head of Cyber Psychology Operations.

"Alexander Mihajlovich Medvedov, you have failed. Their border has not been overrun by millions," she said.

Alexander stayed silent as he was well versed in the futility of speaking when someone had reached this point.

"Take him to Siberia," she blurted as she looked down. "And send the troops into Ukraine and Belarus immediately. Today."

***

"Daddy!" shouted Sara as she leaned to her father from behind the door.

Expecting her to be unconscious still, Temir ran to her bed, surprised with arms outstretched.

As Temir and his daughter hugged tearfully, the doctor said, "She is going to make a near-full recovery. It's remarkable. We can't explain it."

ABOUT THE AUTHOR

Nawtej Dosanjh, PhD, is interested in everything to do with the human story. From our earliest perilous pre-historic adventures in populating the Earth, to how we fare in our near future, he explores power, ambition and the unseen forces shaping our world. With a background in academia, process and organizational transformation, and global leadership, he is a visionary who has spent years guiding institutions and mentoring future leaders. His fiction is driven by experience, weaving together the tensions of decision-making, the weight of leadership, and the complexities of the human desire for autonomy. Whether set in boardrooms, political landscapes, or imagined futures, his narratives challenge, provoke, and reveal. Beyond writing, Nawtej is an academic strategist and innovator, constantly shaping conversations on leadership. Above all he is always searching for the next great story – whether to tell or live.